Steamforged

Books by Eric R. Asher

Shop ebooks, audiobooks, and paperbacks at ericrasherstore.com

The Theme Park at the End of the World

The Steamborn Series

Steamborn

Steamforged

Steamsworn

Skyborn

Skyforged

Skysworn

Stormborn

Stormforged

Stormsworn

The Vesik Series
(Recommended for Ages 17+)

Days Gone Bad

Wolves and the River of Stone

Winter's Demon

This Broken World

Destroyer Rising

Rattle the Bones

Witch Queen's War

Forgotten Ghosts

The Book of the Ghost

The Book of the Claw

The Book of the Sea

The Book of the Staff

The Book of the Rune

The Book of the Sails
The Book of the Wing
The Book of the Blade
The Book of the Fang
The Book of the Reaper
Dreams of the Forgotten Dead
Garden Gnome Graves

The Vesik Series Box Sets

Box Set One (Books 1-3)
Box Set Two (Books 4-6)
Box Set Three (Books 7-8)
Box Set Four: The Books of the Dead Part 1
Box Set Five: The Books of the Dead Part 2

Mason Dixon: Monster Hunter

Episode One
Episode Two
Episode Three
Episode Four

Want to receive an email when one of Eric's books releases?
Visit ericrasher.com to get started.

STEAMFORGED

THE STEAMBORN SERIES, BOOK TWO

By

ERIC R. ASHER

There is more yet to be done.

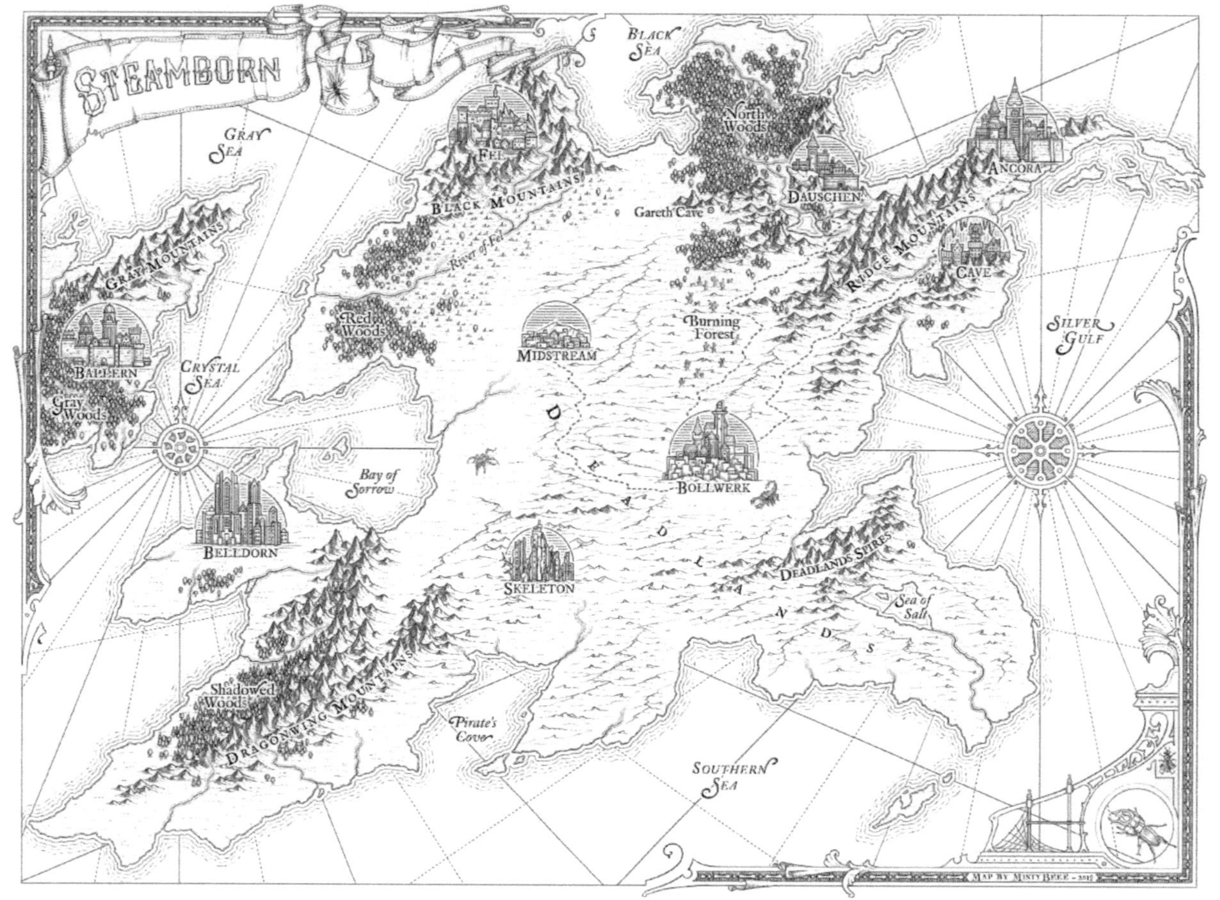
STEAMBORN
GRAY SEA
BLACK SEA
NORTH WOODS
FEL
BLACK MOUNTAINS
Gareth Cave
DAUSCHEN
ANCORA
RIDGE MOUNTAINS
CAVE
GRAY MOUNTAINS
Red Woods
Burning Forest
SILVER GULF
BALLERN
MIDSTREAM
CRYSTAL SEA
Gray Woods
D E A D L A N D S
BOLLWERK
Bay of Sorrow
BELLDORN
SKELETON
Deadlands Spires
Sea of Salt
River of Fel
Shadowed Woods
DRAGONWING MOUNTAINS
Pirate's Cove
SOUTHERN SEA
MAP BY MINTY BEKE · 2017

CHAPTER ONE

J ACOB WATCHED DRAKKAR CINCH A belt beneath the Walker, securing yet another leather saddlebag to the creature's back. The Walker didn't seem to mind. Its forty legs twitched, running from its head back down to its armored tail while its face remained buried in a trough of Sweet-Flies.

Walkers didn't have fangs to impale things with so much as they had built-in spears in their front legs. Drakkar simply pushed those venomous barbs to the side when the Walker grew too curious. The bug's antennae flattened out and then sprang back into the air when it started feasting again.

"Can I help with anything?" Jacob asked when Drakkar stood up and patted the Walker's head.

"I believe we are almost ready." Drakkar smiled at Jacob, and his teeth were a brilliant contrast to his dark skin. "Once Charles returns with Samuel and Alice, I see no reason to linger."

Jacob stepped up on some wooden crates stashed at the edge of the stables. It let him peek through the iron-barred windows where he could see the sweeping grasslands outside the city of Cave. He'd spotted a small cluster of Red Deaths earlier in the day, but nothing moved in the fields now except for a handful of giant Pill-Bugs.

Jacob unwrapped a packet of butcher paper and popped a square of jerky in his mouth. It was chewy, and a bit too salty, but surprisingly not bad at all. "This is really from a Pill-Bug?" Jacob asked, turning back to

Drakkar.

"You sound surprised. Do you not eat insects in Ancora any longer?"

"We do, but not that often. Alice sure likes her Sweetwing Tea." Jacob frowned and scraped his tongue across his teeth while he watched the Walker take another mouthful of Sweet-Flies. "How are you going to keep him fed on the trip?"

"George?" Drakkar asked as he patted the Walker's head again. "He does not need much food. Though he was born in the desert, I do worry about him dehydrating more than starving. This feast will last him many days."

"I can't believe you call it George."

"It is a good, strong name, and a name that does not frighten our Ancoran guests. Would you prefer Impaler or Venom Sword? Those are traditional Bollwerk names."

If Drakkar knew about Bollwerk, he might know about some of the other things Jacob had read about in *The Dead Scourge*. "Drakkar?"

"Hmm?" the guardian said, glancing over his shoulder.

"Have you ever met the Forgotten?"

Drakkar laughed under his breath. "You reveal too much of your intention with your questions. I doubt your tinker and your knight would appreciate that."

Jacob crossed his arms. He hadn't given away anything as far as *he* was concerned. "Well, have you?"

"I have met many people, Jacob from Ancora, as I suspect you will too. I am sure some of those people were, and will be, the Forgotten."

The door behind Jacob creaked open, and Charles stepped into the room with the Walker. George's antennae shot straight up and then relaxed as another mouthful of Sweet-Flies made a sickening crunch in the trough.

Jacob wanted to prod Drakkar for more information, but the more he thought about it, the guardian was probably right about Charles not liking his constant questioning of the man. Maybe he *had* revealed too much. He shook his head to rid himself of the thought.

"What has you so deep in thought?" Charles asked. He paused in front of Jacob, set a large saddlebag beside the Walker, and then dropped it with a grunt.

"It may have been my fault. I mentioned the fact you and the knight may not appreciate his rather revealing line of questions."

Charles blew out a breath through his nose. "You can trust Drakkar, Jacob. Ask him anything you wish, but be wary of men we don't know, especially men who are not pledged to the Steamsworn." Charles rubbed his hands together and looked at Drakkar. "I suppose he already told you about *The Dead Scourge*?"

Jacob's hand flew to his backpack on instinct alone. He had the book with him. It was a rare time he didn't have the book if he had his backpack.

"Not so directly, but his questions of the Forgotten and the lost city of Oase raised my suspicion."

"I didn't say that."

Charles smiled at Jacob and began stuffing his saddlebag into the larger bags on the Walker's back. "Some people are very good at learning what you said, without you saying it."

"Why *do* you seek the Forgotten?" Drakkar asked. He picked up Charles's saddlebag with little effort. Where the old man had struggled to lift it high enough to get it into the Walker's bags, Drakkar moved it like a small sack of potatoes. "Most Ancorans would prefer a great distance between themselves and the men they betrayed." He deftly tied the saddlebags closed.

Charles eyed Drakkar like he was measuring fuel for a Burner. Jacob could almost see the gears turning in the old man's head, choosing each word with great care.

"The invaders?" Charles said.

Drakkar nodded.

"They were driven into Ancora using sound."

"What?" Drakkar asked with a small frown. "That is madness."

Charles shook his head. "You've heard of the amplifiers of Ancora, yes? They use them so one man can speak and most of the city can hear him. It's the same idea."

"I have seen them, in fact. We guardians visit many towns."

The thought of invisible, stealthy guardians creeping through the city sent a shiver down Jacob's back.

"It's the same basic principal," Charles said. "Transmitters were mounted in Ancora, with receivers and repeaters set into a select number of bugs."

Drakkar stared at Charles. "That is not possible."

"I know the men who helped refine the technology."

Jacob thought that was an interesting thing to say. He knew Charles had invented the technology, but he hadn't heard Charles say it had been refined.

The door to the stable flew open and cracked against the wall. The sudden sound made George rear up and hiss at the newcomers. The Walker was intimidating, but Drakkar just shouted at him and pulled on his leg.

"Hey!" he said, yanking on George's leg again. The Walker swung around and looked ready to strike before Drakkar stuffed a Sweet-Fly directly into its mouth. George's antennae twitched, and the Walker dove face-first into the trough once more.

"Umm, sorry," Alice said. She carefully eased the door closed behind Samuel. "I thought the door would be heavier."

"It's heavy," Charles said, "just has some excellent hinges."

"Not such a great doorstop," Samuel said as he made his way to the far side of the Walker and set his precariously stacked armload of boxes and parcels down.

"Were that true," Drakkar said, picking up his conversation with Charles, "someone would have had to place the device on the invaders."

"Talking about the transmitters?" Samuel asked. He slid some of the twine-wrapped parcels into a nearly empty saddlebag.

"Yes," Drakkar said. "Did you see them with your own eyes? It sounds more like some ancient magic than something a man could build."

"Trust me," Alice said. "They work just fine. Besides, it could have been a woman."

Drakkar grinned at her. "I meant no disrespect. I only meant man as in human hands. I would not dare to cross such a capable person."

Alice narrowed her eyes. "I'm not entirely sure if you meant what you said, but I hope you did."

Drakkar nodded. "Ah, that would be an insult to the guardians, my young friend."

"What? Why?"

"They never lie," Samuel said. "Or so the stories say."

"They never lie unless it's convenient," Charles said. He picked up the holster for his air cannon. "That's what the stories *should* say."

"That's true for anyone," Jacob said. He helped Alice load her bags onto the Walker.

Drakkar watched him for a moment. "You are not wrong, Steamborn. You are not wrong."

That wasn't the first time Jacob had been called a Steamborn, but it was the first time he thought it was said with respect.

"Looks like that's everything," Alice said as she fastened the heavy brass buckle on the saddlebag.

Drakkar looked out the window. "The sun is just breaking the mountaintops. We should be able to make Bollwerk before night falls."

"We don't have the gear for a night in the desert," Charles said. "We have to make it. If we freeze to death before someone has a chance to shoot us, we'll feel mighty stupid."

"I still don't see how a *desert* can be cold," Jacob said.

"That's because you never paid attention to Miss Penny," Alice said. She pushed Jacob out of the way and hopped onto the saddle farthest from George's head.

"Still doesn't make sense," Jacob grumbled.

Drakkar motioned for him to come closer. "Help me with the stable door."

Jacob and Drakkar pulled from the south end of the door while Samuel pushed from the north. George the Walker's antennae shot straight up as his body curled and twisted and turned in the ever-widening strip of light.

"That should be enough," Drakkar said. "Alice, I would suggest you duck when George—"

Alice yelped as the Walker shot through the gap in a blur of rolling legs, barely ducking the top of the stone doorway.

"Yes, well, when George does that."

CHAPTER TWO

Drakkar summoned George back, complete with a screaming Alice, by blowing two quick notes on a round, four-hole whistle. It looked a great deal like the silver Spider Knight whistle Samuel had given Jacob, except this was a deep, rich green and didn't look metal at all. Every step the Walker took thundered like a drum, deep within the earth, and the rhythm of the creature's legs turned those drums into a rolling thunderstorm.

Samuel and Charles pushed the sliding stable door closed until it locked with a rapid series of metallic clicks. Each of them wore a backpack with extra canteens and travel-ready food.

"I don't expect to encounter the sandstorms today," Drakkar said, tossing a Sweet-Fly into the air, "but did you acquire the masks?" The Walker tracked the arc of the fly, impaled it on a pincer, and consumed it in one bite.

Charles patted a pocket on his pants. "We did."

"Why do they call them desert pants?" Jacob asked. He looked at the mottled gray and tan patches running across the many-pocketed pants.

"Camouflage," Charles said. "The material is a bit lighter than denim, and should be a lot more comfortable than leather in the heat of the desert."

"Are you ready to depart?" Drakkar asked, gathering the reins behind the Walker's head.

"Come on," Alice said. "It's almost fun, in a terrifying way."

"Right," Charles said. He placed a foot in a stirrup and pushed himself into a saddle.

"I am sure we can keep the pace a bit less … dramatic," Drakkar said, taking the front-most saddle.

"Can't be worse than riding Bessie up a wall," Samuel said before he grunted and hopped into the saddle behind Alice. "Right?"

Jacob wondered how Bessie was. She was an old spider, and he hoped nothing had happened to her since Samuel had left. Either way, there was nothing he could do about it now. He put his foot in a stirrup and yelped when the Walker moved its leg, catching his backpack.

Jacob stumbled forward at the same time George shifted again, hitting Jacob in the chest with a knee. Jacob grunted as he landed on his side, his nose filled with a damp, earthy scent. "Ow." The grass had been soft, and it really didn't hurt that much. He pushed off the wet ground and brushed at his side.

"You okay?" Alice asked. "You shouldn't stand between his legs for too long."

"I noticed," Jacob said. He turned to the stirrup again, hoisted himself up without incident, and settled into the saddle in front of Alice. It was obviously a newer saddle, judging by the way it smelled. The scent of tanning overwhelmed everything else, and the reins—well, handles, he supposed—didn't feel dry and cracked at all.

"The beginning of every journey lights a new path," Drakkar said, drawing Jacob's attention away from the leather. "For honor …" Drakkar paused and glanced back at Charles.

Jacob thought the old man seemed to stiffen for a moment.

"For friends," Charles said.

"For family," Drakkar said with a smile.

"For country."

"Protect those who cannot protect themselves."

"And woe be unto the man who shatters his vow."

"For we are the Steamsworn." Drakkar looked toward the Bull's Horn. "I have not said those words in a very long time." He looked at Charles and exchanged a nod before turning his attention back to the Walker. "Hold on!"

Drakkar tugged the reins and George raised his head before surging forward. Jacob yelped and teetered back in the saddle. He scrambled for the handles, and once he found them, his knuckles whitened from his death grip.

The wind surged by as the Walker's legs pounded the ground in a hypnotic rhythm. George's body pulsed forward, devouring the distance across the field of tall grasses faster than Jacob imagined they could. He guessed it would still take an hour to cross the grasslands, even at their current pace.

Alice laughed behind him, and he turned to find a huge smile stretched across her face. A halo of red hair snapped around her head, and he couldn't help but smile back.

"This is amazing!" she shouted over the roar of the wind and the thunder of the Walker's legs.

The more Jacob adjusted to the Walker's rhythm, the more he realized she was right. He'd been on Walkers before, but they were always slow, methodical trips. He'd never seen one at speed.

"Were the trains this fast?" he shouted to Charles.

"Maybe," the old man shouted back. "We didn't ride on the outside of the damn trains though!"

Jacob grinned at Charles and laughed when George dodged a pond in the center of the field. The motion sent him rocking from one side to the other as he tightened his grip on the handles once more.

The next time the Walker dodged to the side was to avoid the largest Pill-Bug Jacob had ever seen. He looked back at Alice as she held out her hand, just missing the antennae pointed toward the Walker and his passengers.

"Careful," Samuel said. "You touch something at this speed and you'll need one of those prosthetic hands you tinkers like to build."

Jacob frowned at Samuel's words until he realized Samuel was calling *him* a tinker, like Charles. He sat up just a little straighter, as much as the Walker's movements would allow, and reveled in the title. Maybe one day he could be a tinker as good as Charles.

The thought kept him warm against the wind rushing out of the mountains when they neared the pass.

Jacob watched Drakkar pull the reins slightly downward. The Walker slowed. Boulders became more frequent in the field, and the grasses eventually gave way to gray and brown stone, with only a few shrubs adding color to the landscape.

The breeze died down when they crept past the larger stones and entered the narrow path. Jacob felt like he could reach out and touch either wall at once, but in reality, a carriage would have fit through the path without much problem.

"Stay alert," Drakkar said as he turned his head. "We have seen the occasional Widow Maker in the Horns."

"During the day?" Alice asked.

Drakkar nodded. "Sometimes, yes."

Charles reached down to the air cannon holstered between two of the Walker's legs while they pumped up and down like a piston. Charles slid the cannon out and checked the slide before easing the weapon back home.

George's steps weren't very loud while they moved slowly through the pass, but the echoes of the Walker's feet on stone turned the air around them into chaos. Jacob's eyes snapped to focus on anything that moved above them. A Widow Maker ambushing them here, with so little room to maneuver, could make fast work of their entire party.

Jacob's nerves calmed after a while. No one made an effort to shout over the thunder of the Walker's steps, and Jacob had grown accustomed to the constant echo. He still watched every sign of movement with suspicion, but his first instinct wasn't to grab the air cannon away from Charles and kill everything that breathed.

The pass through the mountains made a gradual turn to the west, and they lost the sun for a while. A chill lurked in the shadows, but he knew they'd be in the desert warmth soon.

"How long is the pass?" Alice asked. "I've never been this far south of Ancora before."

"We're about halfway through," Charles said as he pointed toward the steep cliffs above them. "You can see the remnants of an old fortress up there. Used to be built right into the wall."

Jacob squinted and sucked in a breath. The sheer cliff wasn't truly a cliff at all, but a carefully built wall. The construction blended into the stone around it so well that it almost vanished. Jacob counted at least eight battlements perched over the pass. Some bore arrow slits while others showed gaps wide enough to fire a cannon through, and not a little cannon like Charles carried, but a mounted cannon that could destroy a city wall.

"Men thought to control the pass during the war of the Deadlands," Drakkar said. The Walker's legs scraped the sides of a particularly narrow section of the pass.

"Did it work?" Alice asked, leaning forward and grabbing Jacob's shoulder to steady herself.

"For a time," Charles said as he watched one of the battlements pass them by overhead. "A handful of men could hold the pass with very few weapons against an army of their enemies." He frowned while he looked at a particularly damaged section of the wall. "They never expected an attack from above."

Drakkar glanced back at the old man before returning his attention to the path ahead.

Charles stayed silent, and as much as Jacob wanted to prod him for information, he could tell by the old man's slouch that Charles didn't want to talk anymore.

They rode in silence for a while, watching patches of persistent shrubbery growing in the stone of the mountain pass. Jacob kept his eyes on the walls, still wary of what might come down on top of them, but he was still more interested in the old battlements by the time the path split ahead of them.

Drakkar led the Walker to the right. The beast had to place some of its legs up on the loose stones of the canyon wall, creating miniature landslides as they surged past the divide.

"Where does the other path go?" Jacob asked.

"The Sea of Salt," Drakkar said. "Chances are good, if you have ever tasted salt from a trader, it came from there."

"Nothing lives in that sea," Alice said before leaning away from another miniature landslide. George dodged it without issue, having caused it with his own steps.

"There are … things there," Drakkar said.

"Truly?" Charles said. "I've been there before, and it seemed more void of life than the Deadlands."

Drakkar nodded and looked to the southeast. There was only the stone of the pass there now. "Salt harvesters thought to speed the process by plunging into deeper parts of the sea. It was not so dead as they thought. Giant clawed things rose and destroyed the salt barges. I heard tales that they were much like the crayfish you raise and eat in Ancora, only a thousand times larger. The shallows are safe, but you will not find Bollwerks swimming in the waters.

"So yes, young ones, we avoid the sea. This path," he said as he gestured with his right hand, "leads into the desert, across the Scorched Plain to the city of Bollwerk."

"We're going through the Scorched Plain?" Samuel asked, and the apprehension in his voice had Jacob trying to remember what Miss

Penny had taught them about the desert. He frowned and looked back at Alice.

She sat wide-eyed, staring back. "The Scorched Plain borders the forest."

Alice didn't mean a forest of trees, Jacob realized as Miss Penny's words came pouring back to him. "The Burning Forest?" Jacob raised his voice. "Are we going through the Burning Forest?"

He could see Charles chuckling and Drakkar gave him a brief look before saying, "No, Jacob. Nothing goes through the Burning Forest. It is as impenetrable as stone, and far more deadly. Look, the Deadlands are upon us."

CHAPTER THREE

T HEY CRESTED A SHORT RISE, and the desert opened before them, a sweeping vista of golden sands. Jacob squinted against the harsh light. The pass hadn't been dark, but the difference felt as great as noon and midnight.

Jacob frowned as his vision cleared. The land before him came into better focus, and what he saw were clusters of short shrubs and wide, gnarled ironwood trees. Their canopies of tiny leaves spread out in jagged, irregular patterns, dwarfed only by the occasional cacti soaring toward the skies. Some of the ironwood branches had grown back down so they stood only an inch from the sandy earth.

"It's … it's green?" Alice said.

"You expected nothing but sand?" Drakkar asked. He glanced back at the other riders. "It is what most Ancorans expect of the desert. There are parts of the Deadlands that are nothing but sand dunes as far as the eye can see, but we do not live in those places."

"Closer to the Sea of Salt," Charles said, "you'll find barren dunes with little sign of life."

"Why didn't we learn that in school?" Jacob asked. "If people know that, why didn't we learn that?"

"Parliament calls it a control mechanism," Charles said. "If Ancorans are raised to believe there is nothing but sand and death in the Deadlands, they have no reason to go there."

"No reason to defect," Samuel said. "You've told me that before,

Charles, but I don't know that I believed you until I saw this."

The Walker wove its way around a patch of shrubs, and something moved inside, shifting the short branches. Jacob caught a glimpse of beady black eyes and a furry snout before the creature vanished. Jacob frowned, not sure what would be out in the desert other than bugs. As long as it wasn't a Widow Maker, he wasn't too worried about it.

George almost sprinted through a mountain stream before pausing halfway across. The Walker's antennae shot straight up before it dipped its face into the meandering water. Drakkar patted George's head and the Walker took off at a blistering pace.

Cool water splashed up onto Jacob's face, and it felt good.

"It's hot," Jacob said.

"It's the desert," Charles said. He flashed a sideways grin.

Jacob narrowed his eyes, but he couldn't suppress a smile of his own.

Where the wind had been cold against his face on the other side of the Bull's Horn, here it was a heavy heat, laced with sprays of sand as the Walker attacked the terrain with a fury. George's steps whispered in the deeper sand. They still beat a steady rhythm, but there was no thunder or echo in the loose sand, only a whisper of displaced grains.

"The trees are shorter already," Alice said.

Jacob looked around at the old ironwood trees, and they were shorter than those by the stream. "Not that one," he said, pointing to a towering ironwood off to the west.

"Maybe it's by an underground stream?"

"Maybe."

Jacob squinted as the hot, sandy winds tore at his face. He blinked and rubbed at his eyes when George plowed through a low sand dune, sending a spray of grit into the air.

"If you have eyewear," Drakkar said, "this would be a good time to don it."

Jacob leaned to the side and frowned at the uneven pattern of the sands. There were short dunes as far as he could see. He dug into the small pocket just beside his left handle and pulled out the pilot's goggles he'd used when flying the glider. He watched the sands roll by for a time, dirt and grit pinging off the goggles before he thought to ask Alice if she wanted to use them.

He turned to ask, and she already had a thin strip of glass over her eyes. He'd never seen goggles quite like them. The shaded lenses looked more like squares set into wide, cushioned frames.

"What are those?"

Alice pointed to her goggles and asked, "These?"

He nodded.

"You probably don't want to know."

"Why not?"

Alice shrugged. "Suit yourself. They're for Plague Burners."

Jacob's stomach soured, and he wanted to tell Alice to stop right there, but she'd already launched into her story.

"The shading keeps the flames from blinding them, and they have to protect their eyes in case they missed a Plague Bug. Can you imagine if one of those awful things escaped? So, as long as they can see around the fires, they can kill any Plague Bugs that pop out of the corpse.

"The cushion," she said as she pointed to the soft ring around the lenses, "keeps all the ash and greasy bits out of their eyes."

"Ugh," Jacob said. He returned to watching the landscape.

"Hey, you asked!" Alice laughed, and Jacob heard a chuckle from Samuel behind her.

Drakkar led the Walker across the edge of the Bull's Horn, flanking the higher sand dunes and occasionally weaving back between the gray stones of the mountain. The closer they came to the cacti, the more Jacob realized how large they really were. A few had to be twenty feet tall with an untold number of arms sweeping out and up into a needle-coated cluster.

It wasn't until they reached the bottom of the Bull's Horn that Jacob saw the first of the fallen creatures. George surged forward, and then he stopped so suddenly Jacob and the others almost smacked their faces on the saddles.

Jacob could see the creature in the middle of the path when he sat up straighter. It lay on its back with an arrow stuck through its abdomen and another lodged in a multifaceted eye. The arrows themselves were dwarfed by the stinger somewhat hidden beneath its shimmering, broken wings.

"Sky Needles," Drakkar said. He patted the Walker's head. George surged forward again, veering around a boulder close to the Sky Needle instead of climbing over it.

"Look at the size of that stinger," Alice said. "It's as long as a sword."

"They are deadly creatures," Drakkar said.

"This is odd," Charles said. "I've never seen Sky Needles cluster this densely."

Samuel shouted and leaned to the side in his saddle when they cleared a thick cluster of ironwood trees that created a path into the flatter desert. "By the gods, look at them."

Jacob raised his eyes and tried to understand the field of glinting objects strewn about before them. Charles cursed and Alice clamped her hand down on Jacob's arm. He shivered as individual shapes came into focus on an endless field of dead Sky Needles.

"They've been here a while," Alice said, watching the carcasses vanish beneath George's steps. "When did this happen?"

"It was likely intended to be part of the attack on your city," Drakkar said, "but we do not know for certain. If so, Ancora and Cave owe a great deal of thanks to the Mechs that patrol the hills."

"Where *are* the Mechs?" Charles asked.

"Gone back to Bollwerk to tell the townsfolk of the invasion would be my assumption. I would not doubt they left guards behind, hidden in the mountains. We will not see them. Look to the south," he said, gesturing with his left hand. "The shadow on the horizon is Bollwerk."

Jacob looked away from the mass of dead Sky Needles and squinted into the distance. "That little bump to the southwest?"

Drakkar laughed. "Yes, that is the city. We have a good deal of distance to cover before you can see its true face."

"Alice," Charles said, "see if you can find my scope in your left saddlebag. It should give you a better view."

The Walker had slowed to a deliberate pace, weaving through the piles of dead Sky Needles, before Charles shouted for Drakkar to stop. The guardian pulled on the reins, causing George to raise his head and slow to a halt.

"What is it?" Drakkar asked.

Charles slid off the side of his saddle and stepped around the stinger of an enormous Sky Needle.

"Be careful, my friend. A dead stinger can still kill you if you are having an unlucky day."

Jacob thought of the Widow Maker's fang he'd used to kill the soldier, Simmons. Charles had ended the man's suffering with a blast from the air cannon, but it had been Jacob who stabbed him in the neck.

Charles crouched down by the head of the Sky Needle and cursed. He pulled out a knife and sawed away a section of the creature's head. When he stood up, Charles held a transmitter that looked *exactly* like what they'd seen in Ancora.

"I guess that mystery is solved," Charles said. He opened the saddlebag closest to his seat and removed a sack and a length of rope. The transmitter and its gory mount mostly fit into the sack, and Charles tied it to one of the saddlebag's straps before taking his seat once more.

"What do you need that for?" Jacob asked. He eyed the sack swinging by the old man's knee.

"Proof," Charles said. "My word might be good enough for some, but

I suspect there are others who won't hear of it. It will be hard for anyone to deny this technology when we have it in our hands."

Drakkar nodded agreement and urged George into a pulsing, weaving gait.

"Got it!" Alice said.

Jacob turned to see her holding up a bronze scope. She yelped and wrapped her left hand tightly around the saddle's handle when the Walker slammed into another short dune and then scurried over a larger one. Their pace evened out as George found a rhythm that wove them between most of the dunes.

"Can you see Bollwerk?" Jacob asked.

Alice held the scope up to her eye and started sweeping it along the horizon. He turned his attention back to the ironwood trees and cacti spread across the desert. A thick cluster of brush stood in their way, but George had no problems dragging them all through it.

"Around the brush!" Drakkar shouted when the Walker forged ahead, sending woody limbs and needles to scratch at his passengers.

Charles crouched down, and Jacob did the same, thinking to shout "duck" before Alice or Samuel caught a branch to the face. The brush was loud as it cracked against the Walker's legs and snapped beneath his feet. A light scent surrounded them, and it reminded Jacob of the small flowers his mother used to keep on their kitchen's windowsill.

Drakkar cursed at George and called him a great deal of things that Jacob could scarcely imagine the meaning for. "Next time your legs will be coat hangers on my wall."

Alice laughed as she raised the scope to her eye once more, and then she gasped. "I can see it!"

"Bollwerk?" Samuel asked.

Alice nodded. "I think … I think there's a Fire Lizard by one of the small cactuses too. It looks big. You have to see this, Jacob."

CHAPTER FOUR

J ACOB STARED THROUGH THE SCOPE and tried to understand the skyline of the city in the distance. Buildings, impossibly tall, rose from the desert like sword points, and some even glistened in the afternoon sun like a sharpened edge.

Out in front of it all stood a ring of something pale and gray.

"Is that a wall?"

"Yes," Charles said. "If you thought the city wall in Ancora was something, wait until you see Bollwerk."

Jacob frowned. The gray band didn't seem so tall from where they were. Maybe as high as the wall in the Lowlands. Maybe.

"Where did you see the Fire Lizard, Alice?"

"Follow that dry creek bed by the big ironwood trees."

It took a little practice to keep the scope steady while the Walker surged forward in little bursts, rocking him like a child's ride at Festival. He slowly followed the dip in the earth that was the old creek bed, and laughed when he saw the shadowed form lumbering from the stump of one cactus to the huge flowering buds of another in the shade of an ironwood tree.

"It's huge!"

"I know," Alice said. She leaned forward and squeezed his shoulder. "It's amazing, isn't it?"

"I almost didn't think they were real," Jacob said, but there it was. The long snout of the reptilian form opened and snapped a trio of flowers off the nearest cactus. "It's … *eating* the cactus?" Jacob lowered the scope and looked at a nearby flower. It was almost a foot across from the edges of the petals, which meant the Fire Lizard was a monster. "How big are those, Drakkar?"

"They have to be big to survive here," Drakkar said. "The young Fire Lizards are often killed by Sky Needles, and even the Red Death have been known to feast on them."

"What about the adults?" Alice asked.

Drakkar looked back and smiled. "Nothing feasts on the adults, little one. There was a time the Bollwerks hunted Fire Lizards for food and leather. They are protected by laws now."

"Why?" Jacob asked. "It looks like you could feed a city off one of those."

"Bollwerk killed too many," Charles said. "They didn't realize it until it was too late, but the Fire Lizard population kept the Sky Needles and Red Death populations in check."

"That's kind of sad," Jacob said as he raised the scope to his eye again. They were closer to the great lizard now, and it had taken notice of the Walker rushing toward it. It no longer stood in the shade, and Jacob could see its full length, from the tapered head into the bulk of its body and down to the long tail that swished back and forth as it walked. Small spikes stood up along the creature's back. The legs looked small compared to the rest of the body.

"Are they fast?" Jacob asked.

"For short distances," Drakkar said. "They could outrun George if the race was within a half mile."

"Their legs are short, though."

"And powerful. You should see the claws. A Fire Lizard need only get close."

"I've heard they can outrun a Jumper," Samuel said. "Even Bessie wouldn't be able to stay ahead of one of those things."

"Do they *really* breathe fire?" Alice asked.

Charles was already nodding when Drakkar said, "Very much so. It is not a large flame, but it is enough to kill a hapless meal."

"So …" Jacob said, handing the scope back to Alice. "Fast, claws, fire. Not a good pet. Aren't we getting kind of close to it?"

"They are quite docile, so long as they do not feel threatened. I will see if we can get close enough for the beast to send up a warning flare."

"A what?" Alice said. She leaned forward and grabbed Jacob's arm. "What did he just say?"

Drakkar flashed them a broad grin.

✧   ✧   ✧

It wasn't long before they didn't need the scope to see the Fire Lizard quite clearly. As large as it had seemed from a distance, it seemed several times larger as they closed in on the creature. Drakkar urged the Walker ever closer until it looked like they'd come within a few strides of the beast.

The Fire Lizard had glanced their way a few times, but now it raised its head and stared at them, tracking George's every movement. Jacob could tell the legs, which had seemed so short before, were at least as tall as Samuel, and the cactus flowers it ate were twice as large as the ones they'd seen by the Bull's Horn.

Jacob was fairly certain he could stand beneath the lizard's head and have room to spare. The Fire Lizard raised its tail to the same height as its head and thumped the ground in three sets of three quick beats.

"Get ready!" Drakkar shouted. "It will be quick."

The creature curled its body onto itself when George got close enough that Jacob could have thrown a rock and hit the lizard. There were a series of clicks, as though a giant were slamming two stones together, and then the Fire Lizard opened its jaws.

Jacob and Alice both screamed as a ball of flame four feet wide poured from the purple flesh of the lizard's mouth and shot over their heads. It was a brief flash of orange and yellow heat, and then they were past the Fire Lizard. Jacob turned to watch as George—with his antennae flat against his head and Drakkar—put distance between them and the beast. Jacob saw the look on Samuel's face and almost laughed. The Spider Knight seemed just as spooked as Jacob had felt.

"That was *amazing!*" Alice shouted before she laughed and slapped Jacob's side.

Drakkar turned around and smiled. "I would not recommend trying that on your own. We have lost many youths over the years to the ill-advised taunting of a Fire Lizard."

"Oh," Samuel said, "you mean like *exactly* what we just did?"

Jacob could see Charles's shoulder shaking slightly, but the old man didn't turn around. He could hear the laughter in the tinker's voice when he said, "Don't worry, Drakkar. He'll get over it."

The Fire Lizard watched them for a time before returning to its grazing.

✧　✧　✧

"I'D ALWAYS HEARD IT WAS a dry heat in the desert," Jacob said as he wiped a small waterfall's worth of sweat off his forehead. "I thought you weren't supposed to sweat in dry heat."

"It is not so dry here," Drakkar said. "We see rains a few times a year. You must travel far to find the lands without water, past the great canyons of the old rivers and across the pale mountains. That is where the Deadlands truly earn their name."

"I'd like to see it someday," Alice said. "I want to see the whole world."

"You are very brave, young one, or very crazy. If you do journey, I would strongly suggest the airships."

"They travel out to the old canyons?" Charles asked. Jacob could see a small frown on the old man's face when he turned to look toward the southeast. "I can't imagine those balloons making it that far."

"When was the last time you saw a Bollwerk Cruiser?" Drakkar asked. "They are not so little anymore."

Charles fell silent while they rode the Walker, rising and falling with its surging steps.

The shadow of the mountain at their back caught up with them a short time later. The sky looked more like fire than clouds as they closed on the towering iron wall of Bollwerk. Jacob could scarcely comprehend the massive plates of metal, much less the buildings that soared into the sky behind them.

"Look at the wall," Alice said as she tapped Jacob's shoulder with the scope.

Jacob raised it to his eye and stared. Large hexagonal bits of metal protruded at regular intervals. "Are those … bolts?"

"Yes," Charles said. "The government feared the bolts would be the weakest part of the ironwork. The smith that designed the wall was told to build a great barrier with bolts the gods couldn't break. He took their word quite literally. I suppose they're a bit more like rivets, really."

Jacob traced the upper edge of the sheer structure. The only breaks in the gentle curve of the wall were watchtowers that rose up into strange, slanted peaks. Beneath them were the massive bolts, each trailing a river of rust down to the sands below. Jacob knew iron could corrode quickly in the wrong environment, but outside of the rust, the wall looked as solid as a mountain, and just as intimidating.

"Won't the rust bring down the walls?" Samuel asked.

Charles nodded. "Eventually, I'm sure, but those walls are some twenty feet thick. It will be a long time before Bollwerk will need to worry."

"They already worry," Drakkar said. "They have an alchemist who claims to have stopped the rust."

"An alchemist?" Charles said. "And he was doing something useful?"

Drakkar laughed and flashed Charles a grin. "Indeed, my friend. She is not so obsessed with gold as you may think."

"Or maybe she is," Alice said, "and she found an easier way to get it."

"The little one, she is very wise."

"Sounds like she's selling snake oil to a metal wall," Samuel said.

"She may be," Drakkar said with a nod. "I have seen her work, and it does seem to remove the rust at the least. The fleet has kept some of its old iron airships functioning with her help."

Jacob handed the scope back to Alice, who then passed it to Samuel.

"Where's the entrance?" Samuel asked a moment after raising the scope.

Jacob hadn't even thought about it. "That's a good question."

"To the west," Drakkar said. "We will be there soon. You will need to convince the guardian you are here under good will. If he suspects otherwise, he will kill you."

"What!" Jacob and Alice chorused, at a complete loss as to why Charles and Drakkar were laughing.

CHAPTER FIVE

"W E ARE AT THE GATE," Drakkar said as he eased the Walker to a slow crawl.

The sky had grown dark by the time they'd followed the curve of the mountain to the gate that stretched from the rocky mountainside to the smooth iron of the wall.

"It doesn't look like a gate," Alice said. "It looks wide open."

Jacob frowned as he looked at the lone figure standing at the opening. The entrance was, perhaps, ten feet across. The path up to the gates seemed rockier than Jacob expected, and he glanced at one of the larger boulders and almost yelped.

The black shell of the largest Red Death he'd ever seen was split open. One wing had been torn away so Jacob could see the ribbed, unarmored flesh of the beetle inside. Its head was twisted around, nearly severed, but its skull-like eyes still had a haunting reddish glow.

The debris between that awful carapace and the Gate consisted of more bugs, and broken shields and weapons, and even something that looked disturbingly like a pile of shredded, bloodied armor. It wasn't until they got closer that Jacob saw the men, face down in the sand and obviously dead. Not much flesh remained on the hand he could see, and what *was* there was a dry, desiccated husk.

"Halt and state your purpose, travelers." As the guard spoke, he extended a wicked-looking halberd in his right hand, creating a forty-five-degree angle against the gate. The question sounded nearly identical to that of the Cave Guardian, but where that guardian had used stealth, this one used bulk, armor, and presence.

"I am but a traveler from Cave," Drakkar said. "A man from Bollwerk come home to see his family."

"What of your companions?" the guard asked as the Walker came to a complete halt, extending its antennae toward him. Drakkar stopped right next to a corpse, and Jacob tried not to look at it. When no one answered, the guard spun his halberd and cracked the handle against the metal gate. "Lights!"

Two lanterns—like the city's streetlamps but several times brighter—burst into life at the top of either side of the gate. Jacob squinted into the sudden flare of light, and his jaw slackened. Samuel cursed and Alice gasped.

The guard wasn't just a guard—he was a Mech. Deep copper fingers wrapped around the halberd, each adorned with a spike long enough to gut a Widow Maker. The metal of his hand flowed into his arm where plates and wires and a series of hollow brass tubes circled his forearm. Something glinted at his neckline, but Jacob couldn't pull his eyes away from the arm and brass boot that he didn't think was a boot at all.

"What of your companions, guardian?"

"I travel with a young tinker and his girlfriend—"

"What?" Alice hissed. "I am *not*—"

Charles held his hand out in a placating gesture and Alice quieted, though she still grumbled a bit.

"—a Spider Knight, and one of the Steamsworn."

The guard jammed his halberd into the ground and held his fist out. "Forgive me, Steamsworn. I did not realize."

"There is no insult to give," Charles said, "and I take no insult from your words."

The guard banged his fist on his chest, making a distinctive, metallic thump before he bowed slightly to Charles. "Please, enter at your leisure.

Bollwerk welcomes the Steamsworn in all their forms."

Drakkar nodded and patted George's head, sending the Walker and its passengers surging forward when the guardian moved to the side. Jacob watched the man as they passed, and the man met his eyes. Those eyes felt empty. Jacob had only seen it before in the soldiers who fought in the Fall.

The guard nodded to him as they crossed the threshold, and Jacob returned the gesture. Inside the gate stood several more men, two of whom stood sentinel at a smaller gate. The nearest guard, clad in a light cloak not much different from Drakkar's, motioned before the inner gate slowly opened before them.

"Stables are a short distance to the west," the guard said. "You can leave the Walker and your bags if you wish."

Jacob wasn't much paying attention to the rest of the man's words because he'd realized they were now inside the walls of Bollwerk. The great shield of iron and bolts swept up into the sky to his right and made a gradual arc into the distance, wrapping a city of madness up in an almost impenetrable wall.

"Gods," Samuel said, and Jacob knew exactly how he felt.

Jacob stared off to the southwest as the Walker followed the iron wall toward the stables. There were buildings in Bollwerk that towered two or three times higher than the tallest watchtower in Ancora. Many appeared to be brick, but a few bore a dark gray sheen like metal.

"How can they build that high?" Jacob asked, not really expecting an answer.

"It's the iron and steel they use on the inside," Charles said. "Bollwerk has the greatest metalsmiths that have ever lived."

"Jacob, look!" Alice said as she squeezed his arm.

Far off in the distance, bobbing gently, Jacob could see the airship docks. At least a dozen ships were tethered to the floating dock. He'd seen airships before, in Ancora before the trade embargos, but what loomed behind those docks struck him with awe.

Two monsters, for there were no other words he could think of, dwarfed the entire airship dock. They looked like buildings floating through the sky, and it was another impossible sight in a day of impossible things. A broad gray deck lined the base of the craft, following a sweeping line of copper in the fading sunlight. The underbelly curved up slightly, meeting the copper swirls before sweeping down to join at a pointed nose that looked like it could cut through a mountain.

"Warships," Charles said. "They only use them for the defense of Bollwerk, and gods help the world when they change their minds about that. Did they ever add the gliders?"

"Gliders?" Drakkar asked with an air of amusement. "My friend, they added engines to the gliders and can launch them from the belly of those warships."

Jacob stared at the rope-laden bulges riding the sides of the gas chamber near the tail fins. "Are those life boats?"

"No," Charles said. "They're reinforced chambers for ammunition and gun turrets. They can be adjusted like ballast, but keeping the explosives away from the gas chamber helps protect the ship as a whole."

"Explosives?"

"Yes, gunpowder is quite common in Bollwerk."

"They carry gunpowder on the airships?" Alice asked. "That doesn't seem like the safest idea …"

"It's not," Charles said, "but it's the best propellant for the heavy guns. Air cannons can only do so much."

Jacob had been so focused on the airships that the sudden darkness of the stables surprised him. A stable hand motioned to Drakkar and held a tall gate open. There were two troughs inside, and Jacob could see the wingtips of a few Sweet-Flies sticking out. George had seen them too. He sped to the trough and stuffed the nearest Sweet-Fly into his jaws.

"You understand now, Samuel?" Charles asked.

The Spider Knight nodded. "If it *had* been the Deadlands come to invade Ancora, we wouldn't have stood a chance."

"Still putting it mildly," Charles said as he slid off the saddle and started unloading the saddlebags. "With the airpower they have, they wouldn't have to worry about knocking down the walls. They could level the city with *one* of those warships."

"Come with me," Drakkar said. "I will show you to the inn where they welcome outsiders." He paused and cocked his head slightly. "It is somewhat more lavish than what you are accustomed to in Ancora."

"I know where it's at," Charles said.

"They moved it just two years ago, my friend. If you have not been here since, you do not know where it is. Take what bags you need and leave the rest. The stable hands will bring them later."

"Son," Charles said. He waited for the stable boy by the gate to turn around. "I have very delicate tools in these bags. Do me a favor and see they don't get broken?" He handed the boy two silver pieces.

"Sir, absolutely," the boy said with a wide smile. "You will have our best."

"And two more silvers when the bags arrive," Charles said, heaving his overstuffed backpack onto his shoulders. He fiddled with the holster for his air cannon for a moment before finally getting it fastened and slipping the cannon home.

Jacob adjusted his own backpack, and the group trailed toward the front of the stables. He turned to watch the boy close the gate to George's stable. It locked in three places with thick, sliding bolts of iron, not much different from the stables of the Spider Knights. Not even the Walker would be breaking through those.

Jacob stumbled forward under the weight of an extra saddlebag. "How far are we walking?"

"Oh, you would not want to walk to the Tower," Drakkar said. "Not with this load. There, our transport has arrived."

A cloud of steam rose from the back of the … "What *is* that?" Jacob asked as he stared at the stubby gray and black machination.

"They call them crawlers here," Drakkar said. "Not unlike the puffing demons of Ancora."

"That is *nothing* like a puffing demon," Alice said.

"I'm going to have to agree with Alice," Jacob said. "Are those … those aren't wheels, what are they?"

The angular metal chassis of the crawler made a turn so tight it seemed to defy the fact it was even touching the street beneath it. The driver lifted his helmet and waved to one of the stable boys.

"They are treads," Drakkar said. "Far better in the desert than wheels that would sink in the sands."

The tread wound around what looked very much like wheels. A narrow fender partially obscured the whole assembly, the only indication of a door.

"Is this the Tower group?" the driver asked from behind the sharp-angled windscreen.

"Yes, sir," the stable boy said.

The driver nodded. "You all can load your saddlebags and whatever else you'd like into the back. I wouldn't recommend loading the kids into the back though. It can be a bit of a bumpy ride."

"Why would anyone load their kids in the back?" Jacob asked. He hoisted the saddlebag into the rectangular space in the back. A black rubbery material on the floor kept the bags from sliding around.

"He's joking," Samuel said as he tossed his own bags into the compartment before grabbing Alice's and stuffing hers in as well.

"Don't touch the pipes," the driver said. "I've been on the road for a while, and they're likely hot."

Jacob looked up at the two gray exhaust pipes. They angled back over the rear of the crawler, leaking a small cloud of white steam.

"Let's go," Charles said, pulling a black net over their belongings in the back. "I could go with some food and sleep."

Alice pulled open one of the doors and a metal step descended from the frame. She hopped up on it and then slid across the bench-like seat. It was cushioned, more than the saddle on the Walker had been, and Jacob sank into it a bit as he joined Alice.

Drakkar took the front seat beside the driver.

"You all want to go straight to the Tower, or take the scenic route?" the driver asked as he put his arm over the leather seat.

"The Tower, please," Charles said. "The kids have never seen Boll-werk, so even a direct path will be a scenic one."

"Fair enough, Steamsworn."

Jacob looked over at Charles, wondering how the driver knew he was a Steamsworn. The medal Charles usually kept hidden hung in the center of his chest. The tinker glanced down at it before slipping the medal back beneath his shirt. Samuel climbed into the crawler last, and Jacob watched as the step retracted when the Spider Knight pulled the door closed. He imagined it was a simple mechanism, likely accomplished by fastening two braces together, but the effect was stunning.

The crawler lurched and then spun in place until the back became the front and the great city of Bollwerk stabbed into the sky before them. It may have been dark now, but the city didn't seem to notice. Lights of every shape and size peppered the skyline. Some floated so high up Jacob mistook them for stars until the crawler started forward.

CHAPTER SIX

"W HY ARE THERE LIGHTS ON top of the buildings?" Alice asked.

"So the airships do not crash into them at night," Drakkar said as the crawler stuttered forward. The shaking caused the guardian's voice to pulse with the motion before the crawler evened out.

"I was rather hoping that would smooth out," Samuel said. "It feels more like riding a train now."

"You ride a Jumper," Alice said. "How can a few bumps in the road bother you after *that*?"

"That's different," Samuel said. "Bessie knows what I can take."

Jacob leaned over Alice and looked down at the rolling wheels that weren't really wheels at all. "What kind of wheels are those?"

"They're called treads," the driver said. "They're a bit more maneuverable than wheels, and a lot more effective in the desert. Our crawlers used to get stuck in the sand quite often when they rode on wheels."

The skyline of Bollwerk loomed closer, and then they bounced off the rough stone by the stables and onto the smooth brick of the city itself. There were several buildings, at first, that looked like they could have been in Ancora, but then came the core of Bollwerk.

Metal and brick soared higher than the city walls in Ancora. Jacob hadn't put a lot of thought into it while they were outside Bollwerk, but clearly if he could see the buildings from outside that enormous iron wall, they had to be colossal.

The men and women of Bollwerk stayed off the streets. Here, the brick thoroughfares were clogged with crawlers and puffing demons and only an occasional carriage. They paused at an intersection while another crawler rumbled by, a great cloud of white steam billowing out from its exhaust. Their driver made a sharp turn onto another street by moving two levers in opposite directions.

"Look at their dresses," Alice said. She glanced down at her own gray dress before looking back to the pedestrians along the street. "Look at that one." She pointed at a young girl whose dress was made from leather with a thin edge of pale lace on the arms and chest. The materials swept toward the back of the dress and melded together with a series of leather ties and brass buckles at the back. It darkened toward the hem, almost turning black in the streetlights.

The man she was with—her father, Jacob guessed—wore black leather from head to toe. It was cut like one of the fine suits of the Highlanders, but it felt like it had a purpose, almost like a piece of armor. It looked intimidating, and Jacob wanted one. He glanced at his own worn leather vest before he smiled at Alice, knowing exactly how she felt.

"The Council is there," the driver said, raising his voice to be heard over the rumble of the treads as he evened out the levers and pointed to a brick building.

It was taller than Bat's home in Ancora, at least eight stories high, maybe more. Archways decorated the front of the building, each adorned with tarnished copper window frames. The archways on the first floor were several feet wide, and then the pattern repeated on a smaller scale all the way up to the roof. Two monstrous pillars flanked the main entrance, stretching up to support a balcony on the third floor.

"Why did they stop hosting their guests in the Council Hall?" Charles asked.

"The Council has grown too big," the driver said. "If they hosted more than a handful of guests, they'd have no room for themselves."

Charles nodded, glanced at the hall again, and then settled back into his seat.

"How far out is the Tower?" Alice asked.

"Well, technically we're headed *into* the city," the driver said with a smile, "but it's just over there." He pointed off to the right and up. Jacob stared at the massive structure, and Samuel cursed.

If it wasn't the tallest structure inside the city wall, it was very close. Gray metal arches adorned every level of the building, and the arches alternated between being filled by brick and what looked to be a shaded glass. It was hard to tell in the city lights, and Jacob couldn't be sure. The crawler turned another corner, leaving Jacob to sway in his seat as he stared at what hung above them.

This side of the building bore a crest large enough that the entire Square in Ancora could have fit inside of it. Enormous tarnished fingers bulged out of that symbol, a closed fist that seemed to be suspended above them. It was so large it seemed wrong to call it a crest. Monument felt like a much better word. Jacob had seen the symbol before. It was the same as the old man's medal, only on a scale he could hardly comprehend.

"Steamsworn?" Alice whispered.

"They have acquired a great respect in Bollwerk," Drakkar said as he too gazed up at the monument.

"They've always been respected here," Charles said.

"That is true," Drakkar said, "but since they have learned to repel the Sky Needles and use their biomechanics to save lives instead of making war … they are revered in Bollwerk."

"I'm sure you still have problems with Mechs," Charles said.

The driver glanced over his shoulder as the crawler came to a stop before the Tower's grand marble staircase. "We don't call them Mechs anymore. Not in Bollwerk." The guard glanced around. "The word itself is frowned on here, so please, don't use it. The men you speak of, the men who lost their way in their quest for power, we call them Berserkers."

"Some still serve the Steamsworn," Drakkar said.

"On the front lines," the driver said with a nod before removing his goggles. "Those who are not completely mad are invited on patrols in the Deadlands and raids on the Sky Needle nests. Don't cross the Berserkers. Some of them are nigh indestructible."

"Thank you for the transport," Charles said, leaning forward to give the driver a gold piece.

The man's eyes widened. "This is too much."

"It is for your silence as much as our transport. Please, do not tell anyone we've arrived. I know the Council must be informed, but I'd like peace for the evening."

The driver curled his hand around the coin. "I can't guarantee the silence of the stable boys. They may have told half the city already."

"Few people listen to the young," Charles said. "What's your name?"

"Most men call me Jones."

"Dr. Jones the tinker?" Charles asked.

Jones's mouth hung open slightly. "How could you *possibly* know that?"

Charles patted the man's shoulder as they began to disembark from the crawler. "An old tinker knows many things, Jones. It's good to remember that. Maybe you'll understand when you're older."

The driver gave Charles a nod and an amused smile as the rest of the group exited the crawler. "If you need me, ask the innkeeper. She knows where to find me."

Samuel finished unloading the saddlebags from the back of the crawler with Drakkar's help before Jones set the levers and pulled away from the Tower. "Innkeeper?" he said as he glanced up the Tower. "That's a hell of an inn."

Jacob stepped to the smooth marble sidewalk outside, and his eyes trailed up the building until the brick and iron façade faded into the night sky some thirty stories above his head. Their entire group stayed silent for a moment until Alice spoke.

"If I wasn't looking at it, I wouldn't believe it."

Jacob glanced at her, and she had her neck craned back to stare at the top of the Tower.

Samuel cursed and tossed a saddlebag over his shoulder. "How tall is that?"

"Afraid of heights now?" Charles asked.

"No, I'm afraid of it collapsing."

"The Tower has stood for almost twenty years," Drakkar said. "If it falls, it is not likely to be on the one night you are staying in it."

An older man, wearing finely striped pants and a wide-shouldered dress coat beneath a tall top hat, started down the stairs. "You are welcome to leave your bags, friends. We will have them carried to your rooms."

"Sign me up," Samuel said, letting his saddlebag fall to the ground.

"Very good, sir." He stepped to the side and gestured to the Tower's entrance. "Please see the innkeeper. She will show you to your rooms."

Alice led the way up the stairs with Jacob close behind. Two men stood at the wide glass doors. They opened up either side as the group approached. Jacob heard Drakkar thank the men for their assistance, but most of his focus stayed on the room inside the doors.

"Welcome to the Tower," a young woman said as they crossed the threshold into the grandest inn Jacob had ever heard of, much less seen with his own eyes. Their every step echoed on the stone floors. Jacob and Alice stared without restraint at the enormous sculptures decorating the bar. Stone airships and Fire Lizards and great hunched beasts for which Jacob had no name for circled the room. Men and women fought beside giant mechanical constructs on sprawling murals that circled the towering marble pillars.

"How long will you be staying?" the young woman asked. Jacob stared at the strange, smooth cream blouse she wore. It wasn't made from any material he'd seen before. He could scarcely make out a single thread anywhere on it, almost like the silk gowns the wealthiest Highlanders wore at Festival. It was marked with a band of leather sweeping across her chest. A neat braid held her black hair, falling into a series of individual braids across her shoulder, framing the dark skin of her face and the electric green of her eyes.

"They are here to see the Council," Drakkar said. "I would expect them to need no more than one night."

"I believe we are to see the innkeeper," Charles said.

"I am she," the young woman said. She gave a shallow curtsey. "You are most welcome at the Tower. Please, feel free to indulge at the bar and utilize the lifts." She traced a precisely manicured nail across a map of the Tower. "We have openings on the twentieth floor tonight. The rooms are identical, though a few of you will need to share. I trust that is not too great an imposition?"

"Not at all," Charles said. "We are road weary and could just as easily sleep on the floor of your bar."

She offered a small smile before pulling out three keys and handing them to Charles. "Please follow the guard. He will show you to your rooms."

A man wheeled a metal cart through the bar, stacked high with their sacks and saddlebags.

"Follow me," a deep voice said.

Jacob looked up, and then up some more. The guard who spoke was a mountain. His muscles and rich skin tone, combined with the leather-plated armor he wore, gave him a presence unlike anyone Jacob had met before. He thought Drakkar had been intimidating when he first met him. Now Drakkar seemed more like a friendly cat.

"How is life inside the wall?" Drakkar asked as the taller man turned to lead them through the bar.

"It is good, brother of Cave. And life inside the ground?"

Drakkar laughed. "I cannot complain. We saw the fields of Sky Needles on our journey here."

The guard nodded. "We lost some of our own in that battle, but it could have been much worse."

"If the swarm had made it to Ancora, most of the Lowlands would have died."

The guard pulled a lever next to a gate and turned toward Drakkar. "There were some soldiers who wished that fate upon Ancora for what they did to the Forgotten. I try to remind them that the poor decisions of a government are not the poor decisions of an entire people."

"Thank you for that," Charles said.

The guard glanced at the old man and then nodded. "I had heard stories when I was young of a Steamsworn force inside the old city."

"Force may be a strong word," Charles said. "There are a few in the service of the knights, and the Spider Knights."

"What?" Samuel said. "The Spider Knights? You never told me."

"Sometimes it's safer not to know," Charles said with a small frown. "I didn't keep it from you for any other reason."

A small chime sounded when the lift arrived. The guard slid the accordion-like gate open and ushered everyone in. He followed them and threw another lever to close the gate.

"Look at the floor," Alice said as she crouched down. "You can see through it."

"It is a very thick glass. You need not worry."

The lift jerked slightly and then started rising. They passed the third floor before Samuel stepped backward and wrapped his hands around the hand railing.

Drakkar crossed his arms, letting the sleeves of his cloak slide forward to cover all but a sliver of his wrists. "You can close your eyes, Samuel. It will not be so bad."

"It's mostly brass anyway," Jacob said. "Look, even if it broke, I don't think I could fit my foot through the grate."

"It's not the height. *People* built this," Samuel said as more floors vanished into the depths below them. "One mistake, a few poorly cast rivets, and we'll go crashing down to the bar."

"At least we'll die in a bar," Charles said. A wide smile lifted his beard.

Samuel barked out a short laugh. He sighed when the lift slowed and the guard opened the gate on the twentieth floor.

"Rest well," the guard said. He stepped out of the lift and held the gate open. "Your rooms are at the end of the hall to your right. In the morning, you'll face the Council."

CHAPTER SEVEN

"LET DRAKKAR HAVE HIS OWN room," Charles said, handing the guardian one of the room keys.

"Who gets the kids?" Samuel asked. He eyed Jacob and Alice.

Jacob narrowed his eyes. "You know, we aren't *that* young. I'll be fifteen pretty soon."

"I'll stay with Jacob," Alice said as she stepped closer to him. "We have some reading to do anyway."

Charles nodded slowly. "Samuel, why don't you stay with me?"

"So the kids get their own room and I'm stuck in a tiny room twenty stories up with the old man?"

"Yes," Charles said. He flipped one of the keys to Alice. "Be glad I'm giving the kids the outer room so you don't have to look out the window at your imminent demise."

Samuel shut up.

Another lift dinged, and the guard stepped through the gate with their luggage. "Where would you like your bags?"

"Follow me, follow me," Charles said as he wandered to the first door. He worked the key into two separate locks, each surrounded by an ornately patterned metal plate, before swinging the door open. "Any-where on the floor will be fine."

Samuel followed the guard in, and Jacob heard him say, "Two beds? There's enough room in here for ten people!"

"Come on," Alice said as she grabbed Jacob's hand and pulled him down the hall. "I want to see how our room looks." Their room was at the farthest end of the floor. Alice slipped the key into three different locks and tried the handle. "It won't open."

"I don't think that's a peephole," Jacob said as he moved up beside Alice. He pushed the glass orb to the side to reveal another lock.

"That's a lot of locks. Do you think we're in a bad neighborhood?"

"I have no idea."

Alice put the key into the fake peephole and twisted. Something hissed before metal clanked against metal. She tried the handle again, and the door swung open.

They stepped into the room and stared. A fireplace waited in the center of the room with a bath and shower sectioned off to their right. A black leather couch sat against one of the panoramic windows while a desk sat against the other. An inkwell and fountain pens were neatly laid out across the dark wood, but it was the city beyond that struck them speechless.

Jacob and Alice made their way to the window by the desk and stared.

Ancora had a few lights on the street when the sun left its people to darkness, but Bollwerk seemed to be a sun in its own right. As far as they could see, buildings were lit by a network of streetlamps, so much so that no one carried their own lantern. The people walking beneath those lights seemed more like windup toys from Jacob's vantage point.

He felt Alice lace her fingers through his, and he squeezed her hand.

"It's so beautiful," she whispered. "I never imagined."

"I don't even understand how people could have built this." Movement caught his eye and he looked up, angling his gaze to the southwest. "Alice …"

She glanced up at him and then looked to the skies. A slow-moving airship sailed over the city skies. A lantern in one of its portholes flashed a message to the docks, and a dockworker returned an answer with bursts of light.

They stayed there for a time, watching the enormous airship float to one side of the dock before the workers below caught the landing lines thrown from the deck. Eventually, the craft settled into place, secured between two wide platforms.

"Do they leave it in the air?" Alice asked. "Just tied up?"

"It looks that way," Jacob said. He set his backpack on the desk and headed to the other window. Far in the distance, an orange glow lit the horizon. At first, he thought it was the last of the sunset, but then he realized there was darkness beyond it.

"Is that the Burning Forest?" Alice asked, and the disbelief in her voice matched Jacob's own.

"Unless it's another city?"

Alice shook her head. "I don't think so. Dauschen is on the other side of the canyons. That looks too close."

Jacob sighed and turned away from the window. "Oh."

"What?"

"There's … there's only one bed."

"So?" Alice said. "It's huge, and there's no way you snore as loud as my mom."

"Or my dad. He sounds like one of Charles's engines after it blows a gasket."

Alice laughed and slid her backpack off, leaving it by the side of the couch. "Didn't *The Dead Scourge* have something about the Burning Forest? I think I remember reading that."

Jacob nodded as he walked to his backpack and slid the book out. He crossed the room again and flopped onto the leather couch. "This is a nice couch."

"Not really surprising, considering the rest of this place. What do you think of their respect for the Steamsworn?"

"Respect?" Jacob asked as he opened the book. He thought the Burning Forest had been mentioned somewhere toward the middle.

"Yes, even Drakkar seems to have immense respect for them, and he doesn't even live here."

"He used to."

Alice shrugged.

"Here it is," Jacob said. He scooted closer to Alice. He followed the lines with his index finger while she began to read aloud.

> I did not understand why they called it the Burning Forest until I saw it for myself. Formations of minerals and stone had grown from the earth, or perhaps the earth had been eroded around them, leaving behind skeletal, tree-like structures. Clearly, they were hollow to some degree, for an oxygen well beneath filtered through their limbs and fed those eternal flames.
>
> One of the guardians told me of a man who tried to extinguish a burning tree. He went so far as to crush it and bury it, only to discover a brighter flame in its place the next day. Unimpeded by the structure, the fire was twice the height of any of the undamaged trees.

"So they look like trees, but they're not. I wonder if it's like the old bugs and lizards Miss Penny has that are trapped in stone."

"The fossils?" Jacob nodded his head. "They could be, I guess, but shaped like a standing tree? I don't know."

Alice leaned over Jacob and turned a few of the old yellowed pages. "I don't understand how there can be so many things in this book that we didn't learn in school."

"Charles says it's because the winners of every war write the history books, so all you ever get is their point of view."

Alice sank back into the couch and crossed her arms. "That makes sense, but it's awful. It makes me wonder about a lot of things, even in Ancora. Why didn't we know about the underground station? Or the catacombs? Were the invaders *really* why the Lowlands were cut off from the building of the city wall?"

"I don't know," Jacob said. "There's definitely something strange going on with Parliament. The men we heard in the catacombs talked about basically sending all the miners out just to die."

"Not just the miners. All of the Lowlanders."

Jacob looked up and met Alice's eyes. She frowned, and her face was tight.

"Jacob, those men said Ancora needed the miners to harvest fuel for the Highlands. So they can reopen the trade routes with Dauschen?"

He nodded. "Right?"

"Why would they be so afraid of Dauschen allying itself with the Deadlands? Why would Bollwerk have any interest in what happens in Ancora?"

The stories, atrocities, and the respect for the Steamsworn fell into a graphic, terrible image in Jacob's mind. "Oh, gods, they want the Butcher."

"But they could *level* Ancora with those warships. It wouldn't even be a fight!"

"I bet they don't leave in case Bollwerk is attacked," Jacob said. "Think about it, if those ships leave …"

Alice shook her head. "No, no, they still have the wall. I don't think that's it. They aren't worried about being defenseless. You saw what that Biomech had done at the gates."

"There may have been more we didn't see."

Alice raised an eyebrow and cocked her head to the side. "Since when are *you* the optimistic one here?"

Jacob smiled and closed *The Dead Scourge*. "We're just guessing. Maybe we'll find out more at the Council tomorrow."

Alice stood up and stretched before walking over to the bed. "Come on, let's get some sleep. It's getting late."

Jacob sat the book down on a low table beside the couch. His mind worked furiously, trying to find the pieces that fit together in the best possible way. If Bollwerk pursued the Butcher, they could invade Ancora. If Dauschen was out to eliminate their competition, *they* could invade Ancora. And if the two were forging an alliance against the city he called home?

Jacob sighed and shook his head. Every motivation he could think of ended in war and death.

"What is it?" Alice asked.

He squeezed his forehead and shut his eyes against the burning that suddenly threatened tears. "This won't end well."

Jacob jerked in surprise when Alice wrapped her arms around him, breaking his grip on his forehead, and forcing him to look at her.

"It'll be okay, Jacob. We'll get through this. I know we will. We'll get back home and see our families again."

She laid her head on his shoulder and squeezed him like it was the last time they'd ever see each other. Jacob felt her tremble, but when she released him, there were no tears.

"Let's get some sleep." She grabbed his hand and pulled him onto the bed. There was enough room that both of their families could have slept comfortably on that one single bed.

Alice slid over to the center before Jacob pulled a short lever on the bedside lamp, shutting down the artificial light. He kicked off his shoes and flopped onto the bed, twisting slightly until his head was on a pillow.

"What in the world is this made out of?" he asked. His muscles seemed to melt into the soft bedding.

"Sleep?" Alice mumbled into her pillow.

Jacob smiled. He couldn't see much in the room, but the city's lights created a not-unwelcome backdrop to his thoughts. He ran his hand over the blanket until he found Alice's fingers. He squeezed them, and something settled in his nerves when she squeezed him back, lacing her fingers into his own.

For the first time in a while, Jacob fell asleep with a smile on his lips.

CHAPTER EIGHT

J ACOB OPENED HIS EYES, THINKING he'd heard something. Three quick knocks sounded again. He started to sit up, but something held him down.

"What …" he said before he slowly realized Alice's arm was draped across his chest and her leg had his in a stranglehold.

He'd always thought of Alice as more of a sibling than anything else, but lying there beside her with her breath so close …

The knocks came again and Alice let loose a bed-rattling snore.

Jacob laughed and eased himself out of her grip, disentangling himself before making his way across the room. He opened the door and rubbed at his eyes. Charles stood there in his leather vest and backpack.

"Are you two ready to go? They've already taken our bags down to the lift."

Jacob squinted at Charles. "Just woke up."

"Hurry up, then. Meet us downstairs once you and Alice are ready."

"Hurry?" Jacob said, half hoping the old man just had a terrible sense of humor.

"We'll meet you by the doors. The Council will convene in about an hour, and I'd like to be early."

Jacob watched Charles start down the hall before pushing the door closed until it clicked.

"Who was that?" Alice asked, her voice scratchy. She propped herself up on her right arm.

"Charles. We have to get ready."

"Pfff." Alice rolled up in the blanket until she looked more like a sausage with a burst of red cabbage sticking out the top than a girl.

Jacob laughed and tugged on the blanket. "Come on. I'm sure we can sleep later."

Alice groaned and slowly crawled out of the bed to make her way into the bathroom. "How do they get the water up this high?" Alice asked from behind the sectioned-off corner of the room.

"I don't know." Jacob ran his fingers over the silver skull before stuffing *The Dead Scourge* into his backpack.

"It's actually warm," Alice said. She walked out of the bathroom, wielding a hairbrush. "And they left brushes out for us. This place must cost a fortune." She tossed Jacob the brush.

"What are you trying to say?"

Alice grinned. "We're off to meet *the Council*," she said, wiggling her fingers. "You should probably comb your hair."

"I'm sure they'd be thrilled at you making fun of Jacob."

"I don't really care what they think, as long as we get to go home."

Jacob fastened the latches on his backpack before hefting it over his shoulder. "Me too, Alice. Me too."

AN EMPTY BAR GREETED THEM when the lift stopped on the first floor and one of the guards slid the gate open. The innkeeper, as they called her, stood near the front doors. Jacob watched the pillars as he and Alice walked by them, every inch of the old stone revealing another story, another mystery.

"Perhaps it is not so wise to let the children share a bedroom," Drakkar said when Jacob and Alice were close enough to hear him.

"This whole trip is full of unwise decisions," Samuel said under his breath.

"Oh, stuff it," Alice snapped.

Jacob raised his eyebrows at the heat in her voice.

Drakkar laughed and bowed slightly to Alice. "I have heard tales of the fire in the hearts of flame-haired maidens. I begin to think they have some truth."

"Your transport awaits," the innkeeper said, sparing Drakkar from Alice's gaze.

"Thank you, my lady," Charles said. He slid the innkeeper a gold piece.

"I require no compensation, Steamsworn. It is my honor and privilege to serve."

"*My* honor requires that I give you compensation, my lady. So you will take it, or cause grievous wound to the heart of the Steamsworn you so honor."

The innkeeper's mouth hung open, and she silently pocketed the gold coin.

"I'm glad we could come to an agreement," Charles said with a broad smile.

Jacob squinted in the bright light as he followed Charles and Samuel through the doors. Alice and Drakkar trailed behind him. One of the Tower's guards was loading their bags into a crawler. The front end of this crawler bore the crest of the Steamsworn.

"What do you think that means?" Jacob said, gesturing to the crest.

"It is an official transport," Drakkar said. "That is all."

The doors were already open on the transport. Charles didn't hesitate to place his foot on the small step and climb into the crawler. Everyone else followed him in.

"Leather seats?" Samuel asked, sliding across the bench.

"Only the best for the Council," the driver said. "This is their personal transport. You folks must be some kind of important."

"What a waste," Drakkar said as he took a seat beside the driver.

The driver looked around before he said, very quietly, "It's quite refreshing to hear someone speaking some sense." He held out his hand and shook Drakkar's.

"You're all clear. Take them to the temple," the Tower guard said as he latched the net over everyone's luggage.

The driver held up two fingers and snapped his wrist to the side before pushing the crawler's levers forward. They pulled away from the Tower and slipped into traffic behind a puffing demon that looked as though it could have been on the streets of Ancora.

"You all have some time to spare, so I'm going to take you around the heart of Bollwerk. I'd hate to think any visitors to our fine town would miss it."

Charles looked like he was about to protest, but then he shrugged.

"I didn't really notice last night, but that crawler was very squeaky," Jacob said. He leaned over the edge of the door and watched the treads.

"The one that runs to the stables?" the driver asked before he laughed. "Jones is the only driver for that old route. He's a nice enough guy, don't get me wrong, but that old crawler could use an overhaul."

The driver kept talking, but Jacob wasn't paying attention after they turned a corner. The architecture changed so fast it almost felt violent. The buildings two blocks down were all shaped like daggers or spears, streaking into the sky. Rusted iron and old steel peeked through at random intervals, leaving Jacob to think of rot and the ruin of a city.

"What happened?" he asked aloud. "The front of the city's so clean."

"You mean the rust?" the driver asked.

Jacob nodded without thinking about the fact the driver couldn't see him. "Yes, yes, that's what I meant."

"This is one of the oldest parts of the city. It's built on the bones of one of the ancient towns. They left the rust and iron exposed for a purpose. It looks like hell, but it reminds us that Bollwerk will always stand here. Even if the city falls, it will be rebuilt, and it will be greater than it was before."

Jacob liked that. He liked the fact that the city, in some form, had stood here longer than he could even imagine. The city could be a legacy lasting for ages. Even if men and women were lost to memory, their work would live on.

Charles crossed his arms and took a deep breath. "The Forgotten have changed a great deal in a half century."

The crawler slowed, and the driver glanced back at Charles. "Don't use that name here. The Council doesn't like to remind people that they weren't born here."

Charles barked out a laugh and leaned forward. "Isn't their skin enough to give them away?"

The driver nodded. "For a few members, yes, but most have married and had children, and their children's children now serve on the Council. Many of the … the founders are no longer alive."

"What happened to them?" Samuel asked.

"Age, for most of them. Two were assassinated. An attempt was made to assassinate Lady Grey, but she killed her own assassins. She's my favorite, personally. No nonsense, blunt, but never cruel."

"Grey," Charles said as he ran a hand over his beard.

The driver shifted one lever back and one lever forward, turning sharply onto a side street. The sudden movement slammed Samuel into Charles and Alice into Jacob. She reached out and caught his hand, and Jacob smiled.

"Sorry about that," the driver said. "I got caught up in telling you about our fine Council."

It was scarcely a minute before they took another turn, this one much smoother, and the rusted iron of the old town, peeking through the façade of the new city, fell away behind them.

"I can't even see the walls from here," Alice said. "I thought you'd be able to see them from anywhere in the city, like Ancora."

"They staggered the streets just for that," the driver said. "Council didn't want the city folk to feel trapped. Unless you're around the shorter buildings, or closer to the walls, you can't see the wall from street level."

Charles frowned and watched the pedestrians go by. "An illusion of freedom? A caged bird in a larger cage is still a caged bird."

The driver laughed and slowed by an old, modest brick building, mostly square, with a slight slope to the roof. "You see this here, with the old weathervane? It's the oldest building in Bollwerk. The bricks are a different color because we don't make them like that anymore."

"How were they made?" Charles asked.

The driver shrugged. "Actually, I don't know. Jones the tinker just told me they don't make them like that anymore."

"Do you know how old they are?"

"The cornerstone has a date from the old town, but no one uses that calendar anymore. Nineteen something I believe."

"In the thousands?" Charles asked.

"I think it might have been, but I'm honestly not sure."

Charles nodded. "That would be several hundred years past, maybe a millennium."

"Alright," the driver said. "Hold on tight. I'm taking you on the speedway. We'll be back at the hall in five minutes. It's the only road that goes from one side of the wall to the other."

The crawler shot forward and spun onto a wide, flat street. No pedestrians crossed here, and the bricks were so finely laid that they seemed a single piece of stone. Alice twisted in her seat, pressing up against Jacob as she looked behind them. He glanced backward too, and far in the distance he could make out the shrouded iron wall.

"Hold on!" the driver slammed both steering levers forward and the crawler lurched into a sprint. He threw a third lever, and the steam engine rumbled beneath them. Great clouds of white smoke billowed out of the exhaust, and the treads screamed across the stone streets.

Samuel whooped and put his hand outside, catching a blast of hot desert air as it surged by them. Homes and towers vanished in a blur of color outside the crawler.

Jacob and Alice laughed, the wind whipping at their hair. Drakkar and Charles exchanged glances, and Jacob could have sworn they both rolled their eyes. It made him laugh even harder.

Jacob felt happy, truly happy, for the first time since they'd left Ancora. He was glad it was with Alice and their friends. The ride didn't last nearly long enough.

CHAPTER NINE

J ACOB WAVED TO THE DRIVER as he gave them all the same two-fingered salute he'd given the Tower guard.

"Let's go," Charles said, hefting the holster for his air cannon.

"Are they going to let you take that inside?" Alice asked.

"Of course they are. What am I going to do? Shoot an old friend in the face?"

Samuel froze and glanced at Charles. "You're not going to, are you? I'd really like to get back home some day and not be fed to the desert in the meantime."

"I'll try to control myself," Charles said as he turned and winked at Jacob and Alice.

The building had seemed tall the evening before, but after being in the Tower and seeing the city from above, some of that impression had been lost. At eight stories, it rivaled the tallest buildings in Ancora, but here it was only average. Maybe even less than average.

Jacob's gaze traveled from one end of the block to the other. He'd known some brick masons in Ancora, boys and men only a few years older than him, and he had no doubt they'd all be impressed with the consistency of each of the archways.

Jacob followed Charles between the towering pillars on either side of the entrance. A polished copper archway waited behind the tall, iron-braced doors. Beyond that, the hall opened into a grand assembly of pillars.

"It's so high," Alice said as she looked up.

The first four floors were wide open. The only obstruction the thick, tarnished metal pillars placed several steps apart from each other. Their footsteps echoed on the dark wood floors in the cavernous hall. Doors lined the walls to either side, but the guards standing sentinel beside each pillar motioned for them to continue to the lift on the far wall.

Jacob slowed when they reached the center. "Look at them." To either side were titanic flywheels, each as large as a house, slowly spinning and turning in place. Half hidden by the floor, their slow-moving spokes vanished into the shadows of the basement only to return a few seconds later.

"How do they keep the steam from rotting the floors?" he asked.

"They have an exhaust system built in that brings the steam out the top of the roof," Charles said. "They redirect it on the cold nights to help keep the place warm."

Jacob watched the old man for a moment, wondering how much of the hall Charles had seen built the last time he was here. Or, for that matter, how much of it he'd *helped* build.

The last guard, standing before the lift, held his hand up. "We will hold your luggage in the Atrium. It will be safe, so do not worry yourselves about it."

"Thank you," Charles said.

"Of course, Steamsworn," the guard said with a nod of his head.

They all filed onto the lift. Drakkar was last, and Jacob caught an intense gaze exchanged between the man from Cave and the guard.

Jacob waited until the gate closed, a flat piece of bronze engraved with the seal of the Steamsworn, before he turned to Drakkar. "What was that about?"

Drakkar sighed and ran a hand through his black hair. "If I were a man who lived on assumptions, I would guess my skin is not dark enough."

"What?" Alice asked as she scrunched up her forehead. "That doesn't make any sense."

"Shades of gray, my friends. You thought the guardians of Cave had the darkest skin imaginable."

Jacob started to protest, but Drakkar stopped him.

"Samuel told me why you both stared, and there was no offense taken. There are some men from Bollwerk, descendants of the earliest cities, who believe the mixing of the races was a terrible crime. I would guess that guard is one of them."

"I thought you said you thought it wasn't." Jacob rubbed his forehead. "Why would it be?"

"And I stand by that. My grandmother was a full-blooded Fel. She was kind and helpful and better than most men could ever hope to be. Part of her gives me strength, and part of my desert heritage gives me strength. I do not believe this," Drakkar said as he pulled at the skin of his arm, "matters. Different is not bad."

"I do miss the philosophers of Cave," Charles said as he smiled at Drakkar. "I'll have to make it a point to visit more often."

"We would welcome you."

The lift jerked to a halt, and the bronze doors slid open.

Alice gasped and Samuel cursed. Risers flanked the hall, ten rows deep. Men and women and children lined up all along them, watching Charles lead their little group onto the floor.

At the far end waited a grand bench, split into three tiers. A great deal of metal flashed in the light as the men and women of the first tier moved their arms and leaned together to whisper. As he got closer, Jacob realized they were all Biomechs. The eyes in the risers to either side felt like they might bore a hole into his head at any moment.

A row of stoic Bollwerks formed the second tier, dressed in fine leathers with one of each of their shoulders draped in thin golden chains. They didn't whisper, or move; they simply watched the progress of Jacob and his friends.

Above them, at the top of the bench, sat a single man with slicked-back gray hair, a broad mustache, and a finely cut coat. He wore glasses, not unlike Charles's, but with far fewer lenses. His fingers steepled together, and he waited in silence. Jacob wouldn't have thought too much about the man's light skin tone, but considering what Drakkar had said, he guessed it was unusual for Bollwerk. If he'd learned one thing in his lifetime, it was that there were always exceptions. There would always be men and women from the Lowlands who rose to power in the Highlands, and there would always be those who fell.

Charles stopped and seemed to lock eyes with the man at the top of the bench. Jacob assumed they would stand there until formally addressed. Instead, Charles's voice filled the hall.

"Archibald Jones."

The name hung in the air. Jacob and Alice glanced at each other and then stared at the man at the head of Bollwerk, the man who'd written *The Dead Scourge*.

✧ ✧ ✧

SILENCE REIGNED AFTER CHARLES MADE his pronunciation until one of the women on the lower bench stood. "You dare address Bollwerk's Speaker so casually, outlander?"

"Outlander?" Charles laughed and crossed his arms. "Yes, I dare." He raised his eyes from the woman and addressed the Speaker directly. "Archibald, if you mean to let your Biomechs tear us apart, then have at it. If not, I'd like to hear why you've attacked Ancora."

A rumbling of questions and curses and disbelief replaced the silence of the audience.

Charles slid his backpack off and pulled out the somewhat sour sack he'd carried in from Bull's Horn. "You look surprised, old friend. Allow me to change tack." He untied the satchel lifted the gory, crusted bit of a

Sky Needle. "Do you see this? You know what it is?"

Whispers and outrage met his question.

"*Do you know what this is?*" Charles's voice had grown low, dangerous.

Jacob watched in horror as the guards around the pillars stepped forward, each leveling something like Charles's air cannon at them. His heart lurched, and he tried to find an escape route, somewhere they could run, but there wasn't a chance in hell they could make it back to the lift and close the doors.

"If you're going to shoot, shoot," Charles said. "Otherwise, answer the goddamned question, Archibald." He threw the gory piece of technology forward, and it left a slimy trail as it slid across the wooden floor. "You're the only other man who knows the frequencies. I never told anyone else. *Now answer me.*"

Archibald froze for only a moment—his eyes on the metal bar mounted in the carapace—before he leaned back and set his hands on the bench. "Stand down. Guards, stand down. Charles, I would advise you to be more respectful in the Temple of the Steamsworn."

The tension relaxed in Samuel's shoulders when the guards lowered their weapons and returned to their posts. The Spider Knight had been ready to fight, ready to kill, even against impossible odds.

"Understand now," Archibald said, "the only reason you're not on your way to one of the brigs in the warships is because of our history and what you did for our allies in the past."

Charles crossed his arms and stared at Archibald. Jacob had always known the old man could be stubborn as a grumpy Pilly, and he was clearly not impressed by Archibald.

"Speaker," Charles said, and Jacob cringed at the mockery in his voice, "could you enlighten us as to your reasons for all but declaring war on Ancora? The only reason I say you haven't is that I know any one of your warships could wipe Ancora from the earth."

Archibald laughed, and it grew louder before dying away. "You haven't changed a bit, Charles, rash and prone to violence. We're all more gray up top," he said as he ran his hand over his hair, "but that hasn't changed us so much as I expected."

Rash? Jacob thought, trying to fit the Charles he knew into the person Archibald had described. Charles was methodical, almost careful. How could anyone call that rash? Maybe confronting the Speaker in his own hall had been a bit rash, though.

"If it were me," Archibald said, leaning forward, "or my men, do you think we too would be cut off from the medicines of Dauschen? Answer me that, Charles. If we had become the monsters, why would we accept their embargo?"

Charles frowned, and almost whispered, "Why indeed."

"We are not a violent people. That doesn't mean we won't defend ourselves. We'll defend our city from whatever the desert brings to our doorstep. Even you."

The two men stared at each other until the guards grew restless again.

"We have to stop Dauschen," Charles said.

"Dauschen?" Archibald raised his eyebrows. "So, you don't know …"

"Know what?" Charles asked as he took a step forward. The guards between the pillars shifted their halberds, setting them at an angle where they could strike Charles down in a heartbeat. "What aren't you telling me?"

"Fel, on the far side of the trade routes. They've conquered Dauschen, Charles. Most of its people are dead, and the few who survive are traitors to their own city or prisoners. We've taken in a handful of defectors, and the stories are terrible."

"Fel?" Charles frowned and turned to Samuel. The Spider Knight shrugged slightly and Charles gave a tiny shake of his head. Jacob barely caught his whisper of, "I don't think it was Bollwerk."

"Who then?" Drakkar asked aloud, breaking the silence. "If it was not the only other man who knows this *technology*, who would have done it? Who *could* have done it?"

"There is no one else," Archibald said. "The only men with enough skill are in this room. Except ... no ..." Archibald said before he and Charles locked gazes. The name came at once, synchronized between the two men as though they shared the thought.

"The Butcher."

CHAPTER TEN

A COLLECTIVE INTAKE OF BREATH turned the entire room into a hiss before it exploded with shouts and cries of anger. Archibald tried to speak, but the cacophony drowned out his words. He lifted a modest hammer and struck it against a thin bell mounted in the bench. The sound boomed and rang through the hall, bringing silence in its echoing wake. The crowd fidgeted and all eyes turned to the Speaker.

"This session is at a close. Please make your way to the nearest exit."

Whispers filled the room and curious eyes watched Charles as they walked past. Archibald waited until most of the hall was clear before he spoke. "We should have been more tactful in bringing up that monster's name." He sighed and squeezed his forehead before speaking to the guard beside him. "Please leave me to consult with the Outlanders."

"Are you sure that is safe, Speaker?"

"They are not the enemy."

The guard nodded before leading the bottom tier of Biomechs—apparently Archibald's guards—out of the room. Jacob stared after them, admiring the bronze legs and intricate limbs rebuilt from rods and pistons. The precision gear ratios it would take to get a leg to walk like a human's leg boggled his mind. It seemed an impossible task, yet here they were.

Were those Biomechs meant to guard the Speaker from Charles, or from Archibald's own people? Jacob was surprised at the violent response to the Butcher's name. The man was clearly a threat, and he wondered if the people of Bollwerk knew more than he and Alice had learned in their time reading *The Dead Scourge*.

When Jacob turned around, Archibald was alone. He took a deep breath before standing and making his way down off the bench. Archibald disappeared behind the towering construct, only to reappear at its side before joining Charles and the others.

Charles held out his fist, and Archibald eyed it for a moment before wrapping his fingers over it in the greeting of the Steamsworn.

"What brings you here, old friend?" Archibald asked.

"The destruction of the Lowlands," Charles said, his expression steel.

"That was a rumor I hoped was only a rumor."

"How did the Butcher learn to use this technology?" Charles didn't give Archibald time to answer. "Every day that passes raises that madman's death toll."

"What can we do about it, Charles?" Archibald asked. "Level Ancora to kill one man? Start a war that will kill thousands, tens of thousands, to stop him? And no, I don't know how he knows about the transmitters."

"Help us, Archibald," Charles said. "Help us turn the tide in Dauschen. Send some of your people with us, and we may yet triumph. With people from Ancora *and* Bollwerk traveling together, they'll be more likely to believe we all defected. It will be a simple thing to plant new spies inside the city."

"How? How will sending Bollwerks to Dauschen change anything?"

"If we can convince the Butcher that the loyalty to the Steamsworn is cracking, he may lower his guard. He's always feared the strength of Bollwerk. Why do you think he didn't try to forward his agenda here?"

"If ..." Archibald leaned against the nearest pillar, crossed his arms, and looked at the floor. Jacob thought they could have heard the needle of a cactus hit the wood floor in that deafening silence. After a time, Archibald looked up.

"I will not order our people into your service, Charles. You have my respect, and the respect of the Steamsworn, but what you ask could lead to much violence."

"I know," Charles said. He exhaled, seeming to deflate as the breath left his lungs.

"That said, I will not stop our people from helping you. If they wish to travel to Dauschen to help you in your ruse, it will be their own decision."

"Thank you," Charles said as he inclined his head.

Archibald nodded.

"How can we get past the Burning Forest and through the mountain pass?" Drakkar asked.

"How many are you hoping to take?" Archibald asked.

"To create the illusion of a mass defection?" Charles asked. "I hope we can take fifty or more."

"You could fit fifty on an airship," Samuel said.

Archibald shook his head. "The pilots are all loyal Steamsworn, and our enemies know that. Arriving in an airship would give you away."

"A caravan, then," Drakkar said. "Carriages and Walkers can make that journey."

"What about the crawlers?" Jacob asked. "It seems like those could drive over just about anything."

Archibald frowned. "That's not a bad idea, but I can't send them all. And then, even with all the crawlers of Bollwerk at your disposal, you couldn't carry all the people and their luggage."

Drakkar nodded. "I agree, Speaker. I can gather a team of riders, with your approval."

"Sir?" Alice asked.

Archibald turned to look at her after a moment, apparently slow to realize *he* was the sir she was asking after. "Yes?"

"You were at Gareth Cave?"

Archibald's smile died. "Yes. I was."

"What you wrote, about the Butcher? That all happened?"

Archibald nodded. "That and much more, I'm afraid. We turned that awful place into a shrine. I don't think that was in the book. Maybe it was. I have a hard time remembering some things.

"It was good of you to do that," Charles said. "Those people should not be forgotten."

"Neither should your brother," Archibald said.

The two men watched each other for a time. Sometimes there are no words.

Alice turned Jacob by his shoulders so she could root through his backpack. She held up *The Dead Scourge*, and Archibald's eyes widened.

"Where on earth did you find that, young one?"

"This *is* your writing, isn't it?"

Archibald nodded.

"Then why? Why let the Butcher live?"

He gestured for the book, and Alice handed it to him. "I wrote this shortly after the war. Some of it I wrote during the war. War changes a place. It brings out the darkest parts of a land, just as sure as it brings out the darkest parts of its people."

Archibald glanced up and then started rifling through the pages. "When I wrote this, all I knew was death. My friends had died, my enemies had died, and my homeland was in the process of declaring us outlaws to be struck from the history of our own city. I'd had enough of death."

"The Forgotten have never been erased from Ancora's memory," Charles said.

"I always assumed I had the last copies of these." Archibald closed *The Dead Scourge* and handed it back to Alice. "Where did you find it?"

Alice hesitated before spinning Jacob around to put the book away again.

"It was the old train station, underneath the city," Jacob said.

"The what?" Archibald wrinkled his forehead. "I don't remember an underground platform in Ancora."

"From the old train route," Charles said. "They built it into a cavern so they didn't have to breach the walls. It's by the old catacombs."

Archibald shook his finger. "I recall something about that. They tried to build a subterranean rail, like the one in Fel."

Charles nodded. "Until they found the nest of Red Death. That was the end of that."

"They never finished it?"

"No, they barred it off and sealed most of the entrances. Some of the old stores are still there, and that's where they found your book. It was probably just collecting dust for the past forty years."

"Amazing. Just amazing."

"Not as amazing as those airships," Jacob said. "I've never seen one so large."

"Charles has," Archibald said. "He helped me design the metalwork."

"What?" Jacob asked. "How? You didn't have airships like that when Charles was here. Did you?" He looked at Charles.

The old man wore a sheepish grin. He glanced at Jacob and said, "Oh, come now, you know I can't resist a good challenge. I may have met with Archibald once or twice over the years."

"Once or twice," Archibald said with a smile. "We'll leave it at that. Now, you may not be able to take the airships to Dauschen without raising suspicions, but that doesn't mean we can't take the kids up for a time."

Jacob looked to Charles, hoping almost more than anything that the old man would agree to it.

"I don't know …"

Alice slapped her hands together and pleaded with her eyes. Drakkar laughed as Charles visibly caved in.

The old man sighed and looked up at the ceiling. "Gods, I hate flying.

Can you at least fly us over the old city?"

"Me?" Archibald asked. "Gods no, I can't stand flying." He winked at Jacob. "I'll send you up with the best pilot we have. Be nice to her, or she may toss you over the side. We'll get a crawler to take you over to the docks."

"Do you sell tickets for this blasted thing?" Charles asked. "How does that work?"

"Show them your medal, and tell the pilot that the Speaker has requested you get an aerial tour of the old city."

"Why do I think I'm going to regret this?" Charles asked.

Archibald gave him a dazzling smile.

CHAPTER ELEVEN

THERE WERE NO SIGNS OF the crowd, or the panic that had gripped them, when Jacob stepped off the lift and onto the first floor. Everything seemed normal on the streets. No one screamed or ran away as the guards loaded the group's luggage onto the same crawler that had dropped them off.

No one said anything until they pulled away from the curb. The driver, Dr. Jones this time, turned around and glanced at Charles. "You cheated."

"What?" Charles asked.

"You know my father. That's how you knew who I was."

"Oh, he may have shown me a photograph once or twice over the years, Dr. Jones."

The driver laughed as he pulled the steering levers and veered onto another street. "Call me Walter."

"You toyed with this man for what end?" Drakkar asked. No accusation lived in his words; it seemed more an honest curiosity.

"I was rather hoping he'd tell his father about the nice group of people he'd met. I figured Archibald would put two and two together."

"He did," Walter said. "You're just lucky he didn't come up with six."

"What?" Samuel asked. "What does that mean?"

"I'm guessing it means we're lucky Archibald didn't decide we were a threat and have the Biomechs turn us into a snack for the Fire Lizards."

"Oh no," Walter said. "That would be cruel. They probably would have taken you up in an airship and dropped you in the middle of the desert without any supplies. Die a warrior's death."

He turned slightly in the driver's seat and said, "Where was it I'm taking you again?"

"The docks," Charles said.

Drakkar released a loud sigh.

"Don't worry," Walter said with a laugh. "Mary will treat you right. She's the best pilot we have."

The reality of their situation began to sink after the next turn. "We're going up in an airship," Jacob said.

Alice looked at him and blinked. "Did you just figure that out? Just now?"

Jacob smiled and smacked her leg with the back of his hand. "Shut up."

She slouched down in her seat and looked toward the sky. "Look at them, Jacob."

The crawler bounced onto the rougher cobblestones leading to the base of the airship docks, and Jacob stared. One of the warships was gone, leaving a monstrous gap between the floating platforms high overhead. The other still hovered there, eclipsing the sun and leaving them in shadows.

"The men of Cave were not made for flying," Drakkar said.

"If I'm going up in one of those damn things," Charles said, "you are too."

"If I were another man, I would laugh at those words, Charles. As it is I who must ascend into the clouds, I find your humor weak."

Walter slowed the crawler down when they reached the crowds milling around the vendor stalls at the base of the airship docks. People moved out of the way quickly enough, but the crawlers and carriages were far outnumbered by the pedestrians.

"Alright," Walter said, "take the first lift to the top. You'll only see two ships up there. Look for the smaller one with a bronze nose. If you're not sure, ask for Mary."

"What about our luggage?" Samuel asked.

"Good gods, you people worry about your luggage in Ancora, don't you?" Walter smiled and patted the back of the leather passenger seat. "I'll take it to the hotel. It'll be in your rooms when you get back."

"Which hotel?" Charles asked.

"Probably the Burning Bed, but I'll know for sure when I pick you up."

Charles nodded and slid out of the crawler after Samuel. They all followed the old man to the lift, Alice stopping to wave at Walter before he vanished behind the crowds.

"The Burning Bed?" Samuel said. "That's a terrible name for a hotel."

"Everything here is about stuff being on fire," Alice said as she looked around at the sprawl of vendors.

"Once you have been in the city at high noon in the dead of summer, you will understand why," Drakkar said. "It is much like being set on fire."

"It's kind of like Festival," Jacob said.

"Being set on fire?" Alice asked with a sideways grin.

"It's a bit like Festival," Charles said, "but they're far less tolerant of thieves here. Keep your hands in your pockets. We don't need that kind of attention."

Jacob wanted to say something about how the thought hadn't crossed his mind, but it had, so he just nodded.

The vendors here peddled almost every imaginable food and gadget Jacob could think of. Some of their tents seemed to be the size of buildings, stocked to the canopy with raw copper and brass and machinations. One man sold scrap metal that he'd turned into tiny models of airships and Fire Lizards. Another sold windup toys—some of the larger ones looked like soldiers that would run and flip and spark. Only the parents of the wealthier kids were buying those. Jacob could tell they were wealthy by their fine dresses and shoes so polished they glowed in the sunlight.

Those were marks. Back home, when they needed food or money the most, those were the people he'd steal from. Here, he only walked past them, observing the spread of peddlers and pedestrians until they arrived at the lift.

It had taken longer than he thought. The sheer size of the airship docks made them appear closer than they actually were. Jacob tilted his head to the skies, and plain excitement warred with dread, looking at that impossibly tall tower.

Charles slid the gate to the lift open and stepped inside. Once everyone was in, Drakkar pulled it shut and threw the lever up. The lift jerked once and then sped toward the skies.

"It's fast!" Alice said.

Jacob and Samuel both put their arms out to catch their balance.

Samuel groaned and looked at his feet. "Why do they always put grated floors in lifts?"

Jacob looked down at the earth falling away beneath them. He wasn't afraid of heights, but he could understand how the vision of the world rapidly turning into ants would be unwelcome to someone who was.

Drakkar stared at the solid ceiling of the lift. Two small lights on the copper roof were the only feature, dimming as the lift slowed and eventually came to a halt. Drakkar sighed and spared Jacob a smile before he slid the gate open. He struck out with a purpose, and Jacob knew it couldn't be easy for him.

Jacob stepped onto the dock and froze. He could feel it shifting slightly beneath his feet, and his hands wrapped around the tall, thick railing on instinct alone.

"It shifts with the wind," Drakkar said. "Do not worry."

Charles grumbled as he followed Alice out onto the dock. "They balance it, and maintain the floats to keep the stress off the steel and iron. Never get used to it. Never." Charles ran his hand along the railing, pausing briefly to look back over the city.

"Now *this* is where we should launch the glider from," Jacob said as he glanced at Charles.

"Oh, gods," Samuel said. "You're insane, kid."

"Falling off the wall would have killed you just as much as falling of these docks," Charles said, "but that glider would have to work flawlessly for a much longer stretch of time."

"We brought it," Jacob said with a grin.

"Yes, well, we're not going to jump off something that's four times the height of the city wall yet. That's a good way to get dead."

Alice leaned over the railing. "It's a long way down."

Jacob's retort to Charles died in his throat when Alice wrapped her fingers around his arm.

"I think that's our ship."

He looked to where she pointed. There, beside one of the behemoth warships, waited a sleeker airship with sweeping lines that just *looked* fast. Alice pulled him forward, and he didn't hesitate to match her pace.

"We're actually going up in an airship," Alice said. "I've never been in anything more than one of the balloons they have at Festival sometimes."

"My dad took me on a trip around the city wall once," Jacob said. "Back when Dauschen used to bring airships in."

"I think *this* is going to be better," Alice said.

CHAPTER TWELVE

THE SHEER MASS OF THE warships impressed Jacob, and the enormous cannons spread across the decks in sets of three, but something about the little ship with the sharp bronze nose called to him.

"It almost looks like a spearhead," Jacob said.

"That has to be it," Alice said with a glance at the ship beside it. "They both kind of have a bronze nose, but that one's definitely smaller."

Charles cupped his beard and eyed the airship. "I'm surprised it gets enough lift with such a small gas chamber."

Something clanged against the metal dock, and Jacob turned to see a woman walking toward them. She wore dark leather overalls with a black utility belt cinched around her waist. A smear of black grease stained her dark skin, and she wiped her hands on a dirty towel before stuffing it into a pocket.

"Just have to keep the balance right." She tipped her head to Charles, and Jacob saw the pilot's goggles over her close-trimmed hair. "She can be a bit bumpy in high winds, but she can manage almost any storm."

"Do you know where we can find the pilot?" Charles asked.

"I think she is the pilot," Jacob said.

"I like the boy," she said with a wide smile. It surprised Jacob how warm the expression was. With the tools and dirt strapped onto her, he expected someone a bit more … hostile.

"They call me Skysworn Mary."

"Apologies, Mary," Charles said. "No disrespect meant."

She waved her hand in dismissal.

"Skysworn?" Drakkar asked. "I have not heard this term before."

"Don't fret yourself about it," Mary said. "Some Councilman screamed at me one day about being more loyal to the sky than the Steamsworn. One of my crew put the two together. I hated the damn name at first, but it grew on me. Fact is, we named the old girl Skysworn."

"The ship?" Jacob asked. He liked Mary's story, even if it seemed a bit of a ridiculous way to name an airship, but it fit. "Is that why you have the Dragon wings on your emblem?"

Mary glanced back at the wide circle with four insect wings springing from a bronze fist. She nodded. "It is indeed. Enough with the pleasantries. Archibald told me to take you up in the Skysworn, and that's just what I aim to do."

She ushered the group toward the gangplank. The instant Jacob's feet were off the dock and up on the metal plank, he could feel the subtle movements of the airship. He kept one hand on the chain railing as he made his way across behind Alice.

"You all are welcome in the cockpit, so long as you don't touch things." Mary didn't so much as pause before she swung open an iron door with a round porthole and vanished inside. "And pull the gangplank up when everyone's across. Don't need to be tearing a hole in the old girl."

Drakkar and Samuel stood on the other side of the plank while Charles joined Jacob and Alice. The old man looked back to the odd pairing of the cloaked guardian and the armored Spider Knight and smiled.

"For two supposedly brave warriors, you look like schoolchildren panicked about a game of Cork." Charles glanced at Jacob. "Actually, the schoolchildren are faring much better than you two."

Drakkar took a deep breath and crossed the plank in three quick strides, stretching each step as far as he could. The guardian took a deeper breath when he reached the lightly swaying deck of the Skysworn.

"And I thought the Tower was a bad idea," Samuel said, following in Drakkar's footsteps. He glanced over the side of the gangplank and suppressed a shiver.

"Get the plank up!" Mary shouted from the cockpit.

"Where's the crank?" Samuel asked, biting off the words.

"Here," Drakkar said, reaching out to a wide iron ring with a post sticking out of it. "It must be this." He moved the old wheel, and it squeaked before it started spinning. The gangplank retracted into the hull with a few turns of the iron handle, and a solid metal railing rose to block off the edge of the deck.

"The gearing on that must be fantastic," Charles said. "Retracting the gangplank and raising the railing from one wheel? Fantastic."

Jacob slipped by the old man and Alice stayed close behind him. He pushed open the door to the cockpit and almost gasped. Mary stood before a massive wheel. A series of bent levers rose from the floor, and brass and copper gauges he could scarcely imagine a function for lined the windscreen of the Skysworn, embedded in a dark wood dash.

A tinny voice sounded from an array of horns extending from the ceiling. "Ready to disengage."

Mary pulled the horn down and said, "Do it."

There was a loud metallic pop from somewhere below deck, and the airship drifted to one side. Jacob didn't hear any more commands or see any cues, but a burst of steam rose up around the exterior of the cabin, and the Skysworn slowly backed away from the dock.

The city fell away as they rose, and Mary spun the wheel to keep the airship on a gradual turn. Jacob stepped closer to Alice, who had her face nearly on the windscreen, and put his arm around her shoulders.

She leaned against him slightly and then pointed into the distance while Mary shouted commands back and forth with the tinny voice on the horn. A trail of dust billowed into the air, miles outside of the wall. Jacob couldn't tell if it was a beast or some machination from Bollwerk, but it moved impressively fast.

The airship tilted, and then started forward. Mary steered it easily around the docks.

Jacob stared at the warship as they passed by, the cabins, the deck, and the sheer girth of the gas chamber.

"That's quite a sight to behold," Charles said. He opened the wide porthole and stuck his head out. "Truly a feat."

"It is a terrifying feat," Drakkar said. "I do not like the fact that men hold enough power in their hands to level a city. Not even Bollwerk's walls could withstand those cannons."

"Not to mention the fact they're on an airship," Samuel said. "Don't have to worry about walls at that point."

"No, you don't." Drakkar frowned as they passed one of the remote turrets before turning back to the inside of the cabin. Jacob watched Drakkar for a time, wondering why a man who had dedicated his life to fighting would frown at a more powerful weapon. A stronger weapon meant less fighting—at least, that's what his dad always said. He wondered about his parents and hoped they were still okay.

"Where to, ladies?" Mary asked.

Alice looked away from the window and laughed, stepping closer to Mary. "Jacob's hair *has* gotten a bit long."

"Hey …"

Charles smiled and ruffled Jacob's hair.

"You don't have room to talk, old man," Alice said.

"She seems so nice," Charles said, "and then she stabs you in the heart. I need to keep my hair long so when it catches on fire, I have some left."

Mary turned toward Charles and raised her eyebrow. "I couldn't even tell you were lying." She rubbed her hands together and grinned. "I don't think we'll be playing cards anytime soon."

"Smart," Samuel said. "Charles has more of my silver than Parliament. That's saying something."

"It's not like I didn't warn you," the old man said.

Samuel crossed his arms and smiled.

"Can we go to the old city?" Jacob asked, bringing everyone's attention to him.

"The skeleton?" Mary asked. She frowned slightly and then smiled. "Well, that *is* quite the sight." She grabbed one of the horns and flipped a cover off it. "Jimmy." She waited a beat and then shouted, "Jimmy!"

"Yes, Captain!" Jimmy sounded winded and out of breath.

"Deploy the turbines. We're heading to the skeleton."

"Aye, Captain!"

"If you can handle the view from outside, Charles, you might want to watch this."

"Turbines? On an airship?"

"You don't get to be the fastest ship in the sky without taking chances."

Charles sighed and stared at the handle on the door. Jacob didn't hesitate. He pushed the discolored gray latch down and smiled as a blast of cool air streamed into the cockpit.

"You coming?" he asked.

Charles followed him out the door and onto the deck of the Skysworn.

Jacob paused at the railing and watched the vast, open world before them. He couldn't see the airship dock anymore. They'd already left it behind. Mountains rose off to the west, the desert sank below them, and a bright, towering horizon that paled to a bluish gray gleamed in front of them.

Something ground and whined below, and Jacob stared as a huge stretch of the hull rose outside the railing.

"Gods," Charles said as he walked toward the aft. He leaned over the railing, no longer seeming concerned with their immense altitude, and cursed. "They're insane."

"There's another one over here," Alice shouted from across the deck.

A second round cylinder rose near Alice. Two clamps the size of Jacob's leg arched out from the turbine and locked into place with a metallic clank.

"How can they control the pressure?" Charles asked. "On a turbine that big, a failure would tear half the ship apart. They'd have to integrate it into the skeleton, but how can they do that if they're moving?"

Jacob listened to Charles pondering the nature of the turbines for a while before he joined Alice.

"I've never seen anything like it," she said. The giant metal core began to spin faster and faster, and a low whine emanated with a concentrated blast of steam.

"Never," Jacob said. "We never would have seen this if we were still in Ancora."

Alice glanced at him before looking back to the turbine. "I hope our families are safe."

"Charles said they would be, so long as we weren't there. I think we did the right thing, leaving."

"I do too, but I still worry."

A brass horn rattled and clanked above them before Mary's voice came to life. "I'd recommend getting your butts back in the cockpit. We're about ready to go to speed."

"I don't know exactly what she means by that," Alice said, "but I'm going back in."

"Come on!" Charles shouted from across the deck. "If this does what I think it does, we do *not* want to be outside." He ushered Jacob and Alice back through the door where Samuel was gripping the back of a seat so tightly his knuckles were white.

"She said … she said …" Samuel couldn't finish his sentence.

"Hush," Mary said from a chair that hadn't been behind the wheel a few minutes ago. "Don't spoil the surprise. You three, grab a jump seat."

"A what?" Jacob asked.

"Here," Drakkar said, pulling up on a handle set into the floor. A thin metal sheet rose from the deck, and he pushed it back, revealing a seat and a harness.

Alice sat down and Drakkar showed her how to fasten the harness over her shoulders. It clipped into the seat between her legs and she wiggled a bit to adjust it.

Jacob pulled up the handle beside her, and the weight of the thin seat surprised him. He poked his head through the harness and fastened the straps between his legs. In front of him, he could see Mary, and beyond her the wide blue vista of the windscreen.

Mary glanced back, and Jacob figured she was making sure everyone was in their seats. She pulled down one of the horns and shouted into the brass mouthpiece. "Engaging thrusters in ten, nine, eight, seven, six, five, four—"

Jacob stretched his arm out and Alice grasped his fingers.

"—three—"

He smiled and took a deep breath as the Skysworn tilted forward slightly. Alice leaned back in her seat.

"—two—"

The turbines screamed outside the cockpit, and Jacob couldn't hear the last of the countdown. The thrust felt like someone pushing on his chest, holding him down. It slammed him into the back of his seat. Alice grabbed onto her harness and he did the same as the airship shook and accelerated. Mary pushed a wide lever forward, and the Skysworn rocketed ever faster toward the horizon, screaming Samuel and all.

CHAPTER THIRTEEN

"How do you keep the ship from tearing itself apart?" Charles asked when the pressure evened out and everyone's ears began to adjust to the change in altitude.

"I can hear you over the Spider Knight's whimpering now," Mary said. She winked at Samuel.

Samuel glared at her, but he didn't argue.

"The entire length of the gas chamber is reinforced," Mary said. "Even if we get a tear or a puncture, it won't collapse. Not like the old bags we used to fly."

"You don't have enough gas in the chambers to support a structure that heavy," Charles said.

Mary shook her head. "Don't have to. It's enough to keep us floating. The wings give us some extra lift with the main thrusters, and I'm not sure we'd need the gas at all when the turbines are going full speed."

"Madness," Charles said. "Beautiful madness."

Drakkar took a deep breath and blew it out slowly. "It is madness, my friend, but I do not know that I would call it beautiful."

"Our speed should stay constant for a while now," Mary said. "Feel free to take off the harness. If you want to step outside … don't."

"What if you need in-flight repairs?" Charles asked.

"We have tethers, but it's generally a good idea to wait until the old girl slows down a bit." Mary unbuckled her harness and stood up. "We'll be heading over the far range soon. You should stand up for this. You'll never see anything like it again."

"The mountains at the horizon?" Samuel asked. "We're already to them?"

"Almost. Keep your seats up. We'll need to strap in when the ship slows down. It's not the most gradual process."

Everyone unfastened their harnesses, even Samuel, and joined Mary at the windscreen.

They were high in the air, but the two mountains on either side stretched into the cloud bank overhead.

"The clouds are always here," Mary said. "Makes it hard to see if you're about to run into anyone, but I haven't yet."

Samuel groaned when their visibility dropped to almost nothing. The Skysworn shook and rattled as she skipped through the airstreams in the mountain pass.

"None of you have seen the old bones, have you?" Mary asked.

"I have," Charles said. He stared out the window. "Back before the war for the Deadlands."

"Trust me, old man, you haven't seen them like this."

The clouds thinned and then vanished in an explosion of golden sunlight.

"By the gods," Drakkar said. He placed his hand on the windscreen and leaned forward.

Jacob stared, awe warring with horror at the ruins of a city so large he could barely comprehend it. Even now, just past the mountains, they flew over the outlying area where ancient roads peeked through layers of grass and brush. Farther out, towers of iron and brick and stone reached into the sky, but it felt wrong. It felt dead.

"What happened here?" Jacob asked.

"We don't really know," Mary said. "I knew a man that lived in the old shell for a while, deep inside the skeleton. He said they built a bomb so large it killed the world." Mary shrugged. "Maybe that's how it happened, and maybe not. Take your seats and strap yourselves in. We're going to slow this girl down."

Everyone sat, silent in the wake of seeing the old city. They clicked their harnesses together as Mary took her seat and opened one of the horns.

"Pull it back, Jimmy. We're going to circle the city and head home."

"Aye, Captain."

Mary glanced back and said, "Just let the harness do its work. Don't want you breaking your fingers off."

Jimmy's voice started a countdown over the horn, and as soon as he reached zero, Mary throttled the thrusters back.

Jacob yelped as his body slid forward, slamming into the harness as though the airship had run into a wall. He could hear the whine of the turbines lower in pitch before the Skysworn's cabin rocked forward and slightly up.

The pressure lifted from his chest in an instant, and he could breathe easily once again. He glanced at Alice. She stared out the windscreen. When he followed her gaze, he almost cursed. The old buildings looked so close that he could reach out and touch them. Vines and foliage wrapped around and through the ancient structures.

"It's safe to stand up now," Mary said.

"Look at them," Samuel said as he joined Mary at the window.

"They form colonies in certain towers. We don't really know why, but most of the bugs keep to themselves."

Jacob could see the beetles when he stood up, the glint on their long horns a dead giveaway in the sunlight. One tower looked to be coated in them as if they were sunbathing on the old structure. They weren't Red Death; they were the docile creatures used as beasts of burden in Ancora to pull carriages and wagons alike.

Far below the towers were the old roads. The altitude made the roads hard to see, but they looked gray and cracked, and some parts looked to be nothing more than sand and weeds.

Mary steered them closer to one of the tallest towers. One lone pane of glass remained in the side. Most of the stonework had fallen away, left in a sloping pile of debris at the base of the tower.

"I want to show you the old ironwood," Mary said. "It's just around the tower."

Not a minute passed before they made the slow turn, and the largest tree Jacob had ever seen filled the window in front of them. Mary pushed a lever and the Skysworn lowered a bit, swooping toward the tree before she leveled it out.

"Does it have a name?" Alice asked.

"Not really. We just call it the old ironwood."

"You could build a city from that one tree," Drakkar said. "Or so the old stories go."

"I don't think it's quite that big," Charles said, "but it *is* massive."

"Can we land?" Jacob asked. "I just … I want to put my feet on the old city. See the tree up close."

Mary smiled and spun one of the wheels above her head. "The winds are light today. I think we can probably land without a problem." She popped the cover off one of the horns and shouted into it, "Jimmy, let off some heat. We're going to hover for a bit."

"Aye, Captain!" came the tinny response.

"We can't land here," Charles said. "It would take half a day just to get her off the ground again."

"Oh, come on." Mary elbowed Charles in the shoulder. "We won't *land* land. We'll get close enough to throw some lines out, and the kids can have fun sliding down them."

"The old man might not have so much fun sliding down them," Charles grumbled.

"Archibald thought you might turn into a fussy bastard," Mary said. She pulled a tray out from behind the main steering wheel.

"A fussy …" Charles narrowed his eyes.

Mary tossed a two-wheeled contraption at Charles and said, "I think those were your design."

The metal springs squeaked a little when Charles inspected them. "Belayers?"

"We just call them Wheels, but you can call them whatever you like."

Charles ran his finger around the large circular opening in the side of the belayer. Jacob studied the slide mechanism that would close the chamber off.

"That's for a Burner, isn't it?" Jacob asked.

Charles nodded. "How did he get the engine working so it wouldn't burn the ropes?"

"It'll singe them a bit if you run on a long enough rope," Mary said. "You won't have to worry about that today." She pulled out a roll of paper and held it out to Charles. "Archibald thought you might like to see how he did it."

Charles handed the Wheels to Jacob and unrolled the paper a bit. "Exploded diagrams," he said as he squinted at the figures. "Looks like he finally got his handwriting to be legible too. Never would have thought." His eyes roved over the pages for a minute before he looked up. "Brilliant." Charles rolled the diagram up and handed it back to Mary.

"Now you know why I need you each to take a Burner with you," Mary said. She slid the diagram back into its compartment and pulled out a steel box. She pulled the lid back to reveal a small mountain of tiny Burners.

"At least he didn't change the name on that invention," Charles said, plucking a Burner out of the box.

"He gives you credit for them, too," Mary said. "In case you were wondering."

Charles raised an eyebrow. "I wasn't, but that is quite kind of him." He pinched the Burner between his thumb and forefinger and held it up to the windscreen before dropping it into a pouch on his vest.

As Jacob pushed the door to the cockpit open, and the warm breeze above the skeleton rushed past him, he heard Charles whisper, "How safe is it here?"

"As safe as any part of the desert," Mary said. "I'll send Smith down with you, one of my fighters and my best mechanic, but be on your guard."

Outside the cockpit, Jacob heard the low chirps of the beetles below them.

"It's almost like they're singing," Alice said. She leaned on the railing, watching the tree and the tower of beetles beside it. The airship slowly glided closer to the tower and then passed it.

"Full stop!" Mary said from inside the cockpit. "Smith, up on deck."

Jacob heard something shift and clank beneath his feet before there was a quiet hum that joined the beetles' chirping. The Skysworn stilled, swaying slightly in the breeze, but showing almost no other signs of movement.

"What *is* that?" Alice asked, squinting into the distance.

It looked like a cloud of dust in the desert, just outside the tangle of the ruined city, but flashes of light sparked into being before vanishing a moment later.

Mary stepped out of the cockpit and placed both hands on the railing. She pulled a short brass tube out of a pocket on her black leather belt, and stretched it into a sizable scope. She moved it around a bit before focusing on a single point. "Fire Lizards, looks like nine or ten of them. It's probably a nest."

Mary handed the brass device to Alice.

Alice strafed the scope around the desert and gasped. "They're … they're breathing fire at each other."

Mary nodded. "One of the animal doctors, the vetra …" She frowned.

"Veterinarian," Charles said from behind them.

"That's it. One of the veterinarians thinks they do it to stay clean, gets rid of the parasites. They only seem to do it when they're in a nest, like it's a family thing."

Something creaked behind them, and Jacob turned to find a man lifting the main hatch on the deck behind the cockpit. He stood at least as tall as Drakkar when he straightened up, with slightly canted eyes and skin not so dark as Drakkar's. The man was twice as thick as the Cave Guardian, and it was all muscle.

"You're going down with the tourists, Smith."

"As you wish, Captain." Smith's voice was deep, and Jacob half expected it to echo like they were standing inside a cavern. Smith adjusted his black leather vest and hooked his thumbs into the waist of his shorts. He pulled a cabinet open on the wall and lifted out a pair of thick leathers.

Smith strapped the leathers over his legs and turned back to the railing. When Smith appeared beside him, Jacob was surprised to see two long blades tucked into his leathers. A strange vambrace ran the length of his right forearm, circled in bronzed tubes and etched with lettering in a language Jacob didn't recognize. A pair of guns hung in the holster at Smith's waist, and a bandolier of what looked like crossbow bolts rested on his shoulder.

"You keep gunpowder on board?" Jacob asked before he really thought about whether or not it was wise to ask Smith anything.

"Yes," Mary said before Smith could speak. "We do see pirates occasionally out in the Deadlands, and sometimes we need guns for the bugs."

Smith looked up at the sky. "It's high noon, Captain. If we're going down, now's the time to do it. The worst things should be asleep."

CHAPTER FOURTEEN

MARY NODDED AND LEANED DOWN to a coil of rope. The entire mass swiveled up from the deck until it was upright on the edge of the ship. A heavy metal anchor, that looked like a spear tip, dangled in the open air.

"Not a standard mount for landing lines," Charles said, crossing his arms. "Looks more like a boarding line you could launch with an air cannon."

Mary sighed and glanced at Charles. "Let me guess, you helped invent them."

Charles flashed her a broad grin. "You do what you must to survive in the Deadlands. I understand that." He stepped forward, flipped a clasp open on the wheel holding the rope, and then pulled a lever below it that Jacob hadn't even seen. "I may have seen them once or twice."

Jacob and Alice leaned on the railing and watched the rope unravel as it sped toward the earth. There was a whisper of heavy rope on steel before the anchor hit the desert below in a burst of dust. Jacob turned around in time to see Smith dropping landing lines on the other side as well.

"They aren't heavy enough to be anchors," Samuel said, looking over the edge of the airship.

"No," Mary said, "but they help us keep the ship centered and hovering. "Every little bit helps. You ready to take a ride?" She opened a footlocker below the ropes and pulled out a tangle of tightly woven black fabric. She peeled off parts of it and handed some out to everyone.

"These are your flight harnesses. Strap in, and make sure they're tight. Archibald won't be happy if I bring his friends back crushed into little pancakes."

"People don't really flatten out when they fall from a great height, you know," Charles said as he stepped into his harness. "We did experiments dropping … test subjects … off a cliff. Once they reach a certain speed, that's as fast as they get, and it's not fast enough to truly flatten out."

"You threw people off a cliff?" Mary asked. "To see if they'd turn into bloody pancakes?"

"Well," Charles said, "they were already dead. It sounds *much* worse when you say it out loud."

"Eww," Alice said. "That's just gross."

Charles offered her a weak smile. "You're certainly not wrong about that."

"Enough," Drakkar said, tightening his harness and picking up a set of Wheels from the deck. "We do not need to talk about falling from great heights when we are about to leap from an airship."

"Is everyone armed?" Mary asked. When Jacob and Alice shook their heads, Mary picked up a small assortment of narrow black cylinders. "These are collapsible crossbows. Same idea as the bolt thrower on Smith's wrist."

"You only have two shots in each cylinder," Smith said, "so do not miss."

Jacob took two of the crossbows, immediately sliding one into a deep pocket on his thigh. The other he looked more closely at. There was only one button amid the fine metal seams.

"Click the button to arm it," Mary said. "Click it again to fire. It has a counter spring that will reload once, and then you should probably run."

Jacob raised his eyebrows.

Mary smirked and swung a section of the bulkhead inward, leaving a clear path to the landing line. "Smith, go first. Show them how it's done."

The mountain didn't speak as he tugged on a black armored glove. He lined the rope up in one wheel's groove, pulled on the other spring-loaded wheel, and let it snap closed over the rope. He gave Mary a two-fingered salute … and jumped.

Smith howled like a three-year-old with a face full of Cocoa Crunch, and Jacob couldn't help but smile as he watched the massive man sail to the earth.

"Just pull the lever when you get close," Mary said. "That's your brake. Technically, you should be able to survive a drop without using it, but I wouldn't trust it. Same thing when you're coming back up. Load up a Burner and release the brake."

"Just like the lift poles back in the Lowlands," Alice said, looking away from Smith on the ground and back to Jacob. "At least you'll have a harness here."

Charles sighed and then grumbled as he hooked his own Wheels onto the dense rope. "Getting too old for this crap."

"You can always wait here," Mary said.

"I said *getting*, not got," Charles snapped as he checked his harnesses.

Mary chuckled and watched as Charles leaned over the edge. He cursed, took a deep breath, and stepped over the side. The old man remained silent while he streaked toward the earth. His beard caught the wind and half-blinded Charles on the way down, but he made it safely back to solid ground.

"You want to go next?" Jacob asked, turning to Alice.

She glanced at the rope and shook her head. "I want to watch at least one more person go." She pulled the spring-loaded wheel back and frowned. "It makes sense and all; I've just never done anything like that."

Jacob stepped forward and clipped his harness onto his Wheels before pulling the heavy spring back and setting the rope inside the guides.

He glanced over the edge and grinned. Smith and Charles were several stories below them. It really would be like jumping off something higher than the city wall, and without the glider this time.

"See you at the bottom," Jacob said. He jumped out. The rope pulled away from the Skysworn, following Jacob's arc, and then he let go, trusting the Wheels to guide him the rest of the way.

The blast of air wasn't unlike his trips down the lift pole back in Ancora, but here the air scraped at him with a dry, sandy heat. He squinted against the airborne grit as he got lower, switching from admiring the view across the wide plain and the ancient city to cursing about the dust in his eyes. About halfway down, he had the sense to lower his goggles.

"Idiot," he muttered to himself. A few more blinks cleared the dust, and then he could see between the old towers. Things moved in the distance, and the fact he couldn't be sure what they were unnerved him. Mary seemed to think it was safe enough, but when there were shadows shifting, you learned to expect the worst.

Jacob clamped down on the brake and his seemingly reckless descent evened out until he hit the sand with a soft thud. He unhooked his Wheels, clipped them onto his belt, and stepped away from the rope.

"You do not even seem disoriented," Smith said as Jacob joined him and Charles.

"There's a pole in Ancora I slide down sometimes." He looked up at the airship and shaded his eyes. "It was probably about half that height."

"At least," Charles said. "It's a wonder you never did more than twist your ankle."

Something moved in Jacob's peripheral vision, and his eyes snapped to the giant old ironwood tree. Charles and Smith kept talking, but Jacob kept his eyes on the low, sweeping branches until a happy scream caught his attention.

Jacob looked up and smiled. A trail of red hair twisted in the wind as Alice rode the Wheels and the rope down to the earth. The Skysworn looked small behind her, and it wasn't long until Alice braked and slowed before she landed on the sand beside the line.

"I'm ready to go again," Alice said. She shook out her hair and adjusted the denim pants she wore. "Is that why you always take the pole?"

"Might be," Jacob said.

Samuel followed next, cursing so loudly that they could hear him on the ground before he was even a quarter of the way down the rope. By the time he landed, Jacob had learned about fourteen new strings of swear words he never would have thought to put together.

"I feel like I just received an education from the most foul-mouthed professor ever to walk the land," Smith said.

"Ha!" Charles said, patting Smith's shoulder. "We do like to give him some grief."

"Sweet land. Sweet, sweet land." Samuel bent down on one knee, and Jacob wasn't sure if he was kissing the sand or just resting his forehead.

Drakkar followed Samuel down the rope in complete silence. The Wheels skimming on the rope made far more sound than the Cave Guardian himself.

Samuel looked up and glowered at Drakkar as he landed. "You didn't have to push me."

"You insisted on going before me, yet you would not move." Drakkar unlatched his Wheels and clipped them onto a rope belt beneath his cloak. "Mary instructed me to do so. Although, if one was to judge by the look on her face immediately afterward, she may have said it in jest."

Alice snorted a laugh and then covered her mouth.

Samuel sighed and looked at her. "You too?"

"How you can ride a Jumper," Charles said, "yet be so afraid of heights, I will never understand."

"That's different!" Samuel said as he pointed at Charles. "When I'm riding Bessie, I know she has enough sense not to make a misstep and fall of a cliff with me on her back. I don't have the same confidence in my own footing.”

"Your knights are a strange folk, tinker," Smith said.

Charles blew out a breath. "This is not the typical Spider Knight."

"You don't have to talk about me like I'm not standing right here," Samuel said. He started walking after Smith.

Jacob fell into pace beside Alice.

"Where are we going?" Alice asked.

Smith pointed off to one of the towers, and Jacob was *fairly* sure it wasn't the one being swarmed by beetles. At least he hoped it wasn't. Docile or not, that was too many bugs.

"There is an old tinker's shop there. I thought you may like to have a look around. See how the world used to look."

Charles frowned and crossed his arms as he slowed to a stop. "Sometimes the past is best left in the past."

"Let's go!" Jacob said. "Maybe you can find a new tool, or a blueprint or something."

Charles blew a breath out through his nose. "Fine, fine." He slowly relaxed his arms and matched Samuel's pace.

Something shifted in the old ironwood tree off to their left. Jacob glanced at the movement, but he saw only bark and leaves and the eerie shadows of the ancient tree—until it moved again.

"What the hell?" Jacob said, stepping under the tree's branches and starting toward the branch that seemed to move on its own. The shadows felt like a leafy cave. Jacob paused and stared at the dried-out tree branch before he took another step closer. It looked dead among the bright leaves of the ironwood tree. Maybe something had eaten away its leaves.

"Jacob!" An armored hand came up from behind him and grabbed his shoulder in a vise-like grip.

Jacob yelped and his heart pounded away in his chest. He glanced back to find Smith's left hand on his shoulder and his right fist extended toward the dead branch.

"Stay away. That is a Tree Killer."

The massive dead branch shifted again, and a pair of faceted eyes appeared in the dim light of the leafy cave. It lowered its head into another shadow and vanished, blending seamlessly with the bark of the ironwood.

"They are deadly creatures, but will normally not attack unless you wander too close."

"Ambush predators," Drakkar said. "I am surprised to see them here, and so well adapted."

"I as well," Smith said. "They normally stay in the forests." He kept his arm raised and walked Jacob backward, out of the tree's shade. "Let's keep a reasonable distance from that tree."

"Kind of hard to do when it's grown over the entire area," Samuel said. He glanced up at the branch arching over the party's heads.

Smith glanced back at everyone, wearing a strange expression. Jacob wasn't sure why until the Bollwerk lifted his collar and held a button down. "Mary, come in."

Something crackled to life on Smith's shoulder. "Are you concealed?"

"No, I'm with the group."

"Goddammit, Smith, I told you not to show our hand."

"There are Tree Killers in the old ironwood."

"What? *What?* Get them back here *now.*"

"There aren't many, Mary. I will keep them safe."

"You damn well better. I'll keep watch from above. I'll be the least of your worries if something happens to Charles. Archibald will flay your hide and then let the Fire Lizards cremate the rest."

The static from the speaker on Smith's shoulder died. He grimaced and folded his collar down.

"Did you get that from Archibald?" Charles asked.

Smith didn't hesitate before he nodded.

"That's the same technology we used in the war. Same wavelength as the transmitters used to overrun Ancora during the Fall, if I'm not mistaken."

Jacob's legs locked up and he stared at the mountain in front of him.

Smith sighed and looked back at Samuel. "It was not us."

"Why did you try to hide it from us, then?" Alice asked. "It's not that I don't believe you, because I honestly don't see how you'd benefit from an invasion of Ancora."

"And what do you know of politics and the maneuvers of war?" Smith asked.

"I read *The Dead Scourge*," Alice said. "Jacob did, too. We know Bollwerk didn't build the warships to invade another city. They were built to protect your own walls in case Ancora declared war on *you*, or Dauschen, or Fel.

"Your entire city has flourished by trade, not by war."

Smith stared at Alice for a moment while he walked. "Those are not the words used in *The Dead Scourge*. You are wise for one so young, and you are correct."

Jacob wondered how in the world Alice had gotten *that* from *The Dead Scourge*. He was already on his second read through, and he hadn't picked up on all of that.

"So why hide it?" Samuel asked. "Are you afraid Ancora will adopt it? Some of the knights in the Highlands already have it, but I'm guessing you knew that. Or at least guessed it, since Charles is with us."

Smith nodded and said, "We hide it because we are not supposed to have the technology. Archibald and the Council have outlawed it in times of peace."

"We won't speak of it," Charles said. "I'll try to put Mary's mind at ease when we get back. What's the punishment for possession?"

"She would be stripped of her ship. For her, she may as well be dead."

"Why would she risk it if she could lose her ship?" Jacob asked. "I don't get it."

"Because, they are pirates," Drakkar said with a wide grin.

Smith exhaled loudly, and it almost sounded like a growl.

"Oh, cool!" Jacob said. "We know pirates."

Smith slapped himself in the face with his palm. "I will never hear the end of this."

CHAPTER FIFTEEN

O NCE THEY'D LEFT THE SHADE of the old ironwood tree behind, the sun felt like an open flame. Air rose from the sands and blasted them with a terrible heat.

"This is awful," Jacob said. "It's so hot. I should be sweating, but I'm just hot."

Alice lifted the canteen to her mouth that Smith handed her. "Still cold, so good."

"We are here," Smith said as he took the canteen back.

Jacob looked up at the tower. The upper floors were gone, only rusted iron remained to reach into the sky like a dead hand, but the bottom few floors were intact.

"This is one of the few that collapsed outward," Smith said. "You can see the stone and glass around the sides of the structure. Several of the buildings collapsed inward, destroying their contents completely. Many more are tangled rubble beneath the sands."

A small path had been carved through the rubble, leading up to the entrance. Someone had built a rough wooden door and mounted it in the old doorway. A trail of rubble, higher near the door, gradually spread into the old broken street.

"What's the street made out of?" Jacob asked. "It doesn't look like cobblestones or bricks. It's all jagged."

Charles paused and studied part of the street that wasn't buried under the desert sands. "I'm not sure. It looks like small stones held together in some kind of gray mortar."

"It is called concrete," Smith said. He pulled the wooden door open.

"How do you know that?" Charles asked. "Is that the name the pirates came up with?"

Smith didn't even flinch at the tone of the question. "No, it is in the old books. What few survived the end of this place."

"Book?" Charles asked, his voice changing to open curiosity.

"Books," Smith said, emphasizing the plurality of his statement. "They are stored in the old tinker's shop. Come."

Smith held the door open for everyone. Jacob entered last, and Smith pulled the door closed behind him. A little light crawled into the room from the clear desert skies, but it wasn't until Smith ignited two lamps that they could really see.

Ten workbenches and a hundred tools Jacob couldn't imagine a use for filled the massive room. Giant metal beasts with jagged points and levers and saws danced in the flickering lamplight. The floors reflected the lamps where they weren't obscured by dust, like a polished stone.

"What is this place?" Charles asked. "This is no tinker's lab. There is space for fifty men to work."

"We believe it is where they built the bomb," Smith said.

"That doesn't fit the stories," Charles said. "The bomb they speak of is said to have destroyed the world. A payload unlike anything the earth had ever seen."

Smith bent down to a small gray box and spun the dial in an alternating panel. Jacob didn't realize it was a safe until he heard a click and the door swung open. "We found the combination carved into the workbench by the bones of a tinker."

When Smith stood up, he gingerly held an ancient book. Yellow pages looked like a strong breeze might cause them to fall apart. "This is some of what we found."

Charles took the book from Smith and laid it on the nearest workbench.

"There are a few more books," Smith said. "The rest are so much dust."

"How many were there?" Alice asked.

Smith glanced down at her. "There is a roomful of lost knowledge farther out in the skeleton. We only found fifteen books and a few manuscripts that were still intact. A handful were in a language we understand. Do you know these letters?"

"This is a journal," Charles said as he opened the cover. "And yes, I know these letters. It's a dead language. I doubt you'd know the name."

"If it is like the others, there is knowledge in that journal no man should have," Smith said.

"Why me?" Charles asked. "Why not destroy the books?"

"I know of your legend, Charles von Atlier. I know what you lost to the war, and I know what you would do to prevent it. What if there are great things hidden behind the madness in that journal?"

Charles frowned slightly and turned his attention back to the book. "If you know so much about me, you know that I've done things I'm not proud of."

"We all have, Steamsworn. We all have."

Jacob kept listening to the banter between Charles and Smith with one ear while he walked toward the other side of the room with Alice. Smith wasn't nearly old enough to have been around in the Deadlands War, but he sure seemed to know a lot about it. Drakkar and Samuel stayed near the door, fiddling with one of the upright machines that looked like some kind of saw, but bigger than anything Jacob had seen before.

"How can a whole city just disappear?" Alice asked. "Someone must have survived whatever happened here, don't you think?"

"Maybe," Jacob said. He ran his hand over the nearest workbench. A series of tensioners stuck out in alternating patterns. He opened each one up, trying to envision the design of what they were used to create, but there didn't seem to be a pattern at all. "What would they have used this for?"

"An assembly line?" Alice asked.

Jacob almost smacked himself. "Of course. The bench is wide enough for three or four men to work. Can you imagine a room this big full of tinkers? The things they could have built?"

"It's like a carpenter's workshop and tinker's lab all rolled into one," Alice said. "Look at those saws."

When Jacob turned to look at the room again, keeping the idea of an assembly line at the forefront of his thoughts, the layout made much more sense. The blacksmiths and the tinkers and the woodworkers would have assembled their various parts and builds before the last of the workers finished whatever the other men had created.

A bluish square caught Jacob's eye. He turned and stared at the faded photograph on the wall. There was sand, yes, but beyond the sand waited a blue infinity. "What is this?" he asked, pointing to the photograph.

"That is the ocean, my friend," Drakkar said. He stepped up behind Jacob and Alice. "Far to the southeast, beyond the barren wastes, is the closest ocean I know of."

"Some of the airship pilots used to talk about the ocean when they came to Ancora," Alice said. "They had stories of islands full of treasure and ancient ships that used to sail the seas."

"Now we have ships to sail the skies," Drakkar said. "It is different, yes, but not so very different. We still have pirates, after all."

Smith shot Drakkar a sour grin.

"Are there more floors here?" Jacob asked.

Drakkar nodded. "There are, but they are not so well protected. With Tree Killers around, there are likely Widow Makers, and those darker shadows are the sort of place they would nest."

Jacob didn't bother to ask to see the second floor after that revelation.

He'd seen enough Widow Makers to last him a lifetime in the Fall, and then in their escape from Ancora. He followed Alice around the room for a while, poking and prodding at the strange tools set up around the tinker's shop, until he found a workbench with an arrangement of tubes and springs.

"Looks like the thing on Smith's arm," Alice said.

Jacob nodded and picked up one of the narrow tubes. One sat partially assembled with a damaged spring. Jacob could see a lever and counterweights inside. The springs were taut, hard to budge without a tensioner. He glanced back at Smith and frowned.

"It looks like it would shoot something."

"The crossbow bolts?" Alice asked.

Jacob nodded slowly. "That could work. Yes, yes, I bet you're right. This just doesn't have all the parts you'd need to make it work."

"We should burn this book," Charles said, drawing everyone's attention to him. "These men learned things that no man should know. And then the fools wrote it down? So some hapless inventor, or a crazed madman, could rebuild their Great Equalizer?"

"What was it?" Smith asked. "Do you know?"

"You know of it too?" Charles asked.

"It was mentioned in one of the books written in Old Bollwerk. They did not give detail so much as warnings that it should be avoided at all costs."

Charles nodded. "They harnessed the stones from the Cavern of the Dead Light, and they *weaponized* it. *That* was their great *achievement*." Charles almost roared as he stood up. "That was their damned fool *Great Equalizer*. They called death down on every man, woman, child, and beast living in this city."

"How do you know they used the stones from the cavern?"

"Look at the description," Charles said. "It glowed in the darkness without light. The men grew ill. The miners died within months. This was a bomb that could do a good amount of damage, yes, but it was a bomb that killed every living thing, even if it didn't die at the blast site. And those things, those people, died in *terrible* agony.

"The words he uses? Casualties, misfortune, limbs compromised, skin *failure*—these are the words of a man who can't justify his invention in his own mind. He knew what he did was evil. He condemned a civilization to a slow, agonizing death.

"We should burn this book."

"We cannot," Smith said after a brief hesitation. "It is a record of the Deadlands history. A record of the skeleton."

Charles tore a handful of pages out of the journal. He crumpled them up, flakes of paper falling from the edges where it was more brittle. "It cannot leave this place."

Smith frowned and watched the paper fall. "Please stop."

"You want to keep the journal? Fine, but we're destroying the detail on how to build these bombs. It was lost, and it should stay lost." Charles flipped open the book again, found the part he'd torn out, and carefully removed two more pages.

"Give them to me," Smith said.

Charles took a step back and narrowed his eyes.

Samuel and Drakkar took a defensive stance, and Jacob tried to understand what had just changed. The air almost hummed with tension.

"Don't do this," Charles said.

"Give them to me." Smith's voice stayed firm, commanding.

Charles slowly handed him the paper. Samuel started to draw his sword until Charles shook his head slightly.

"What is *wrong* with you all!" Jacob shouted. "Are you going to kill each other over this? The knowledge in that book helped destroy an entire civilization, and it could do it again." He slammed his hand down on the bench and stormed out of the workshop.

"Jacob, wait," Alice said, following after him.

Charles didn't take his eyes from Smith.

Smith picked up the crumpled paper from the floor and added it to the sheets in his right hand. "I am not a fool, Charles von Atlier." He leaned over and set his lantern on the floor before he opened the top of it. Smith dropped the papers inside. In seconds, they were gone, nothing but ash and a wisp of black smoke.

"I am glad we share the same opinion on these things," Smith said.

Samuel blew out a breath, and Drakkar visibly relaxed as Charles nodded.

"What concerns me," Smith said, "is that we don't know what was in the other manuscripts."

"Do you even know who has them?" Charles asked.

"Most are kept in the vaults beneath the Council with the few texts that have survived throughout the ages. Some are children's stories, no more, but others are like this journal, filled with numbers and symbols we cannot comprehend."

Charles closed the journal and held it out to Smith. The larger man took it and stared at it before taking off his backpack. He wrapped it in a leather cloth before sliding it into a pocket on his pack. "You cannot imagine what men have done to keep our history from our own people."

"I can," Charles said. Smith looked up and met his eyes. "I remember what the Forgotten did, and how many they saved, before Parliament turned them into traitors and exiles."

"They brokered a peace with Bollwerk unlike any that had been offered before," Smith said. "Without them, the wall would not be what it is today. Our city would not be the haven it is today."

"The truth is always buried in the lies of rulers," Charles said. "As much respect as I have for Archibald, I'm sure even the Council obscures the truth to better suit them."

"I have no doubt." Smith pulled his pack over his shoulder, adjusting the bandolier of crossbow bolts once he settled the narrow leather sack.

"Come, let us return to the Skysworn. We can ask Mary if she knows where the other books are. I would prefer to hear your interpretation of them."

Charles nodded. "I'd be happy to provide it."

CHAPTER SIXTEEN

S TEPPING BACK INTO THE SUN felt like placing his face in a frying pan. Jacob squinted at the bright light. It wasn't directly overhead anymore, but that didn't seem to have cooled things off.

"Shouldn't we wait for the others?" Alice asked.

Jacob shrugged. "It's not like we don't know where the ship is. I'm not staying behind to watch that ridiculous argument."

"What if they need our help?"

Jacob glanced back at Alice and shook his head.

Someone shouted in the distance behind them. Samuel and Charles led Smith and Drakkar out of the old building. At least they hadn't killed each other.

Alice skirted the edge of the ironwood tree's shadow. They stayed as far away from the trunk as possible, though some of the lowest hanging branches still arced over their heads. Jacob kept a constant vigil, watching for movement in the tree.

Voices rose behind them, and Jacob slowed, grabbing Alice's arm as he turned to look back at the others. They were running. He finally made out the word Smith screamed: "*Run!*"

The warning came far too late.

Jacob cursed when something cracked beside him and tugged on his pants. A sudden burst of pain exploded in his leg, but then he felt nothing as he toppled forward, wondering how he'd lost his balance. The pinch had been horrible, and the pain that followed after that brief moment of numbness felt like a white-hot flame flaying his skin. It wasn't until Jacob tried to stand up that he screamed.

He looked down at his pants, at the trail of blood leading back to the lowest branch, and the Tree Killer with its gory prize.

"Oh, gods, Jacob," Alice said as she hooked her arms under his shoulders. "Your leg, your leg, your leg … it's gone."

He didn't answer. He couldn't answer. A small black cylinder waited in the bloody sands. Jacob snatched it up and hit the button. A cap flipped open and the sides sprang out. The first bolt glanced off the Tree Killer's claw. The second struck it in the eye, and the creature collapsed into the sand.

Jacob shook as Alice dragged him away from the mottled brown Tree Killer that had devoured his leg. All the world was pain, and blood, and pain. The venom from the Tree Killer started working its way through his body. He tried to lean forward, to grab at the stump that arced blood across the sand, but the pain was too much. Shock should have deadened his nerves, but the venom brought them to terrible life. His vision swam, slowly darkening into a tunnel, but not before he saw them. It was like the cave beneath Ancora all over again, only this time it was a swarm of Tree Killers descending on his friends. Then there was nothing.

✧   ✧   ✧

THE SECOND TREE KILLER ALMOST caught Jacob's other leg, stalking forward on those horrible scythes. Alice aimed the collapsible crossbow and pressed the trigger with three quick clicks. The recoil threw her aim off, but not enough to miss her oversized target. The bug twitched, two bolts sticking out from its faceted eye, and then it stilled.

Three more of the creatures dropped to the earth and stalked toward her. The next volley of crossbow bolts didn't drop any of them, bouncing harmlessly off broad armored heads. She pulled a pair of throwing knives from beneath her vest and sent another Tree Killer into the dirt. Never had she been so thankful for Jacob relentlessly dragging her to play Cork.

Alice stared at Jacob's limp form, her throat caught somewhere between a sob and a scream. Smith was suddenly there, far faster than he should have been, raising his arm as the cylinders around his wrist began to spin.

A storm of crossbow bolts fired in rapid succession, peppering the tree wherever Smith swept his arm. "Tie it off!" he shouted, as another Tree Killer fell from the ironwood, looking more like a kebab than a bug, with all the bolts stuck in it.

"More!" Drakkar said as he slowly caught up to Smith. "To the left!"

Drakkar and Samuel engaged another Tree Killer in Alice's peripheral vision. She unfastened the belt at Jacob's waist and pulled it off as fast as she could. Alice lifted the stump of his leg high enough to slide the belt underneath it and then pulled it tight, tying a knot just like her father had shown her so very long ago. The blood slowed, but the wound continued weeping. There was so much blood. She put her hands on Jacob's pale face, but he didn't respond.

Samuel and Charles burst through the lowest branches of the ironwood. Samuel hacked at every thick limb that could potentially hide a Tree Killer. The Spider Knight dodged one of the scythe-like limbs of a Tree Killer before Charles pulled the trigger on the air cannon. The thing's head broke open like a ripe melon in the thunder that followed. Its body collapsed.

The entire tree came to life with the sudden report of the gunshot. A horrible, high-pitched chittering rose from the center of the ironwood tree, and Smith cursed. "Get back to the ship! *Now!*" He clicked the transmitter on his collar. "Mary! Tree Killers everywhere. We need support!"

Alice looped a hand under Jacob's shoulders, her other under his thighs, and picked him up as if he weighed nothing. She wiped her eyes on his sleeve, stumbling only once as she ran as fast as she could, back to the landing lines.

Samuel caught up with her there. "Put him down. Put him down. You did the tourniquet?"

Alice nodded and set Jacob on the sand. He felt so limp, and she fought the tears away again.

"It's good," Samuel said. "We'll just tighten it a bit more." He pulled a metal bar out of a sheath on his back and slipped it into the knot Alice had made in the belt. Samuel twisted, and what blood had still been flowing was cut off.

"Here," Charles said, pulling a loosely woven cloth out of a pocket on his pants.

It took Alice a moment to even register what it was. She squeezed her eyes shut, trying to focus in her panic for Jacob.

Samuel placed the bandage over Jacob's wound and tied it around the tourniquet.

Reports thundered methodically from above, each blast dropping a Tree Killer to the dirt.

Smith took down two more Tree Killers as he fell back to their position. He didn't see the third coming as he loaded a fistful of bolts, and no warning could have saved him.

Drakkar struck faster than any man had a right to move. His blade severed the scythe of one Tree Killer before the follow-through removed the head of the next. The body twitched, and Drakkar cut it in half. Another of the monstrous things reached out for him only to be taken down by one of Mary's shots.

"Wake him up," Smith said as he and Drakkar joined the rest of the group. "We can't let him fall asleep. The venom is not fatal, but the blood loss will be. Start boarding the airship."

"I will go," Drakkar said, stepping to the landing line and connecting his Wheels. The flash of a Burner came to life before the Wheels dragged Drakkar back into the air, his cloak snapping in the wind.

"He is going to need a cap on that leg," Smith said.

Alice stared at the bandages, already soaking through with a bright red stain. "Just help him."

"I will," Smith said. He locked his Wheels onto the rope. "Hand him to me."

Charles gently slid his hands underneath Jacob and lifted him up. Alice shut her eyes against the sight of Smith taking Jacob's limp form over his shoulder. She heard the crack of the Burner's igniter and the whizz of the man's ascent.

"Gods," Samuel said, his face turned toward the ironwood tree. "What do we do?"

"We get him to a doctor," Charles said. "We don't have much time. Go."

Samuel didn't hesitate. He turned around, snapped his Wheels onto the rope, and held his arm out to Alice. "Come on."

She didn't argue. She didn't want to have to concentrate too long. She only wanted her friend back, whole and alive and taking things he ought not take. Alice buried her face in Samuel's neck. The Spider Knight's grip was firm around her waist. Wind rushed past her, but Jacob's screams and his severed leg were all she could hear and see.

"We're here."

Alice opened her eyes. It was just a short stretch onto the deck. Mary grabbed her hand and helped her through the bulkhead. She did the same with Samuel.

Charles's shock of white hair appeared beside her a moment later, and the circle of friends felt more like a funeral. Alice gritted her teeth and squeezed the sides of her head, trying to rid herself of a dark, terrible thought.

Jacob was going to die.

✧　　✧　　✧

Something spoke to Jacob in the shadows. A voice. It was a familiar voice, but he struggled to focus on it. Light slowly returned to his eyes, and the panicked faces of his friends and Smith greeted him as an awful pain shot through his leg.

"—at me! Look at me!" Smith shouted as he unbuttoned his vest. "Stay awake, Jacob! You need to stay awake."

Jacob could feel himself nodding off. He didn't understand how he could be so tired and in so much pain all at once. All he knew was that the world was on fire, and people were shouting. Smith grabbed him by the shoulders and Jacob ground his teeth together, choking back a scream.

"You're hurting him!" Alice pulled on Smith's arm, but she could barely budge the mountain. Instead, she slid behind Jacob, propping him up as Smith let go.

Smith cursed and ripped his vest off, severing the thick threads of the last three buttons and dropping his pack and bandolier. "Look at me, Jacob!"

A tremor ran through Jacob's spine and his head felt heavy, but he still raised his eyes. Alice held him from behind. He knew that was Alice, but there was only pain. "What … what happened to you?" he asked through a clenched jaw. "I'm sorry I ran out."

"We can save you."

Jacob stared at the bronze and copper metal melded into Smith's chest. A series of slim pistons moved when the man shifted his arm.

"I don't want to be a Berserker! I don't want to hurt my friends!" Pain slammed through his body in another surge of agony, and he shook in Alice's embrace.

"You won't be, dammit! Hold still. Would you rather be dead? I will *not* let you die, boy. You have not lived long enough, have not loved long enough. I will not let you die. Let him go, girl."

Smith picked Jacob up, and the pain sent his world into the black.

"HOW LONG?" CHARLES ASKED. HE looked at the blood on his hands, and then back to Mary.

She ran a bloodied hand through her hair. "Gods, he's just a kid."

"*How long!*"

"Even at full speed, almost two hours back to Bollwerk."

"We can help him," Smith said as he reappeared at the hatch in the deck with Alice. "We are the *Steamsworn*, brother. It's better now, while the wounds are fresh. I have caps. It will keep him alive, and we can rework the leg back in the city."

"How can we make that decision for him?" Charles said as he looked up. The tears in the old man's eyes sent a chill through Alice's bones, even as she felt the warmth flow down her cheeks—and then a fire took hold in her gut.

"There isn't a choice!" Alice screamed, and Charles winced at the blood on her hands. "You save him, you keep him alive, and screw the goddamned consequences!"

"I'm with Alice, Charles," Samuel said as he stared at the crimson-stained deck. "He has a better chance with a Biomech implant."

"If he survives," Drakkar said, "he will adjust."

Charles let out a string of curses that made Smith flinch. The old man pulled off his vest and slammed it onto the deck before he walked through the puddle of Jacob's blood. "I swore I'd never do this again."

"Some things are worth breaking your oaths for," Smith said. He vanished down the hatch behind the cockpit, and Charles followed him into the shadows.

CHAPTER SEVENTEEN

Alice stayed by the stain on the deck. She hung her head and rocked as she heard Jacob's screams tearing their way through the deck below her. She tried to cover her ears, but it only smeared the sticky blood into her hair. Jacob's blood.

She felt someone wrap their arms around her, but still she rocked back and forth.

"They are helping him, child." It was Drakkar's voice. Some part of Alice felt surprised at the Cave Guardian's kindness. The rest of her could only hear Jacob's cries.

"We're ready," Mary said.

"Come," Drakkar said. He pulled on Alice's hand. "The lines are secured and the engine is primed. We must get Jacob back to Bollwerk."

Alice sniffed. She placed her hand in the edge of his blood. It still felt warm. She knew that was probably the sun's doing, but she still worried it might be the last time she ever felt his warmth. The last time she ever saw him alive.

"Can I get you a towel?" Mary asked.

Alice looked up at the captain of the Skysworn. She dragged her hand across her dress, leaving a bloody streak on the gray fabric.

Mary didn't say anything else. She only pulled Alice's seat up for her and helped her fasten the harness.

Samuel squeezed her shoulder before he sat down, and Drakkar took the seat beside her.

"Have faith in the gods, child. Tragedy can make us stronger."

"Tragedy also created the Butcher," Alice said, and her voice was low.

No one spoke as Mary guided the ship around the buildings and straightened out the nose.

✧　✧　✧

CHARLES WATCHED SMITH WORK. HIS skill was plain to see, but the lack of anesthetic left Jacob to scream through the pain when he wasn't blacked out. Charles had wrapped a small block of wood in leather as a sort of bite stick, but it could only do so much. He held Jacob's hand when Smith didn't need his assistance, and the tremors almost brought him to tears.

Seeing that boy laid out across the workbench like he was a god-damned experiment was too much. Charles had seen horrors in the war, seen what men could do to themselves, and to families, and to children, but this was Jacob.

Jacob passed out again, and Charles closed his eyes. When he opened them, he looked at the shadowed ceiling above him. A mass of copper and silver and brass pipes stretched the length of the deck overhead. One curved down and met a rubber hose mounted to the workbench with a decorative spigot.

Smith worked his tools through the flame leaping out of that silver Fire Lizard's head to sanitize them. He kept the tubes embalmed in some kind of fluid that he swore was almost as good as fire.

"He's like a son to me," Charles said.

"The worst of the bleeding is stopped," Smith said. "Keep pressure on that artery. We almost have the tubing finished." He fished another section of clear tubing out of the tub and laid it into the cap. "Extra reservoir, takes some of the pressure off the knee."

The horn above them rattled, and Mary's voice came over. "We're ready to engage the thrusters."

"One minute," Smith said. "I need to wire the cap, and he should be able to survive the jump."

"Shout when you're ready."

Charles's eyes shifted between the wound on Jacob's leg and the deft movements of Smith's hands. The man had quite obviously worked with Biomechs a great deal. Charles wondered if he'd helped build some of the Berserkers, the men who never came back to themselves.

The pile of flesh that Smith had sawed off kept catching the old man's eye. Pieces of Jacob they'd removed to better fit the cap. Smith had cauterized the smaller veins and arteries, and the largest were now connected to a snarl of tubes that led into the cap.

Jacob's eyes fluttered open. "Done?" he asked, his voice was a whisper.

"Almost," Charles said.

"You are a brave man," Smith said to Jacob as he worked on clamping the tubes of blood into the metal half-sphere. "I have to attach the cap to your bones. This … it is going to hurt."

Charles knew what it was when Smith picked up the gun. He fumbled with the bite stick and placed it between Jacob's teeth. "It'll hurt like hell. Be ready for it."

Jacob nodded, and Charles could see the leather bulge when the boy bit down. Jacob looked pale, so very pale. Charles's breath quickened, and it was all he could do not to weep in front of the boy.

"Do it," Jacob said through gritted teeth.

Smith's bloody hand clamped down on Jacob's leg. "It will be fast. Remember, there is pain with life—embrace it."

He pulled the trigger. There was a blast of heat from the vent on the side of the brass gun before the heated rivet slammed through the cap, burrowed through Jacob's flesh, and lodging in his bone.

Jacob grunted, and Charles could have sworn he heard the bite stick crack.

Smith moved to Jacob's other side and fired another rivet through the cap.

Jacob screamed through the pressure he kept on the leather-wrapped wood.

"Two more," Smith fired again. The bite stick fell away, and Jacob screamed so loud the gods themselves could hear him.

The last was too much, and once more Charles watched the boy pass out when Smith fastened the cap. Smith took a deep breath and looked up at the old man. "It is done. We can only wait and see if his body is strong enough to adapt."

They tied Jacob down to the bench using wide restraints before Smith tapped on the brass horn and said, "Go!"

Charles barely had his harness on in the seat beside the bench before the force of the thrusters crushed him into the chair. The sudden change in velocity caused blood to run off the bench and drip onto Charles's shoes.

The sight of Jacob's blood running so freely was finally too much. Charles lowered his head and wept.

✧   ✧   ✧

"HE CAN'T DIE," ALICE SAID as Bollwerk appeared on the horizon.

Mary glanced back and offered a weak smile. "Smith is one of the best biomechanics I've ever met, hon."

Alice thought it nice of Mary to be positive, but she'd read *The Dead Scourge*. Sometimes Biomech bodies rejected implants, or infection set in, or the Biomechs went insane. It all led to one simple fact: if it didn't go well, they died.

"He can't die," she whispered, squeezing her eyes shut.

Something clanked on the horn by Mary's head and she opened the speaker. "Go ahead."

"It's Charles," the voice said. "Jacob's awake. We think he might make it."

Alice's lip trembled, and then she broke down. She felt arms on her shoulder as she shook, and when she raised her head, she found Samuel with tears in his eyes.

"Lowlanders are too tough to get taken out by a little thing like losing a leg, right?" Samuel said.

Alice smiled despite the tears. She caught the tail end of Mary's question.

"—stopped the bleeding?"

Smith's tinny voice replaced Charles's. "He has lost a lot of blood. We will have to wait and see, but he may well be the first Ancoran Biomech."

Mary cursed and closed the horn. "And where the hell does that leave him?"

Alice didn't think those words were meant for her ears, but where it left him was *alive*, and that was all that mattered.

✧ ✧ ✧

"ARCHIBALD, THIS IS THE SKYSWORN, come in." Mary released the button on the podium beside the steering wheel and waited. When no response came, she pressed the button again and shouted, "Get off your ass, you old bastard. The boy's been hurt and we're coming in hot. We need every deckhand you have so we don't overshoot the docks."

Silence.

Mary cursed and glanced back at the men sitting behind her. They seemed stable enough, but the girl looked like she was on the edge. If they lost the boy … gods only knew what these people might do.

Smith could help keep her safe, but that lunkhead seemed more interested in talking with the old Steamsworn tinker than paying attention. How could he have let that boy get his leg taken off? Mary's knuckles whitened as she strangled the wooden steering wheel.

The horn above her crackled, and relief almost sent her to her knees.

"Skysworn, this is Tower Two. How bad?"

"Smith is capping his leg," Mary said as quietly as she could while still being heard by Archibald. "Poor kid was screaming about not wanting to be a Berserker."

"Is he stable?"

Mary sighed and closed her eyes. "I think so. He survived the jump."

"He has a chance then."

"He needs blood," Mary said. "Smith said he's white as a sheet."

"I'll get the transfusions ready."

"We don't know his type. We don't have any kits on board to check."

"Smith will donate," Archibald said before his voice broke in a burst of static. "I'm sure of it."

Smith's blood was a rare type, Mary knew. He could donate to anyone, and the transfusions always took.

"Mary!"

She blinked and glanced up at the little mesh box hiding the speaker inside the horn. "What?"

"I asked, how hot are you coming in?"

"Thrusters on full."

"Cut them off two miles out. I'm raising the net."

"But …" she knew if they hit the net at that speed, it could collapse the gas chamber, or crack the struts inside it.

"I'll pay for any damage, Mary. Just get him here alive."

The Skysworn shook beneath the power of the thrusters, but Mary didn't slow their pace. She heard Alice sniff behind her, and she ground her teeth. This was not a day for dying.

CHAPTER EIGHTEEN

Samuel watched Mary flip another horn. "Smith."

Something clanged, and then a voice came back. "Yes?"

"We're going to hit the net after cutting the thrusters two miles out."

Smith hesitated, and then said, "It is going to hurt, but the hull should be able to handle it. We may need some repairs to the gas chamber afterward."

Alice was quiet now, but Samuel could still see where the tears had carved a path through the blood and dirt on her face. He knew she was a strong girl, but the way she held herself together to help Jacob … He remembered the first time he'd lost someone to an invader in Ancora. He'd always thought people died quickly after a mortal wound, but they could scream and suffer for hours before death took them like a mercy.

"What do they mean by a net?" he asked Drakkar.

Alice glanced up, but then her gaze returned to the clouds rolling by outside the windscreen.

"It is as they say." Drakkar folded his hands across his lap. "It is a giant net made of spider silk. You should feel right at home."

"Large enough to catch a ship like this?"

"It is large enough to catch one of their warships if needed. The silk is flexible but strong as steel. Not that I need tell you. I know the armor your mount wears is made from the same silks."

Samuel nodded. Drakkar was right. Bessie's armor was forged from a fabric woven out of the silk of Widow Makers. He always found it odd, fashioning armor to protect lives that was made by a creature so deadly.

"Strap yourselves in, Smith," Mary said as she pulled her harness over her shoulders. "We're about to find out how right you are."

The captain of the Skysworn stared at her hand. It was on the wide brass lever that powered the thrusters.

"What are we waiting for?" Samuel asked.

"This side of the wall is about two miles from the docks. As soon as we hit it, I'm cutting the thrusters. We'll slow, but it's still going to be a hard hit on the net."

Samuel leaned forward. The wall came up fast, and far in the distance, he could see a gray fog with sharp edges that looked entirely unnatural. "Is that it?"

Mary didn't answer his question. "Hold on!" She slammed the lever for the thrusters toward the floor until it locked. The ship lurched forward when its propulsion suddenly died off. Samuel grunted against his harness, and when he looked up, he saw the net coming ever closer.

"How hard will this stop be?" Drakkar asked.

Mary glanced over her shoulder. "Keep your hands and fingers out of the harness. No sense in getting them broken."

"Hard, then," Drakkar said. He folded his hands onto his lap and closed his eyes. "The boy will survive, child."

Samuel wondered why Drakkar had said that until he looked at Alice. Tears flowed down her face and her body shook again. He wanted to comfort her, tell her Jacob came from a strong bloodline, that if anyone could survive this, he could.

The Skysworn reached the net faster than he imagined possible.

Samuel thought his eyes might pop out of his head, and he shouted at the sudden pressure assaulting his body. The windscreen held as the silk cables stretched in front them, but he could hear the creak and buckling of metal above.

"Come on, hold!" Mary ripped her harness off as soon as the inertia lost its strength. She dashed out the cockpit door and Samuel followed.

Smith was handing Jacob up onto the deck already, into Charles's waiting, bloody arms. Samuel froze when he saw how white Jacob was.

"Help me with the lines!" Mary said.

Samuel rushed to the nearest coil and pushed the assembly up and over the railing. A metallic clunk sounded, and the ropes released, speeding toward the dock full of people below. Samuel blinked as he ran to the next landing rope. There had to be three hundred men and women down there.

The Skysworn lurched to one side, and before he could fully register what was happening, the ship started to descend.

Smith stood at the open railing, waiting, with Jacob clutched in his arms. Samuel watched as the mountain of a man put his ear to Jacob's mouth and frowned. "His breathing is slowing. He needs blood."

"We don't know his type," Mary said.

"He can have mine. Bring them to the hospital, this is close enough."

Samuel stared, slack-jawed, as Smith leapt off the side of the airship. The Spider Knight ran to the railing and looked over. Smith was already on the ground, and moving at impossible speeds. Samuel couldn't be sure, but he thought the man might be able to outrun Bessie at a sprint.

"He's fast when he has to be," Mary said. "And damned powerful."

"I saw the implants," Samuel said as he turned to Mary. "The stories I've heard … the stories we've all heard in Ancora."

"About Mechs?"

Samuel nodded.

"Have you heard *our* legends?" Mary asked as the airship tilted. Samuel had to put his hand on the railing to catch his balance, but Mary only swayed slightly.

"What legends?"

"Of Ancora," she said as she looked down at the crowd hauling them in. "Legends of men riding invaders so large that they could level

Bollwerk in a single charge."

"That's ridiculous," Samuel said, crossing his arms.

"My point, exactly."

Samuel frowned and stared off into the distance, down the street where Smith had disappeared. Charles had told him more than once that truth could change with one's point of view. If Smith was truly one of the monsters—a monster fighting so hard to save Jacob—where did that leave the old stories?

Samuel turned and watched Charles for a moment. He was a tinker, a soldier, a Steamsworn, and an old man comforting a terrified girl. If Samuel died half the man Charles was, he could go into that great sleep without regret.

Samuel started toward Alice when she sobbed again. The red hair reminded him so much of his little sister. He held his hand out and helped pull her up from her seat on the deck beside the cockpit door. She leaned away from Charles and grabbed Samuel's hand.

"Where are you going?" Drakkar asked.

"To find our friend," Samuel said when Mary began rolling out the gangplank.

Charles took a deep breath. Drakkar extended his hand and helped the old man up. They all followed Charles to the break in the railing and waited for the gangplank to fully extend. A great many faces watched them from the docks, clearly concerned, or at worst, curious.

Samuel felt Alice start to fall when her legs wobbled. He put his arm around her waist and hoisted her up as if he meant to carry her across the threshold at a celebration. Only there was no celebration here. There were only the girl's warm tears on his neck and the bloody arms of his friend leading them down the gangplank.

✧　✧　✧

DRAKKAR FOLLOWED HIS NEW COMPANIONS through the streets of

Bollwerk. Mary's concern about Jacob's well-being surprised him. He knew her reputation well, and she was a woman who would not hesitate to kill if it would benefit the city, or her crew. She had all but commanded him to report back when they knew more of Jacob's condition.

An airship captain attempting to give orders to a Cave Guardian? If he hadn't been concerned for the boy, he may have laughed at her.

Charles von Atlier still concerned him. It was obvious he had ties to Archibald, ties that one could use to exploit the other. No matter how much his brother's warnings about the savagery of Ancorans echoed in his mind, he had seen firsthand the love and concern on the old tinker's face. Perhaps Atlier had only been a soldier in the war, and not the monster Drakkar had been warned about. Stories within stories, it grew hard to know who to believe.

Of one thing he was certain: Ancorans could be evil or good, just as the people of any other culture he'd encountered. Perhaps there were gluttonous wastes in the Highlands who would better serve the world as corpses, but that same city harbored Samuel and Charles and Jacob, and the angry young girl who amused him so.

Drakkar watched the shock of red hair hung about Samuel's shoulder. A Spider Knight! He showed such concern for the children of Ancora—children in the eyes of Ancora, but at fifteen, they would be men and women in Cave. Spider Knights were the evil in stories that crept in the darkest corners of Cave, but Samuel was not an evil man. Samuel ... he was a good man in a terrible situation.

The world was changing. It was always changing, for better and for worse, but Drakkar could feel it in his bones. His beloved city of Cave wouldn't be able to hide behind its walls forever.

"You alright?"

Drakkar blinked and looked up into the eyes of Charles von Atlier. "Yes, I am well."

"We're at the hospital."

Drakkar glanced at the red cross circled by a white sphere, cut through by a black sword.

"Did you want to wait here?" Charles asked. Drakkar felt no sense of pressure in his words.

He noticed Alice watching him, still tucked up against Samuel's chest. Drakkar despised the hospital, with its corrupted smell of the sick and the dying, but he found himself saying, "No. I want to see my friend."

And with that, the monster he knew as Charles von Atlier led him into a house of death to see his Ancoran friend.

CHAPTER NINETEEN

Alice stared into the white room, its only color the blood running between Jacob and Smith. Archibald sat in the corner, constantly turning a hat in his hand by the edge of its brim. A woman with short brown hair and a long white coat twisted a knob on a glass container filled with blood.

"Charles," Archibald said. He looked up. "The transmitters—"

"Enough," Charles said. "I *cannot* express to you how much I don't care. I know you didn't attack Ancora. What I care about is him," he said, pointing to Jacob.

"He should survive," the woman said as she patted Smith's shoulder. "Smith here is like magic. I've been a nurse here for a few years, and I've seen his blood work with everyone we've tried. It's just as good as the biomechanics he builds."

Charles frowned. "So, with his Biomech skills, you would call Smith … a smith?"

Smith smiled. "I prefer to be called a tinker. It is less confusing."

"Tinker's a good name," Charles said as he stroked his beard. "People expect less of you for some reason. Keeps the pressure off."

The color in Jacob's face looked better, and for the first time, Alice thought he might really have a chance. "Has he woken up yet?"

The nurse shook her head. "His pulse is stronger, and that's usually a good sign. I won't lie to you. Sometimes the shock takes a life, even when they would otherwise survive."

"He is a strong man," Drakkar said.

Alice looked up at the Cave Guardian. He wore almost no expression, but something burned behind his eyes. Some concern, or dread, or bottled emotion barely contained by Drakkar's cool façade.

Charles nodded. "He survived the Fall in Ancora, and not for hiding behind its highest walls."

"Getting a little light-headed," Smith said.

"A moment to check his vitals," the nurse said. She checked a band around his arm and looked at a tube mounted to a dark wood board. A silvery liquid rose and fell beside a series of marks as she adjusted a knob. The nurse scribbled something and then followed down the page with her finger.

"Well, he's been quite stable for the past ten minutes. I think it's safe to stop."

The nurse twisted a silver knob on the glass tank with blood in the bottom, and then another closer to Smith. She slid a needle that looked as wide as a drinking straw out of his arm before placing a loose cloth over the wound.

Smith held it in place while the nurse returned to Jacob. She waited for the blood in the tank to lower before closing the knob near Jacob's arm as well. She slid the needle out, and a small trail of blood ran to his elbow and dripped. Alice winced when the drop smacked against the floor.

The nurse made a few quick movements and wrapped Jacob's arm in the same type of cloth she'd used on Smith. "He'll likely be unconscious for a while." She pulled the sheet up, exposing the brass-colored cap where his leg should have been. "I'm not seeing any leakage here, so I'm quite confident that the blood loss was staunched."

"Of course it was," Smith said. "You think I'm getting sloppy in my old age?"

"Old age," Charles said with a snort. "You've got a good fifteen years before you can say that."

Smith spared him a smile before he looked back at the nurse. "Vitals are still normal?"

The nurse glanced at the glass bulbs and tubing beside Jacob before she nodded. "A little low, but that could be his natural baseline. We don't know."

A groan sounded somewhere in the room, and Alice looked around to see who it was. Drakkar met her eyes and shrugged before he snapped his head back to the bed. She followed his gaze and saw Jacob's head move. His eyes fluttered open, and closed again.

But in that moment, Alice could have sworn he'd focused on her.

✧   ✧   ✧

CHARLES BREATHED A HEAVY SIGH when Jacob's eyes fluttered open. Even with a full recovery, Jacob wouldn't be going anywhere anytime soon. That meant they had other problems to address. A full recovery? What did that mean, now? Charles frowned and looked up at the rest of the group.

"We need to talk. Archibald, is there a room we can use? Away from the boy?"

Archibald nodded. "Follow me." His cloaked billowed out as he stood and walked to the door.

Charles turned to Smith when the larger man grunted and stood up. "What are you doing?"

Smith glanced at Charles while he started tying off his bandages. "I already have the measurements on Jacob's cap. I am going to start building his leg."

Charles stared at the man. "Why would you do that? We've offered no payment, made no requests. You owe us no oath."

"Sometimes we do what is right, and we do it because it is right. I do not always need a reason beyond that."

Charles furrowed his brow before he nodded. "You have my thanks, tinker."

"The thanks of a Steamsworn is no small thing."

"Come," Archibald said, and they followed.

Archibald didn't walk, he strode down the hall, leading them around a corner to a corridor on the right. Worn wooden floors and reinforced doors flanked them every fifteen feet.

"What is this place?" Charles asked.

"The last bastion," Archibald said. "When all else fails in Bollwerk, this place will be nearly invincible."

"Nothing is invincible," Drakkar said. "Nothing but death."

Archibald glanced back at the Cave Guardian. "You're not wrong, my friend."

Drakkar's lips quirked up at the use of a guardian's phrase. It was a term of respect, in so much as a reference to a true friend.

They reached the end of the hallway after another minute of walking, and Archibald pushed open the door. Charles was a bit surprised to see Alice follow them in before the door clunked closed behind her.

"No one can hear us in this place," Archibald said. "There is stone in every wall, which is why you see no windows. There is stone in the ceiling and the floors."

"It's a good insulator," Charles said, "but I'd imagine a determined man could still hear every whisper."

Archibald crossed his arms and leaned against a dark wood table that looked sturdy enough to support a house. "It's the old Council room, from before we expanded and had the bench finished. There are other defenses in place, Charles. No one will hear us in this room."

Charles narrowed his eyes at Archibald. "You make it sound like you have lethal deterrents around this room."

"We do."

Archibald was serious, and where a sane person might think that was terrifying, Charles thought it was fantastic. They needed to talk, and being overheard could lead to an uprising, or worse.

"Then talk," Charles said.

"There are rumors," Archibald said. "I have many spies, in Dauschen, Fel, Ancora, Cave, and even the far townships in the wastelands."

Charles heard a sharp intake of breath from Samuel and a grunt from Drakkar, but he wasn't surprised in the least. Archibald had always been a smart man, but sometimes his actions betrayed a foresight no mere mortal could have without spies.

"You do not seem surprised."

"Tell me what you've learned," Charles said.

Archibald glanced away for a moment before returning his gaze to the group. "There is a rumor coming from Dauschen, and it carries a portent so vile I can't stomach the thought it might be true."

"What could possibly be worse than being taken over by Fel?" Alice asked. "I'm sure there was fighting then, and people were killed, and families died."

Archibald nodded. "There is a rumor that the new King of Fel is none other than Gregory Mordair."

Charles almost choked on his own heart. "Mordair?"

"The surviving brother of the Butcher."

Alice gasped, and the others cursed.

The old tinker ran a hand through his hair and looked up at Archibald—really looked. Heavy bags and lines etched into his face made him look older than he was, and his hair looked like a small breeze might lift what remained from his scalp. The man still had a stiff posture, but Charles feared it couldn't last. Archibald had looked into the eyes of the Butcher and lived. Archibald had looked into the eyes of the Butcher and hadn't killed him. That was a regret he'd take to his grave.

"If they own Dauschen and Fel, there is *nothing* to stop them from taking Ancora."

"The Butcher has played puppeteer to Parliament for decades," Archibald said with a nod. "It may be he's decided to remove them and reinstate the crown."

"He can't do that!" Alice said.

"He can," Charles said before he cursed. "That bastard has been setting up the infrastructure for ten years, and I didn't even notice. *That's* why they kept me out of the city, and I was *so* happy to stay out of their political maneuvers." He curled his right hand into a fist and punched his left palm.

"What's your plan?" Charles asked, raising his eyes back to Archibald. "If they take Ancora, Cave will fall. Once Cave falls—"

"They come for Bollwerk," Archibald said. "I know."

"Then what do we do?"

"We follow your plan. I won't have you take anyone but volunteers, but take them you shall. Go to Dauschen. Take the long roads through the Burning Forest. The season is dry, and the worst of the swarms are hibernating without water. Find out what their plan is. Find their weaknesses. If our worst fears are realized …" Archibald bared his teeth as he said, "I'll correct a mistake I made fifty years past."

Part of Charles felt elated that Archibald had come around. The other, more sane part of him realized that this could be the end of the cities he'd come to love. Without the trade alliance, war would ever be the answer.

"We have to stop them," Charles said.

"Yes."

CHAPTER TWENTY

C HARLES STARED AT THE SYRINGE pinched between his fingers while Smith hammered on something behind him in rapid, high-pitched bursts. The old man turned around and watched the younger tinker work. Smith beat a disc out into a rounded cone shape. The work should have taken a great deal of time, with a forge and a pair of blacksmiths to create, but Smith simply set it in a mold and hammered away.

Charles glanced at the needle again and asked, "What will it do?"

Smith glanced up. He adjusted a lever on the biomechanics in his chest before taking one vicious strike. "It will deaden the nerves around the wound. Like an anesthetic, but it can last for over a month."

"I never thought the venom of a Widow Maker could be put to good use."

"Highly refined and diluted venom, but yes, it is venom still." Smith held the tiny, rounded disc up to a lantern before nodding and dropping it onto a pile of similar pieces. It slid and rolled across the rounded pile and clunked onto the top of the workbench.

"How many of those do you need?"

"I will not really know until I start building."

Charles set the needle on the upper shelf, beside a vial marked with a red skull. "How long do you think it will be before Jacob can walk? You said the venom will help, but how much?"

"It will still take time," Smith said. "I am hoping to have the boy walking by the time you return from Dauschen."

Charles turned and stared at the man. "That's insane. It used to take three months, or more, for a man to heal enough from a Biomech procedure to even attempt it."

Smith shrugged. "A month is average. If the boy heals fast, it could be a few weeks. We will know soon enough."

"How long does it take to cross through the Burning Forest in a caravan?"

Smith pulled out another disc-shaped blank and glanced at Charles. "It is always different, depending on the mounts, the rains and the fires, and the mountain pass. Two days, maybe four if you are very unlucky."

"In my world, 'very unlucky' usually means dead." Charles frowned and tapped his fingers on the workbench. "I'd rather stay and help you with Jacob."

Smith shook his head. "Let us take care of him. When he is healed well enough, we can join your quest against the …" Smith paused and glanced at the door to his workshop. "Your quest against our enemies."

Charles looked at the door, its heavy ironwork towering over them in the lantern light, cutting off the workshop from the rest of the building. "How often is he going to need a new leg?"

"I do not think he has much longer to grow. Maybe a year or two at most? Foot plates are always a good solution to adjust the height, but I think I have a better idea."

Charles waited, but Smith didn't embellish. "Well? Are you going to tell me about this grand idea?"

Smith cracked a tiny smile as he hammered out another cap. "No. I am going to surprise you with it. Make your plans for the travel to Dauschen, and meet me here tomorrow at high noon. Alice is bringing Jacob."

Charles watched Smith adjust the lever on his biomechanics again before the old man turned and left the younger tinker to his work.

✧   ✧   ✧

CHARLES WALKED THROUGH THE CORRIDORS of the Council Hall, his only company the echo of his footsteps off the stone walls. Sometimes the only way to think, the only way to clear his mind, was to step away from the rest of the world. Gods knew he needed time to think.

He ran his fingers through his hair as he passed a gold-embossed door for the fifth time. It was a holy place, revered by the Steamsworn and emblazoned with the symbol of a raised fist. It surprised him that anyone remembered what had happened there, or much less that they built the Hall on top of it.

His pace slowed and he set his hand on the old emblem. The war lived in the distant past, but it was never far from his mind. Charles read the inscription, and memories of the friends he'd lost came flooding back.

> *Upon these grounds stood the Steamsworn.*
> *Bollwerk burned around them, but not so*
> *Brightly as the fire burned within their souls.*
>
> *Upon these grounds stand the Steamsworn.*
> *Woe unto those who cross their swords.*
> *Peace unto those who bury their brothers.*

It would seem a silly arrangement of words, but for the story behind it. Charles remembered the screams of the women, and the men, and the children. The screams when Ancora and Dauschen rained hell upon that town.

Charles's lip quivered before he snarled and slammed a fist into the fist of the Steamsworn. "You cannot have Jacob. You understand me? No one hurts that boy."

"I don't intend to hurt him."

Charles moved his gaze from the tiny trickle of blood on his knuckles to the cloaked man at the end of the corridor. "War brings death, Archibald. It brings much more than hurt."

"Pacifism without preparedness brings death," Archibald said as his own footsteps echoed through the Hall. "That's what really happened here." He wiped the blood off the golden emblem. "If they'd fought back, they could have killed us all. They outnumbered us five to one."

"We should have killed him, Archibald. We should have killed him fifty years ago."

"I have always believed in giving men a second chance to do good things." Archibald sighed and turned to Charles. "You know what he lost. You understand it better than most."

Charles knew the death of the Butcher's brother wasn't *really* his fault, but he still winced at the comment.

"We're all fools and martyrs when we're dead."

"I can't go to my grave knowing he still walks this earth, Archibald."

"Nor can I."

"What of your oaths?"

Archibald's lips lifted in a sad smile. "The oaths were broken the instant I sent spies into the world. I believe the Steamsworn can survive a few broken oaths in their history."

"Second chances," Charles said. He shook his head. "That got you a knife in the ribs, best I recall."

Archibald's hand moved slightly to a spot near the base of his ribcage. Charles knew that was where he'd been stabbed by one of his own men after he revealed his plan to defect to Bollwerk. "Everyone deserves a chance."

"Not everyone," Charles said. He pressed on the golden fingernails set into the door and moved his hand in a pattern that seemed surprisingly familiar after so many years.

Peace ... unto ... the ... Steamsworn.

Charles twisted the handle and forced it open, and a small cloud of dust ballooned up from the ground, betraying just how long the shrine had been kept locked.

Archibald sighed and followed the old tinker through, his cloak billowing slightly and then falling in the shadowed room.

Charles stood at the altar and stared into the glass coffin. What was inside was barely a skeleton anymore. He had been the first of the Steamsworn, before they'd had a name, and he'd been the first to die in the war.

"I used to think he was so old when he died," Charles said with a half smile. He and Archibald had long since passed that age.

"Forty years old?" Archibald said. "Sounds ancient to me."

Charles lost his smile when he turned back to the glass coffin. "Jacob can't become one of these," Charles said as he laid a hand on the dusty glass. "He can't be a Berserker, Archibald. That boy has too much to live for."

"Biomechanics aren't the same as they were in the war. Smith is the best we have. He's the best we've *ever* had, Charles."

Charles nodded. "I've seen him work. I have little doubt you're right."

"Then why are you here?" Archibald asked. "What is your intention?"

"I wanted to be sure the journals were all still here."

"No one has set foot in this place in a decade."

Charles ignored Archibald and walked around the coffin. It stood on a brass base, and the base itself seemed to be built from a thousand levers. Charles threw three random levers, and there was a quiet crack as the bolts withdrew on the floor safe at Archibald's feet.

The Speaker sighed, pulled up his cloak, and bent down, his knees cracking as he got to the floor. Charles watched him pull open the safe, and something untied itself in his gut when he saw the old yellowed parchment right where he'd left it.

"They're here," Archibald said. "What do you want?"

Charles flipped through the pages, found the few he needed, and slid them gently out of the pile. "A fighting chance, Archibald. I want a fighting chance."

"You're going to bring back weapons this world hasn't seen since the war ended," Archibald said as he replaced the remaining journals and manuscripts and locked the safe. Three new levers shifted, creating a new sequence that only Charles and Archibald knew.

"Those kids deserve a better world than what we left them with."

"It doesn't always have to end in violence, Charles. It doesn't *always* have to end in war."

Charles frowned as he slid the journals into his vest. "You may be right, but this is not the time to sit back and let the world eat itself alive." Charles turned to leave.

"Wait."

He hesitated with his hand on the door.

"You should know we had twenty volunteers. I know it's not as many as you hoped …"

"It's plenty. We'll make a convincing ruse, gather what information we need, and you'll inadvertently be placing new spies in Dauschen."

Archibald crossed his arms. "They won't just be spies. Some of them are Steamsworn, Charles."

Charles turned fully back to Archibald, a dozen questions churning in his mind.

"I've taken the oaths, but that does *not* mean I will let this city fall to some outdated obligation."

"I've never heard you speak of pacifism so … poorly."

"It could get us killed, Charles. I'm afraid Berserkers will be more at home in the coming days than any *true* citizen of Bollwerk."

"The warships," Charles said.

"Fully functional. Not one cannon is just for show anymore."

"I would leave them docked if I were you," Charles said as he pulled the door open. "If our plan is discovered, or one of your spies talks, you could have an army descending on Bollwerk in a matter of days."

Charles glanced down at the footprints they'd left in the dust, as though he'd stepped back into another time and walked through his own ghost. Just before the door clicked closed behind him, he could hear Archibald whisper, "Gods help us."

CHAPTER TWENTY-ONE

J ACOB SAT IN ONE OF the wooden wheelchairs he'd seen in the corner of his room. Alice pushed him down the hall, whistling some irritating tune and being far too chipper for his current thoughts. A blanket lay across his lap. He didn't know why they'd bothered. It wasn't like everyone didn't know his leg was missing.

"Where are we going?" he muttered.

"It's almost high noon," Alice said. She patted his shoulder. "I'm taking you to see Charles and Smith. They have something for you."

Jacob sighed and let the patches of light wash over him in the dim corridor. He was glad Alice was with him, and his leg didn't hurt nearly as bad since the nurse had given him that awful shot. He still frowned when Alice stopped before a towering door adorned in enough ironwork to build a carriage.

Alice knocked. Footsteps approached before metal clinked against metal and the door swung open. Charles stood there, and the old man didn't look much happier than Jacob felt.

"What's wrong?" Jacob asked.

"Nothing, boy. I was just talking over some designs with Smith. He's as stubborn as you are. Come in, come in."

Smith leaned over something that reminded him of Charles's air cannon but much thinner. He looked up when one of the wheels on the chair squeaked.

"Hello, Jacob," Smith said. "Alice."

"So, what are we doing here?" Jacob asked.

"Paying debts." The voice sounded behind Jacob, and he jumped in his chair, not having heard anyone approach. The cloak flowed around the man as he slipped past Alice, and then Jacob realized it was Archibald.

Smith tightened a screw on his project and then set his tools down on the bench.

"The cap I made for your leg," Smith said, pointing toward Jacob's blanket. "It's a Biomech interface."

Jacob frowned and looked at Smith, trying to understand what he meant by that.

Smith took a few steps to a table covered in a rough wool blanket. He whipped the covering off, and the bronze machination beneath glinted in the steady lantern lights. Smith grunted as he picked it up and held it out for Jacob to see. "It's your new leg."

"What?" Jacob stared at the thing, half in wonder and half in confusion. "I'm a Biomech?"

"You are now," Smith said with a smile. "You have blood flow to that cap on your leg. Once it latches on to this," he said as he hoisted the leg, "your own blood will keep it lubricated. You had enough muscle left in your leg for us to build a working knee. When you move—well, when you think about moving as if you still had a leg—those muscles will flex. It pushes on the actuators in your cap, and the cap triggers these." He angled the leg down so Jacob could see a virtual forest of levers inside the joint. "A little practice, and you'll be up and walking again."

Smith thought he might know the cause behind the worried Ancoran expressions around him. "It has been a long road. We have learned what alloys will drive a man insane, and what he can wear for a lifetime without succumbing to the fury."

"Simply put," Archibald said, "we no longer build Berserkers like you remember, Charles. It was the metals in their own bodies that created the rage and the insanity."

"By the gods," Charles said. "I didn't realize you'd come so far."

Smith glanced up at him and nodded.

For the first time since Jacob woke up, he thought he might still have a chance. A chance to help Charles and Samuel and Alice. A chance to help free up the trade routes of Ancora and see his family, his friends, and get the medicine and foods they so desperately needed.

Jacob had only half listened to the conversation. He looked up at Smith and asked, "Can we put it on?"

The mountain of a man glanced down at the leg before he looked back up to Jacob. "We can, but it will hurt. You'll need more shots to deaden the nerves, and more time to rest before you will be able to walk regularly."

"Do it. Put it on me."

Jacob felt Alice squeeze his shoulders. He didn't want her to be wheeling him around like some kind of burden. He didn't want to be a burden on his parents. He wanted to be normal, but then his thoughts trailed back to the kids and the boy at the hospital. Was he any less normal for losing his hand? Jacob grimaced and rubbed his forehead. There were too many emotions for him to sort out, and he'd worry about the philosophical side of things later.

When he looked up again, Smith was kneeling before him and pulling the blanket off Jacob's lap.

"A little help?" Smith asked.

Charles leaned over and raised Jacob's stump. It was the first time Jacob had really studied his cap, and it was only then that he realized how complex the mechanism was.

"You put that on me in the *desert?*"

Smith smiled and angled the leg over Jacob's cap. "Yes, I have done many implants. Now, brace yourself."

A dull pain throbbed through his leg when Smith tilted it up and something snapped together. The real pain, like someone had jammed a white-hot poker into his very bones, came when Smith forced the mechanism down and the cap engaged.

"Hnnnnn." Jacob couldn't form the words, couldn't form a scream. His hands locked onto the armrests of his chair, and the wood creaked beneath his grip. And then the pain subsided. He panted and hung his head.

"You did great," Charles said.

Something touched the side of his face. Something cool and soft, and when he opened his eyes, he saw Alice's burst of red hair and blue eyes a few inches from his face.

"Are you okay?"

"Your eyes are beautiful."

Alice dropped her hands and stood abruptly.

"He might be a little loopy from the medication," Archibald said. "It will normally only last a few hours."

Something in Jacob's mind told him he wasn't supposed to say that out loud, but what did his mind know, really? Instead, he watched his new leg come to life. Tiny panels shifted while Smith inspected its progress.

"Your blood supplies lubrication, as I already told you, but there are tiny turbines inside your leg too. They generate enough power to move the mechanisms, and enough power to give you strength beyond what your old leg was capable."

"You like to ramble like Charles," Jacob said with a small smile. He watched Smith chuckle as the larger man slid a large plate around Jacob's new calf.

"He will be light-headed for a time, until his body can produce enough blood to compensate for his new leg. I would have preferred to wait, but I did not think his constitution was going to hold out much longer."

"More words," Jacob said. "We should be sleeping instead." His eyes fluttered closed.

He heard someone laugh.

Someone squeezed his arm.

Then he was asleep.

✧   ✧   ✧

ALICE WATCHED JACOB WHILE CHARLES and Smith fussed over his new leg. She knew a thing or two about gadgets and machines and engines, but the leg Smith had built was beyond anything she'd ever seen. She studied the muscles in the man's arms as they would move and shift with the pistons and plates of his biomechanics, like watching an insect more than a human—alien, fascinating, and a little frightening.

The nurse from the hospital came and went, administering two more shots to Jacob while he slept. Alice watched her with purpose. The older woman had a strong stomach. She always looked composed, even when blood splashed across her white clothes. Alice wondered how she could keep from panicking. Had the woman truly seen that much blood?

"Gods, it's amazing," Charles said as he looked up at Smith.

Smith shifted the leg up and down and to the side before he nodded. "It is good work, but perhaps not my best."

Charles leaned back in his chair and slouched. "You don't just save lives. You're saving his entire lifestyle."

Smith adjusted a lever on his hand. The mechanism had been hidden behind a flesh-toned glove before, but now he left his biomechanics exposed while he worked.

Alice almost gasped when he bent a steel rod between two fingers, refitting the slide for a plate on Jacob's leg.

"You can say that again." Charles smiled and looked up at Alice.

Maybe she'd done more than almost gasp. She picked up the cool, water-soaked cloth in her hand and dabbed at the sweat on Jacob's forehead.

"He'll be okay?"

Smith squinted and leaned in to look at the flesh where Jacob's new leg met his old one. "He has absorbed the venom well. Sometimes skin does not react so well. It is a good sign."

Alice grimaced. She'd seen what could happen when a man was bitten by a Widow Maker. She'd seen a Spider Knight all but dissolve right in front of her when he met a Widow Maker head-on, saving her during the Fall in Ancora. She never knew his name, but she would always be thankful for his sacrifice.

The two tinkers fussed over Jacob's Biomech implant for another two hours. Archibald vanished for a while, but when he returned, he had food and drinks.

"How is he?" the Speaker asked.

Smith glanced up and nodded at Archibald. "Pulse is strong, the venom has done its work, he is a survivor."

"Lucky thing," Archibald said as he passed a plate filled with diced potatoes to Alice. "Most of the folks around here are terribly allergic to the Tree Killer's poison. More than a graze, and they can't survive without immediate care at the hospital."

"Thank you," Alice said as she turned her eyes back to Jacob. "He's … he means a lot to us."

Archibald smiled and handed Alice a glass of Sweetwing Tea. "Any friends of Charles are always welcome, and always watched over."

"Steamsworn," Smith said as he raised his cup.

"Steamsworn," Charles and Archibald echoed as they raised their own pewter steins.

Alice felt silly, raising her glass of Sweetwing Tea, but she did it anyway. "Steamsworn."

Jacob's eyes fluttered, something clicked in his leg, and his metal foot flexed.

This time, Alice didn't hide her gasp.

CHAPTER TWENTY-TWO

JACOB STARED AT THE INTRICATE web of metal that formed his leg. The outer plates gave him the basic shape of a leg, but when Smith pulled one open, Jacob could see the machinations of a madman inside. How someone could build a machine so precise, and keep that machine working, was beyond his understanding.

"See the tubes here, and here?" Smith asked. He pointed into the cavity behind the plates. When Jacob didn't answer, he looked up. "Well?"

Jacob nodded slowly.

"Good. Those are filled with your blood. You break a gasket or sever a tube, and that is all manner of bad things. If it happens, and it will someday, just remember the tourniquet built around your interface."

"I will." Jacob remembered Smith showing him the levers built into the cap—the interface, as he called it. Jacob liked that word much better than stump. He felt like stump was an ugly word, like a dead tree. Interface spoke of movement and machines and life.

"There is nothing you cannot do, Jacob." Smith paused until Jacob raised his head and met his eyes. "So long as you keep your wits about you, use your mind along with your gut, there is nothing you cannot do." Smith laid a Biomech hand on Jacob's new foot.

"What happened?" Jacob asked as he looked at the network of bronze and copper and steel that made up Smith's hand.

Smith offered a small smile before he pulled the thin, flesh-toned glove back over his hand. "That is a story for another time. Get some rest," he said as he stood and squeezed Jacob's shoulder. "Walking will be a little different for you, and you will need to be rested before you learn."

"Will he need footplates?" Archibald asked between sips of his drink.

Smith shook his head. "This is a newer design." He slid plates open on Jacob's leg and pointed to the notched bars and rivets. He looked up at Jacob. "You are young, and still have a year or more to grow. You can adjust your leg as your body changes, without having to replace it."

"Won't the joints be weaker?" Charles asked. "The tubing?"

"No. There is enough extra tubing to stretch almost three feet. The joints themselves may be moderately weaker than a solid leg, but understand …" Smith pivoted and set a sheet of steel across his largest vise. He flipped a lever on his chest, and then two in his hand, just beneath the glove.

Jacob watched in fascination as the man's arm began to shake, and then Smith punched through the steel plate in a rending squeal of metal. The man returned the switches to their original positions and looked up.

"Moderately weaker will still be far stronger than any mortal joint."

"Your color looks better," Alice said as she brushed Jacob's hair back behind his ear.

He looked up at her and smiled.

"I thought we'd lost you."

"No …" Charles grunted as he stood up. "Looks like we're stuck with the sneak thief for a time."

"Sneak thief?" Smith asked.

Jacob felt the blush crawl up his neck. "I used to be."

"Used to be?" Alice asked. "Like a week ago?"

Smith chuckled. "Well, perhaps part of my story need not wait." He tapped a wrench against his hand and it clinked on the Biomech implants. "That is how I lost my hand, taking things that did not belong to me."

Jacob tried to imagine that. A tinker, without his hands. His life, his entire passion, would be crippled without a hand.

"Yes, you can imagine what that did to me." Smith frowned and began putting away the tools on his workbench. "I had a few dark years. I will not hide that from you.

"I studied Mechs and Berserkers, and mostly by accident I discovered what drove them mad—or thought I had. I needed to prove it to myself. With the help of an old Biomech tinker—long dead now, I'm afraid—I built this to prove my theory." He flexed his hand and rolled his fingers. "None of the toxic metals, or the welds or bolts I thought may be contributing to their insanity, were placed in this hand. Fifteen years now, and I am still the same man I was."

Charles stood up and smiled down at Jacob. "I guess you won't be going crazy anytime soon."

"That ship has sailed," Alice muttered.

"Hey!" Jacob said with a small smile. He looked around the room before it finally registered that some of their people weren't with them. "Where's Samuel? And Drakkar?"

"They're gathering supplies and wagons," Charles said. The old man crossed his arms and seemed to hunch in on himself a bit. That was usually followed by news Jacob didn't want to hear, and this was no different. "We're taking a caravan to Dauschen. You have to stay here."

Jacob wanted to argue, to say he could make it, he could keep up the pace, but he knew he couldn't. The pain in his leg was still substantial, and the thought of walking made him cringe. "I wish I could go."

"Me too," Charles said. "I hope to be gone a few weeks at most. We'll come back for you."

"You are stuck with me, I am afraid," Smith said as he closed and locked one of the many metal drawers beneath his bench. "I will teach you to walk and run and fight as only a Biomech can."

"Can you show me how to work on it?" Jacob asked. "I mean, to keep my leg in good working order?"

"I plan to."

Jacob's disappointment lifted slightly at the prospect of learning more about biomechanics with Smith. It felt odd, how only a few days before, he'd thought anyone with a Biomech implant was one of the Berserkers, the mad warriors of Bollwerk. But now he had his own, and … he still felt like himself.

"You're hopeless, kid." Charles smiled when Jacob glanced up at him. "Doomed to be a tinker."

"Not only a tinker," Smith said as he handed Jacob a thin leather-bound book. "You are a warrior now, Jacob. The Steamsworn will be here for you like a family, and you can join their ranks if you wish. It is the right of all Biomechs."

"Steamsworn?" Jacob said, stretching the word out and letting it roll across his tongue. Him? A Steamsworn? It would be like his childhood dream of becoming a Spider Knight, and the thought sent a bolt of excitement down his spine.

✧   ✧   ✧

Jacob said goodbye to Charles before the old man left. He hoped it would only be a few weeks before they came back to Bollwerk. The thought of being able to walk by then, while every movement was still sending a sharp pain into his leg, was almost unimaginable. Smith said it was possible, and Smith knew more about Biomechs than Jacob ever would.

Alice stayed with him for a short time in his room near the hospital wing. It wasn't long before he said goodbye to her as well. Jacob looked at the two volumes stacked together on the wide, dark end table. The room was stark, undecorated but for a few nonsensical sculptures and a steel bed that looked like it had been poured rather than carved or formed by human hands.

Jacob locked the wheel of the chair and lifted himself onto the edge of the bed. Smith had said it was safe to move, but gods did it still hurt. He pushed *The Dead Scourge* to the side and picked up the thinner, darker tome from Smith. He opened the first page and stared at the title, *Basic Biomechanics and Practical Applications.*

"A textbook?" Jacob asked as he frowned. He flipped through a few random pages before a picture caught his eye. He cracked the book open wide and stared at the mass of cables and tubes and plates. One page showed all the individual pieces, while the next showed how to assemble each one. He turned to the next diagram. It showed a completed leg, not unlike what Smith had given Jacob.

In tiny print, below the diagram, were the initials C.V. and Atlier. "Charles?" Jacob squinted at the page and pulled it close to his eyes. "*Charles?*" He looked up at the lamp built into the ceiling. The light inside swelled and dimmed in a slow, constant rhythm. "What did Charles have to do with the Biomechs?" Jacob turned the page and read until he could no longer hold his eyes open, and sleep took him.

✦   ✦   ✦

Alice stood in the doorway to the stables, watching Samuel and Charles, and just listened.

"I can't believe we're leaving the kid here," Samuel said. "Why would you want to do that?"

Charles looked up as he finished buckling one of the dark leather saddlebags. "I don't *want* to leave him behind, but we have to move. We have to find out how bad it is in Dauschen, and we need to know what's heading toward Ancora."

"I don't like it," Samuel said.

"Neither do I, but I don't see a choice here. I can't see relying on information from Archibald's spies. There's a good chance some of them are already compromised. Look, Jacob should only need a few weeks to recover with the … with the changes.”

"They're turning him into a Mech," Samuel said.

"No, they aren't. They're giving him what he needs and no more. He can live a normal life with that leg, and the only thing he'll have to worry about is close-minded, intolerant fools." Charles poked Samuel in the chest with his index finger as he said, "Don't be one of those fools."

"I'll stay with him," Alice said.

Charles paused and turned away from Samuel. He didn't seem surprised by her arrival at all. "Are you sure?"

"I'm not leaving him here alone."

"I don't like the idea of leaving both the kids here," Samuel said.

"You keep calling us kids, but we're only a few years younger than you."

Samuel smiled and looked at Alice. "When you're my age, you'll think kids your age are just kids too."

"Alice," Charles said. "Please, consider coming with us. I trust Archibald, I do, but I don't know who else, or what else, may be here. I wouldn't want you to end up being ransom."

"But it's okay for Jacob to be ransom?" Alice snapped.

Charles shook his head. "That's not what I mean, and you know it. Jacob can't travel yet. The leg Smith built him has a chance to give the boy a normal life. I think that taking a chance of leaving him alone is well worth it."

Charles could make awfully good sense when he needed to, Alice thought, but the idea of leaving Jacob alone frustrated her. Her eyebrows drew together as she frowned.

She remembered the boy who'd stood up for her in the Square the first time they'd met. The boy who stepped into a circle of hecklers and told them all to piss off. She remembered the boy who smashed a stolen peppermill on one of the heckler's heads. She still wondered why he'd stolen a peppermill, of all things, as she ran her fingers through her fiery hair. It had been the hair that caused her so much trouble. The zealots thought she was evil incarnate. Jacob was one of the few people who treated her like a normal person, even when he was incredibly annoying.

Alice looked up at Charles and said, "I'm staying."

"Jacob needs time to heal," Charles said. "He'll be working with Smith quite a bit—"

"I'm not an idiot," she said, cringing at how effectively she'd interrupted Charles. Her mother would be mortified. "I'll give him the space he needs. Did you even think to find out what the rest of Bollwerk thinks about what's happening? Is Archibald saying what the people think, or is he just as misleading as Parliament?"

Charles stared at Alice and blinked.

Samuel laughed and a grin split his face. "You have to admit, they're pretty smart for kids."

Charles rubbed his face and sighed before he nodded. "Alright, but be careful. It's pretty obvious you aren't from around here. Try not to stay in the sun too long either. It's a lot harsher here, and you won't like a desert sunburn, I can tell you that."

Alice turned away and then hesitated. She took a few quick steps up to Charles and hugged him. "Be careful." Charles ran his hand over her hair. It made her feel a bit like a furry pet, but it also reminded her of the family she'd left in Ancora.

She disentangled herself and hugged Samuel in turn.

"Take care, kid. We'll be back before you know it."

"Tell Drakkar to be safe, too," Alice said. "I know we don't know him all that well, but I like him."

Charles smiled before Alice turned away. As the door closed behind her, she heard the old man say, "Me too, girl. Me too."

CHAPTER TWENTY-THREE

ALICE SKIPPED THE CRAWLER RIDE back to the Hall. Her mother always told her the best way to get to know a place is to put your feet on the ground. She pulled a small change purse out of a pocket on her leather dress and nodded. It was plenty to buy lunch before she checked on Jacob.

The streets of Bollwerk reminded her of the Highlands, but the people here were kind. She smiled at the younger children who waved, and the older folks who only acknowledged her with a nod. They didn't seem to judge her in a single glance for wearing an old threadbare dress with her leggings and boots. Archibald had offered her new clothes, but she felt safer in her own inside a new city. Some Bollwerks seemed curious about her pale skin, and her hair caught a great deal of attention, but no one was rude about it. No one except the girl, but Alice didn't much mind her.

"Is your head on fire?"

Alice stopped and blinked. "What?"

"Your hair," she said as she pointed at Alice's head. "It's so bright!"

Alice ran her fingers through the ends of her hair and smiled. "No, it's always like this."

The girl kept walking beside Alice, even as Alice wove through the crowd and walked up and down the block with no real destination in mind.

"But it's so bright."

Alice smiled and looked at the girl. Her skin was dark, not so dark as Drakkar, but much darker than anyone she knew in Ancora. She hadn't seen many folks with a complexion like that since the trade routes shut down. The girl pulled some sort of copper clip out of her black hair, quickly piled the mass on top of her head, and refastened it.

"Do you know any good places to eat?" Alice asked.

"What's your name?" the girl asked.

"Alice. What's yours?"

"I'm not sure I should tell you," the girl said, narrowing her eyes. "You seem nice enough, but you're not from around here."

Alice held back a laugh. She'd had the same thought about people back in Ancora when she didn't know them. "I'm from Ancora. Is there someplace good to eat around here?"

"Might be."

"What do you like to eat?"

The girl's mouth twitched to the side. Alice wasn't sure if she was thinking about where to eat or whether she should run away from the outlander.

"I think …" the girl started. "I think you'd like The Fish Head."

Alice frowned. "That doesn't sound very appetizing."

"It's the best fish in Bollwerk! They buy it from the mountain fishermen in the mornings, and when they run out they close the shop for the day."

"Are they expensive?"

The girl shook her head. "No more than any fish stand on the streets, and you never know how old *that* fish is. Until you taste it." The girl stuck out her tongue and shivered.

"Why don't you show me where it is? I'll get you some fish too."

The girl's eyes darted to the ground before returning to Alice. "I'd like that. My name's Gladys."

"It's nice to meet you, Gladys. Now let's get some food."

Gladys relaxed a bit as they walked another block and passed one of the massive towers of Bollwerk. Alice looked up, still not quite able to grasp how a building could be so tall and withstand the winds and storms.

"That's one of the Council buildings," Gladys said. She led Alice around the corner. "They leave us alone for the most part, as long as we aren't causing trouble."

"Who? The Council?"

"Well, the Council is always nice, but sometimes the policemen can get a bit nasty."

Alice remembered Jacob's story about the knight who came to cut off his hands. He said the man looked happy—*really* happy—about the idea of cutting Jacob's hands off. She hoped they didn't have that kind of madness in Bollwerk.

"Are they violent? Do they hurt people?"

"Oh, no," Gladys said as if that was the stupidest question she'd ever heard. "They'll just take you home to your parents faster than you can blink. That's where the real trouble is."

"With your parents?" Alice asked with a small smile.

Gladys nodded and stepped around an elderly couple beneath a light-colored parasol. "Oh yes, I've been locked in my own house for an entire week before with nothing but books."

"Not even food?" Alice asked in as serious a voice as she could.

"Well, of course I had food. They weren't trying to kill me. Nothing but food and books for a week! Not very friendly of them, if you ask me."

"It sounds nice," Alice said. She thought about staying indoors for a week and reading. "It sounds very nice."

"You're one of those weird folks who like to read, aren't you?"

"Maybe a little."

"At least you're not boring to talk to," Gladys said. She pointed at something down the smooth stone street. "See it?"

"See what? Oh," Alice said as she found what Gladys was pointing at. A giant fish head of rusted iron hung over the sidewalk. Its jaws were open wide, looking as though it would eat any who dared walk underneath it. It may have looked a bit more threatening if its eyes hadn't been X's.

As they got closer, Alice could see that great care had been taken when someone etched out the design. Every scale and wrinkle and lip was covered in extraordinary detail all across the sign. Between the jaws hung the words "The Fish Head."

"Come on," Gladys said. She pulled the door open and ushered Alice inside.

Alice followed Gladys up to a pale wooden bar. The shop felt smaller than the entrance suggested, with a few tattered banners hung along the walls. A surprising number of patrons ate and talked inside for the middle of the day.

The man behind the bar turned around and Alice raised her eyebrows slightly. He was the first Bollwerk man she'd seen with skin as dark as Drakkar. She almost asked him if he knew Drakkar, but caught herself when she realized that would be a rather silly question.

"Hello, princess," the man said. He laid a fish out on a wide stretch of butcher's block. "What can I get you?"

"I told you not to call me that here," Gladys said under her breath.

"A princess is a princess no matter where she finds herself," he said as he set a roughly hewn ironwood bowl in front of them, filled with seeds.

Gladys grabbed a handful and scowled as she chewed.

"Now, my princess, what would you like?"

Alice crunched down on the seeds, which she then realized were some kind of roasted sunflower seeds, before she froze. "Gladys?"

The girl looked up and then followed Alice's gaze to her wrist. Gladys quickly covered her bracelet and huffed.

Alice kept her voice quiet and asked, "Are you an *actual* princess?"

"See, George?" Gladys said with an even deeper scowl. "You can't just go around saying that."

The chef smiled as he wove his knife through the fish's flesh. "I apologize, Princess."

Gladys almost growled at the man, and Alice choked back a laugh.

"Not you too," Gladys said. "I *was* rather liking you."

Alice popped another handful of sunflower seeds into her mouth.

"And who is your new friend?" George asked.

"This is Alice. She's from Ancora."

"Truly?" George said. "I would have guessed you to be from one of the island nations far to the east. It is the only place I've seen hair so red." George never stopped moving his knife. Before Alice could even respond, the iridescent skin came off the fish and George pulled the bones out with two quick sweeps of the blade.

"Maybe my great-great-grandparents," Alice said. "We're not sure. Most of our family history was lost in the war."

George nodded. "The Deadlands War stole many histories."

"Gladys is truly a princess?"

"Oh yes," George said with a broad smile. "Most everyone here knows it, but we try not to rub it in."

Gladys snorted. It was the most un-princess-like thing Alice thought she could have done. And it was hilarious.

Alice laughed so loudly that some of the other patrons turned to look at them before she slapped her hands over her mouth. "Sorry."

"I rather like your new friend, Princess."

"Great," Gladys muttered.

"We rode a Walker into Bollwerk named George," Alice said.

The chef pursed his lips and nodded. "I'm sure it was a loyal, steadfast Walker that would do anything to protect its princess."

Gladys groaned.

Alice grinned before she asked, "Where are you from? If you don't mind my asking, of course, Princess."

George belted out a deep laugh as he handed each of the girls a glass of Sweetwing Tea.

"Our home is gone," Gladys said, sobering George's demeanor in a heartbeat. "We lost it to a great battle with the warlords."

"It was called Midstream," George said. "It was a small city to the north. What wasn't burned to the ground was overrun by warlords. If not for a small band of Steamsworn, the royal family would have perished in the battle." George untied the top of the leather tunic beneath his apron and pulled it open, revealing a large tattoo of the Steamsworn fist.

"That's why it's on your bracelet too?" Alice asked. "I thought the other was a royal crest, but I wasn't sure."

"It was," Gladys said with a sad smile. "It was our house crest." She rubbed at the bracelet hidden beneath her sleeve.

Alice wasn't sure what to say to all of this, so she only said, "It's an honor to meet you both." She bowed her head slightly, and when she looked up, Gladys had tears in her eyes.

CHAPTER TWENTY-FOUR

J ACOB SETTLED IN BY SMITH'S workbench. He'd thought about waiting for Alice, but he needed to get used to maneuvering the chair on his own. He'd be stuck in it for a few more weeks, most likely, so there was no sense in making everyone else push him around.

Jacob swung his backpack off the chair and into his lap. He pulled out the biomechanics handbook and set his pack on the ground. Jacob studied the intricate diagrams. The name came back to him earlier that morning. Charles called them exploded diagrams. He raised his leg onto a stool so he could lean over it without having to bend down.

The panels slid open easily when you knew where all the latches were. Once he had the leg open, he wiggled his toes. A small gesture, but it still brought a smile to his face. He didn't really have his own toes anymore, but Smith's leg was an amazing contraption. Jacob watched the little rounded plates that capped each piston and actuator. He could see how the mechanical side worked, but the tubes of blood and wires were still a mystery to him.

Jacob wasn't sure how long he'd been comparing his leg to the exploded diagram inside *Basic Biomechanics and Practical Applications* when someone knocked at the door. "It's open." Smith never bothered to lock his workshop. In some ways, he was the opposite of Charles. If Charles so much as left for lunch, he'd bolt down the old observatory so nothing but a Jumper could squeeze in. Unless you knew where the crawlspaces were, of course.

"How are you?"

Jacob turned and smiled when he saw Skysworn Mary standing in the doorway. She wore leathers again and had her pilot's goggles perched on her head. Jacob suspected she slept in those goggles.

"I'm alright," he said. "How's the Skysworn?"

Mary returned his smile. "A bit worse for wear, but nothing we can't fix. Now that Smith is done stitching you back together, at least. It was slow going without him."

"Is he coming back?"

Mary nodded. "Oh, yes. I've heard all about his plans to turn you into a Biomech tinker. They'll make you into a proper Steamsworn, I'm sure. Even if you don't stay in Bollwerk, Archibald likes to have allies spread across as much of the world as he can.

"It makes sense," Jacob said. He slid the panels closed on his leg. "If you don't make allies, someone else might."

"You aren't wrong there," Mary said. She hopped onto one of Smith's stools. "How's Charles doing?"

"Charles?" Jacob asked.

"That old tinker has a terrible guilt over what happened to you."

"He shouldn't," Jacob said. "It was my own damned fault for getting too close to the tree." He ran a hand over his leg and shivered. "Well, lesson learned."

Mary let out a humorless laugh. "Tough way to learn a lesson, kid."

"My dad always said the toughest lessons are the best lessons."

Mary raised an eyebrow and pointed at his leg. "I kind of doubt *that* was what he meant."

The door squeaked as it opened and closed. No one had knocked, so Jacob wasn't surprised when he looked up and found Archibald. Other than Smith, Archibald was the only one who didn't knock.

"Mary," he said with a nod. "How are you feeling, Jacob?"

"Better. My leg still hurts though."

"I'm afraid that's going to last a while. Smith tells me he wants to start teaching you to walk again."

"It's not like I forgot."

Archibald pushed the hem of his cloak to the side and raised the cuff on his dark gray pants. Beneath flashed an intricately etched plate.

"You have a Biomech leg?" Jacob asked.

"More than a leg, my boy. Much more than a leg."

"How did it happen?"

Archibald smiled and pulled up a chair. He sat lower than Mary. Jacob liked that. It was something the Highlanders in Parliament would never allow. It made Archibald seem a little more like everyone else.

"That's a question you'll need to get used to, Jacob. How did it happen? Did it hurt? Are you going to be like a crazy person now?"

"Of course it hurt," Jacob said. "How could losing a leg *not* hurt? It got *bitten off.*"

Mary laughed and slapped Archibald's shoulder. "I think the kid's got that one down."

"Be patient, Jacob," Archibald said. "You'll answer the same questions many times, but people don't mean to be rude. They're only curious."

"I don't mind. People used to ask how I could be a good Cork player growing up in the slums. They weren't the slums to me. They were home."

"The Lowlands were the best part of Ancora, if you ask me," Mary said as she stood up. "None of that uppity attitude you got in the Highlands. Hell, less of an attitude than most of Bollwerk."

"Are you leaving?" Jacob asked.

Mary nodded. "I told Smith I was coming by to check on you. I can't leave him alone for too long. He likes to fix things that don't need to be fixed. You know what happens when you fix something that doesn't need to be fixed?"

"It breaks."

Mary grinned. "I knew I liked you, kid. Take care of yourself."

Archibald gave Mary a brief wave as she stepped outside and closed the door with a click.

"Do you know whose initials N.V.B. are?" Jacob asked.

A tiny smile appeared on Archibald's face as he leaned forward and his shoulders sagged. "Yes, I know whose initials those are."

When Archibald didn't respond for a time, Jacob said, "Well?"

"A very long time ago, Jacob, he was our friend, mine and Charles's. His full name is Newton Victor Burns."

Jacob leaned back in his chair and stared at Archibald. "He was your friend?"

Archibald nodded. "Until he became a monster, until he became the Butcher, yes, he was my friend. For a very long time, Newton was the best smith I ever knew, next to Charles."

Jacob ran a hand over his leg. "I'm going to have to vote for Smith."

Archibald smiled and drummed his fingers on the workbench. "Smith is the fastest I've ever known, and that's about the best you can ask for biomechanics. It's easy to lose someone when you're working in blood."

"Charles told me a Berserker killed one of the Butcher's brothers."

"So he hasn't hidden everything from you?" Archibald narrowed his eyes and nodded. "That's good. You're deep in this mess now, Jacob. You need to understand what we're up against."

"Between what you wrote in *The Dead Scourge*, and what Charles has told me, I know we're up against a monster."

"He is that. He is most definitely that. Jacob, when you can walk again, I want to take you to Gareth Cave."

Jacob's forehead creased. "Why?"

"It's something you need to see in order to understand. At least, I think it is. The slaughter at that cave helped forge the identity of our entire city. There isn't a man, woman, or child who doesn't know it. We've all stepped into the shadows of that place."

Archibald stood as he finished speaking. "Practice your walking with Smith. I know it may seem unnecessary, and painful, but it will help a great deal. There's far more power in that leg than you had in your flesh-and-bone leg."

"I will," Jacob said as Archibald started to leave. Before he left, Jacob asked, "How far of a walk is the cave?"

Archibald paused at the door and turned around. "We'll have Mary fly us out. I'd rather not risk going on a pilgrimage and missing a communication from Charles."

"You think they'll be gone long?"

"I wouldn't expect to hear anything for a few weeks. If it's sooner, that's wonderful, but expect a few weeks so you don't worry. Take care of yourself, Jacob." Archibald pulled the door closed behind him.

Jacob ran his fingers over the initials N.V.B. below the exploded diagram. "Why Gareth Cave? Why would you do that?"

✧　✧　✧

JACOB WASN'T SURE HOW LONG he'd been staring at the text, but there were calculations inside that were too far over his head for him to do much more. He found another book on basic engineering tucked away in Smith's workbench that explained some of the formulas, but he felt like it had melted half his brain.

Jacob almost sighed in relief when another knock sounded at the door. "It's open!" He turned his head over his left shoulder and watched the iron-wrapped door swing open. He smiled when Alice's shock of red hair slipped into the room.

"How are you?" she asked.

"Not bad. Anxious to get walking again."

"Do you mind if a friend joins us?"

"No," Jacob said as he frowned slightly, wondering why she'd need to ask that.

"Come on in," Alice said to the crack in the door.

A girl, slightly shorter than Alice, with black hair and skin darker than most of the folks he'd seen in Bollwerk, stepped inside.

"This is Gladys."

The girl waved, and Jacob nodded to her.

"Did you need something?" Jacob asked.

"I told her about your leg," Alice said, "and she was hoping to see it."

Jacob couldn't put his finger on it, but that bothered him. It wasn't that Alice wanted him to meet her friend; she wanted her friend to see his leg? "I'm not a Festival attraction, you know."

"I meant no offense," Gladys said, catching on to Jacob's irritation in the blink of an eye.

"It's okay." He'd probably had his nose stuck in a book he didn't understand for too long. Jacob rubbed his face and took a deep breath before turning his chair to face them. "Sorry, I think I'm just tired."

"No need to be a jerk about it," Alice muttered as she pulled a chair up beside him.

"Are you sure you don't mind?" Gladys asked.

Jacob summoned a smile and shook his head.

"Gladys is a princess," Alice said.

Jacob's irritation flowed away in a moment. He knew Alice's voice well enough to tell she wasn't lying, or at least she believed she was telling the truth. "Of Bollwerk?"

"I thought we weren't talking about that," Gladys said, looking at Alice.

"Not telling 'anyone' doesn't include Jacob and Charles," Alice said. "I guess I should have told you that. They're the closest thing I have to family here, and I trust them with my life."

Gladys said something else, but Jacob didn't catch it. He watched

Alice out of the corner of his eye. He thought of their little group the same way. They practically *were* family, and he'd do anything to keep them safe.

"Jacob?"

He blinked and turned his attention to Gladys. "Sorry, what was that?"

"Are you hungry? We have some leftovers from The Fish Head."

"Fish heads?" Jacob asked with a frown. "Nasty. I thought princesses would eat better."

Gladys laughed and shook her head. "No, no, it's a restaurant. It's called The Fish Head. She picked up a small paper bag and handed it to him. Inside was a packet of seeds and what looked like a rice ball. It smelled delicious.

"What's in it?"

"Sunflower seeds," Alice said. "The rice ball has some kind of mashed-up fish in it, but it's good."

"Mashed-up fish?" Gladys said. "You don't worry much about making things sound good, do you?"

"She doesn't worry about much of anything," Jacob said as he stuffed a piece of the rice ball into his mouth. It was slightly salty and crunchy, and he guessed it would have been even more so when it was fresh. "It's good, thank you."

He took another bite and waited to swallow before asking, "What are you a princess of?"

"You wouldn't have heard of it," Gladys said. "It was a little province called Midstream."

Jacob frowned, because as much as Gladys thought otherwise, he *had* heard of it. "That's close to Gareth Cave."

"How do you know this?"

"I read it in a book," he said as he looked at Alice. "Apparently I paid closer attention than some other people who read the book."

Alice stared at him, dumbstruck. "I forgot! I forgot that was in there. And shut up, I was most definitely paying attention."

Jacob smiled and tossed back a handful of sunflower seeds.

"You argue like married people," Gladys said, scratching her arm. Jacob saw a line of scars above her elbow before the princess lowered her sleeve again.

He thought about asking her what it was from, but if it was something bad, he didn't want to dredge it up. Instead, he opted for stuffing his face with the rice ball.

"So, what are you doing today?" Alice asked.

"Learning to walk, apparently," Jacob said with a small frown. "Whenever Smith gets here. That's what Archibald says at least."

"Archibald the Speaker?" Gladys asked. She leaned forward and rested her chin on her hand.

"Do you know him?" Alice asked.

"I know of him, of course. I've met him on more than one occasion, but he is still a stranger in many ways. The Speaker gave us sanctuary inside Bollwerk after our own city fell to the warlords."

"What happened?" Jacob asked.

"Do you know of the warlords in the far reaches of the Deadlands?"

Jacob shook his head and Alice said, "No, not more than what you mentioned."

Gladys leaned back and curled her hands into fists before relaxing them again. "The worst of them are Mechs, driven insane by whatever toxic thing their implants were made of."

Jacob tugged on his pant leg, trying to cover the bit of his biomechanics that was still visible.

"Don't," Gladys said as she tapped on her leg. "We don't fear the Steamsworn and the new Biomechs. I've lived here long enough to know the difference. You don't have to hide your leg."

"I already told her you'd exchanged it for a better leg, anyway," Alice said with a straight face. Her façade cracked slightly as she fought a smile.

"That's one way of putting it," Jacob said under his breath. He studied the half-eaten rice ball and took another bite.

"Most of the old Mechs …" Gladys said before she hesitated. "The men who would be as old as Charles or the Speaker now. They're long dead. Driven so far into insanity they could not function, or they had to be struck down by their own kind. The Berserkers who replaced them, they became warlords in the Deadlands.

"Mostly they stay in the remote parts of the desert, but there are times when they'll come into the cities. They do … terrible things to the people. We barely escaped the village outside Midstream—our refuge prior to Bollwerk—before it was burned to the ground."

"The entire city?" Alice asked.

"The town around the castle, yes. There's a warlord who calls himself the Butcher who lives there now."

"Not the real Butcher," Jacob said.

"What do you mean?" Gladys asked.

"The real Butcher, the one from Gareth Cave, ended up in Ancora."

"That madman is long dead, thank the gods. It's the warlord I worry about now. His name's Rana, and he's been hunting my family for ages. George is my guard, but he's also a good cook."

"He made this?" Jacob asked as he held up the rice ball.

Gladys nodded.

"Yeah, he's a good cook alright."

"The best," Gladys said with a small smile. "He keeps the warlord from claiming me as a bride too. He may be a great cook, but I don't think that's my favorite thing about him."

"Like an arranged marriage?" Alice asked. "I've heard of those in Fel before."

Gladys recoiled. "No! Gods no. My father would *never* condone that sort of arrangement." She shivered and grimaced. "It's … it's more like slavery. A warlord claims you, and from then on he owns you. He can do whatever he likes, even kill you, and it's accepted by his people."

"That's wrong," Jacob said. Something cold stirred in his gut. "How can something like that still exist? We've had peace for fifty years."

"Some people have had peace," Gladys said. "Other people have been murdered in their homes in these times of *peace*. That's … I didn't mean to ramble like that. What it comes down to is George keeps me safe from the Butcher. I love him for that."

Jacob and Alice exchanged a glance while Gladys played with a bronze ring on her finger. Alice gave a sharp, quick shake of her head, and Jacob nodded. He didn't think this was the time to tell Gladys that the real Butcher was alive and well.

CHAPTER TWENTY-FIVE

A LICE AND GLADYS STAYED WITH Jacob until he finished eating. They might have stayed longer, but Smith arrived before they could find anything to lighten the mood. Gladys had terrible stories about what had happened to her people, and what could happen to her if the warlords ever found her.

Smith glanced at the paper bag on the floor and smiled. "They bring you something from The Fish Head?"

Jacob nodded. "Best rice ball I've ever had."

"Best everything you have ever had. The Fish Head is one of the best-kept secrets in Bollwerk." Smith sat down in the low chair and rolled up Jacob's pant leg. He opened the panel over the calf and peered inside at the mass of tubes and metal. Smith poked and prodded and checked various parts of Jacob's leg with everything from a thermometer to a strange pair of spikes. A wire ran between the spikes, and a gauge on top of one of the spikes seemed to fluctuate up and down with Jacob's heartbeat.

"Looks good, Jacob. You are generating your own power now."

"What?"

"This," he said as he raised the spiked mechanism, "measures the current inside your leg. You press it to the open contacts, and it shows you what's going on."

"What's the current do?"

"It runs an internal heater so you can survive in the cold, for one. It also engages some optional gearing if you need it. Press the buttons above your knee in series, front to back. It will put extra power into your kick, or let you jump higher, or even run faster."

"Run faster?"

Smith nodded as he closed Jacob's leg. "Yes, but be careful with that one. You only have one Biomech leg. That means the strides on your right leg will be much longer and much faster than your left. It will make it very easy for you to fall down and break your face."

"Thank you?"

Smith grinned. "I do not know much about the humor in Ancora, but the sarcasm? I do like it, Jacob."

"Now, how has the pain been?" Smith asked as he flexed Jacob's foot.

"Not too bad as long as I keep pressure off it. It's been … it's been kind of like a toothache, but in my leg."

"That is good." Smith slid a thin greasy tool under the edge of Jacob's knee. Smith apologized when Jacob winced.

"What was that?"

"It will help numb the pain for a short time," Smith said. "Now, I'm going to push on your leg. Let me know if the pain is too much."

Jacob braced himself against the burning needles of agony he expected, but he only felt a dull ache. He slowly released his grip on the wheelchair's armrests and stared at Smith. Smith wore the closest thing to a smirk Jacob had ever seen on him.

"I think you are ready. Come, let us be rid of your chair." Smith extended his hand and Jacob grabbed it. The tinker pulled him to his feet with little effort and let go.

Jacob wobbled and flailed for a moment, but then something whirred and clicked in his leg. He felt stable and took a tentative step closer to the workbench so he could support himself with his hands.

"How is the pain?"

"I can handle it. It's weird though. I can feel my leg—the pressure around my knee, at least—but I know it's gone."

"That is not unusual," Smith said. "You will likely have some ghost pain for a time. I will ask you again, now that you are standing. Are you ready? We will walk to the Council chambers and back. It is not far, but it will be a struggle." Smith walked to the door and pulled it open. When Jacob didn't reply, he asked again. "Are you ready?"

Jacob frowned and gritted his teeth. His instincts screamed at him to hold on to the workbench. Part of his brain knew damn well there wasn't a leg to stand on. He almost laughed at the thought, and in that moment of distraction, he let go of the bench.

He felt like he was falling at first, but then his body was rocked by the impact of his new leg on the hardwood floor. He didn't have to think about moving his left leg; it followed as naturally as if he still had two legs.

"That is it," Smith said. "Walk as if you have two legs, for in fact you do."

The third step caused Jacob to stumble as his Biomech foot caught the edge of a stool. He almost caught his balance before he overcompensated and landed on the floor. Jacob gritted his teeth. The pain wasn't as bad as he expected, but whatever Smith had done to numb his leg only went so far.

"Three steps," Smith said. "I am impressed. Most people cannot walk three steps for weeks after getting their implants. I think you can do more." Smith extended his arm once again, and Jacob grasped it.

"Three steps isn't much," Jacob said before he grunted and stood up. "I need to be able to walk and run if I'm going to help my friends."

"And you will," Smith said. "Practice will be all you need. A little time walking to the entrance of the Council Hall and back, and you will be ready to try jogging."

Jacob narrowed his eyes. "That doesn't seem very likely."

"Perhaps a week. I have faith," Smith said. "You are healing at a remarkable rate."

Jacob glanced back at the chair and frowned. "It doesn't feel like it."

"Come, walk with me." Smith paused at the door. "Wait outside a moment, yes?"

"Sure," Jacob said. His Biomech foot clanked onto the stone floor of the corridor. He stood and watched the door until Smith pulled it open again.

"This may help," Smith said. He held up one of Jacob's shoes. "You have been off balance, and still you managed three steps. It is more impressive than you believe it to be."

"I forgot my shoe?" Jacob asked of no one in particular. "How did I do that?"

"You have an excellent focus," Smith said, bending down to help Jacob slide his foot into the leather shoe. "Sometimes, when you focus too hard on one thing, you forget the rest of the world. Archibald used to tell me that was the sign of a good tinker. It is also a sign of someone who walks into walls."

Jacob bent down to tie his shoe. He wobbled slightly as he stood up, but caught his balance quickly. Smith was staring at him when he glanced at the tinker.

"I think you are going to do fine, my Ancoran friend." Smith patted Jacob's shoulder and started down the hall.

With both his shoes on, Jacob had less trouble balancing. He still stumbled a few times when the mechanism around his knee didn't move exactly as he expected it to, but he only fell once. One time onto that cold stone floor was enough.

When they rounded the corner into the Council Hall, Smith wore a wide grin. Archibald stood inside, his jaw slack and his eyes wide.

"You're *walking?*"

"Well, more like stumbling," Jacob said. "I guess you could call it walking."

"Was it the injections?" Archibald asked as he glanced at Smith.

The tinker shook his head. "He heals much faster than anyone I have worked on. I do not know if it is his age, or his bloodline, but it is a good thing. I also numbed his injury for this."

"Keep practicing." Archibald turned to Jacob. "If you can already walk, even if it's stumbling," he said with a smile, "you'll be ready for our little excursion when it comes time."

"I will," Jacob said. "Come on, Smith, let's walk back to the lab."

He heard the tinker follow him as he turned away from the Hall and its massive bench. He couldn't stop a tiny smile from etching its way across his lips. If what Archibald and Smith had said held true, he really *was* healing faster than the average Biomech. Maybe he'd get to meet up with Charles and Samuel sooner than he'd thought.

Jacob started down the corridor with a renewed purpose. He wasn't going to leave anything to chance. He was going to be rested, healed, and ready as fast as humanly possible.

✧   ✧   ✧

SMITH FOLLOWED JACOB BACK AND forth from his workshop to the hall for almost twenty solid minutes. Jacob's stamina impressed the tinker. The boy was adapting to his leg faster than Smith expected—a lot faster. He already had plans to teach Jacob about maintaining his biomechanics, and even building some, but now he was almost excited about the prospect. If Jacob proved as sharp as Charles claimed, in time, he could become a master smith.

They made it back to the workshop for the sixth time when Jacob grunted in pain and nearly collapsed.

"Wait," Smith said. He could see the grimace on the boy's face, and it wasn't just out of frustration. His leg was starting to hurt, and that was no surprise at all. "There is something I would like to show you in the lab."

"I don't have to stop," Jacob said through gritted teeth.

"I am sure you do not, but this is important."

Smith pushed the wheelchair closer to Jacob before stepping farther into his lab, passing the largest workbench in the center of the floor, and eventually stopping at a large wall, dripping in such an array of tools and parts that even he had a difficult time remembering all their uses.

Jacob lowered himself into the chair, even though Smith could see the reluctance on the boy's face.

"Close the door, please, and lock it."

A flicker of amusement kindled in his gut when Jacob visibly perked up at the request. The boy was curious, of that there was no doubt. It was a trait that would likely lead him to great discoveries, or an early grave. There weren't many more options in Smith's experience.

"What are we doing?" Jacob asked.

"This is the most advanced biomechanics lab in the world."

Jacob looked around, and Smith didn't think he looked impressed. "It is … nice," Jacob said, not without a great deal of hesitation.

Smith pushed up on a rack holding a series of rubber belts. That released the slide lever, which he grabbed and pushed to the left, causing another rack to shake at the end of the wall. "Push that up, would you?"

Smith watched Jacob as the boy wheeled closer and put his hand on the shaking shelf. Jacob pushed the rack of hoses up and nearly jumped when the wall began to part. The floor rumbled with the movement of the stone, but considering the mass being moved, it was remarkably quiet.

"As I was saying," Smith said. The doors widened enough to allow access to the lights. He flipped the switch, and the large oval-shaped room snapped into focus. Every wall stood covered in silver, brass, and copper pieces. Jars and crystalline drawers filled with fittings of every imaginable type lined the shelves. Smith figured there were enough parts to build twenty men from head to toe, and that didn't account for the warehouse.

He turned to Jacob and said, "*This* is the most advanced biomechanics lab in the world."

Jacob gawked, and Smith let a slow smile spread across his face.

CHAPTER TWENTY-SIX

JACOB WAS IN GOOD HANDS with Smith, Charles knew. He hated leaving the boy behind, but they didn't have much of an option with Jacob's injuries and the recovery he would have to endure. He'd still have Alice to keep him company, and that was a good thing.

Charles glanced back at the shadowy egg of Bollwerk on the horizon behind them. He found it reassuring, being able to see civilization while you were in the desert. The view wouldn't last long. No more than another hour and they'd be skirting the line between the Burning Forest and the mountains, making their way to the western gap.

The clouds rolling in from the west concerned him. Tall gray floating giants cast impossible shadows across the landscape. He glanced at the other men and women riding on the back of the cart with him. They all had their eyes to the sky. From what he could tell by their mutterings, they thought the clouds were a positive sign. At least the carriage rode more smoothly than the bumpy stride of a Walker.

"Doesn't look good," Samuel said as he pulled up beside the carriage and raised his hand, blocking the blowing sand.

"Smith told me the seasonal storm is late," Charles said. "I'm afraid we're about to ride into it. Where's Drakkar? He might have a better idea what we're in for."

Charles squinted into the distance as another gust of wind rose around them. He took a deep breath and then sighed. "Damn. That smells like rain."

"I think I see him," Samuel said. He urged his mount forward, a tall Desert Stick. It had a narrow tan body, and only six legs, but it could move at speeds to rival George the Walker. A string of saddlebags sat between the creature's rear four legs, and Samuel leaned forward in the narrow saddle behind its front legs. A towering pair of antennae searched the air in front of them while the Desert Stick accelerated.

Charles watched the Spider Knight close in on Drakkar. It wasn't long before the dizzying blur of George's legs slowed, and the carriage on which Charles rode caught up to Samuel and the Cave Guardian.

"It looks to be a bad storm," Drakkar said, raising his voice over the constant thump of George's steps. Thunder rolled and crashed in the distance. Drakkar raised his goggles and looked to the west. "I cannot be sure how bad, my friend, but it will not make for pleasant travels."

"How can you be sure?"

"We have not seen a single Sky Needle. Only storms would keep them away from a caravan of this size."

Charles glanced at the ever-darkening skies. He wasn't sure what he'd rather deal with. At least you could kill a Sky Needle. The storms of the Deadlands were legendary, and you can't run a sword through a cloud.

Charles knew the man beside him was a guard from the airship docks. That's how he'd been introduced earlier that morning, but he couldn't remember the man's name. Instead of bumbling around, trying to recall it, the old man just tapped him on the shoulder.

"What is it?" the man asked as he adjusted his pale gray jacket.

"Did everyone pack rain gear?" Charles asked.

"Not likely."

Charles nodded. "We may want to consider stopping at one of the caves in the foothills if it gets bad."

"The floods run south," the man said. "We should be fine so close to the Burning Forest, even in a hundred-year storm."

Another cascade of thunder shook the air. Charles didn't share the man's optimism.

BOLLWERK VANISHED BEHIND THEM BY the time the storm clouds stained the sky, and lightning ignited the mountain passes. Drakkar slowed once again as the orange glow of the Burning Forest drew closer. A few drops of rain started to fall.

"Be on your guard," Drakkar said to Charles. "One of the scouts spoke of Tail Swords being seen in this area."

"Perfect," Charles muttered. "Where's Samuel?"

"I already told him of the danger, my friend. He is near the front of the caravan, speaking with two of the Bollwerk knights. They are not Steamsworn, but they are skilled." Drakkar nodded as he urged George forward. The Walker almost seemed annoyed, as it had its head pointed at the sky while the rain splashed against its face. Drakkar motioned again, and George finally shot forward, weaving through the caravan.

The thought of Tail Swords unsettled Charles. The thought of meeting them in the open desert was one Charles didn't want to entertain. Sometimes you had to ponder terrible ideas to keep yourself alive. He sighed and watched the Burning Forest brighten as the skies grew darker. They had enough men to fight Tail Swords off, and he still had his air cannon strapped to his back, but if they encountered a bed of them, men would die.

The rain started to hit harder, and it wasn't long before he heard the hiss of the water striking the fires of the Burning Forest. He pulled his goggles out of a pouch on his vest and lowered them over his eyes. The rain wouldn't be good for the leather, but he could worry about that later. Right now, he just needed to see clearly.

He was distracted from the rain as the caravan closed in on the Burning Forest. It had grown considerably since last he'd seen it. Geysers of flame cut through the tree-like pillars of stone and arced through the air in a steady cone of fire.

Most of the pillars in the forest looked like long dead trunks, with no branches to speak of, but others had intricate branching systems that made the stone look more like a dormant tree in winter. Flames didn't shoot as high into the air from the pillars with branches. The majority barely had a flame on the top of the trunk, but the branches themselves held a thousand little pockets of fire. It was a beautiful sight.

They stayed on the edge of the Burning Forest, but even there, an occasional pillar of fire would flank them, and they'd have to weave the caravan through part of the forest. Many of the pillars were small at first, no more than ten to fifteen feet in height, but as the rains grew heavier, and they covered more distance, some of the true giants lit the skies far above them. If not for the fires erupting above, the canopy would have been lost in the clouded sky.

Charles had never been in a desert storm that darkened the world like this. It was a sight to behold, but it set his nerves on edge. No matter how far removed he was from the Deadlands War, some instincts never left him.

Dark pockets appeared in the mountainsides, lit from a distance by the Burning Forest. Charles knew some of those were caves. Some of those caves would be havens if the storms grew too severe. Others would slope downward, swallowing water and men and creatures, only to drown them at the bottom. The desert floods could be terrifying.

Lightning broke the darkness above them and someone screamed a few carriages ahead. A series of bolts struck one of the burning pillars. A gout of flame burst out of the tree, ripping across the top of a carriage before it receded. No one had been on top that Charles could see, but it had been a close thing.

The warm glow of the fires revealed Samuel's Desert Stick making its way back to Charles once again. It was a graceful creature, taking easy strides as it moved over sand and rock.

"The men saw movement in the mountains," Samuel said.

"Could be a trick of the light," Charles said. "It happens in the storms. If you see movement in the sands, that's when you should be concerned."

Samuel nodded. "Drakkar tells me the rains will wake things up that would otherwise be sleeping."

"That's one way to put it."

A brilliant fork of lightning crashed into a tall cluster of cacti, and the thunder of the gods followed in its wake. The sky opened as though someone had split a thousand water barrels above their heads.

"Do we take shelter?" Samuel shouted over another roll of thunder.

"No, push harder! Tell the front of the caravan!"

Samuel nodded as he snapped a rein on the side of the Desert Stick. The creature's strides lengthened, and Samuel vanished into the downpour.

Charles dug through the sack at his side until he found a visor to clip over his goggles. He wiped the water away as best he could. The Spider Knights swore the goggles let you see in absolute darkness, but that wasn't true at all. The lenses were a very rare stone, cut extraordinarily thin and reinforced with shaded glass that helped magnify the light.

The Burning Forest burst into brilliant life when he cleared the streaks of rain rolling down his goggles. It matted his hair and brought the sharp scent of the skies with it. Nothing moved within the forest. It was a small consolation in the downpour, but it was something.

Charles felt the carriage surge forward a few minutes later, and he knew Samuel had delivered the message.

"Do you have guns or swords?" Charles shouted to the man beside him.

The man nodded. "We do, but they are packed away. We did not want the guards in Dauschen to be tipped off."

Charles returned the nod. It was smart, in theory, but it could also get them all killed. Water began to lift the sands, forming an arcing spray around the wheels. It wouldn't take long for the sleeping things to awaken, and he hoped they could make it into the mountain pass before anything hungry came hunting *them*.

CHAPTER TWENTY-SEVEN

CHARLES THOUGHT HIS EYES WERE playing tricks on him when something surged beneath the flowing river. It seemed to cut through the sands, but he suspected it was most likely a piece of cactus caught in the storm.

The second time he saw it, Charles didn't ignore it. The air cannon slid easily from its holster on his back.

"Something's out there," Charles said.

"What?" the man beside him shouted.

"Something's out there," Charles said. He motioned with the air cannon and raised his voice. "Watch the waters. Do you have some way to signal the leads?"

The two people who had heard him shook their heads.

Charles almost growled. He turned his eyes back to the river of water edging the trail they followed. It appeared to deepen with every passing moment. He knew one way to get their attention. He pumped the air cannon three times and then released the safety clasp on the back. It let him pump the lever twice more. It wasn't the wisest thing to do, since the safety was made to prevent a chamber failure, but it would get the job done.

He leveled the barrel at the water and waited for the next surge. It didn't take long. Something glinted in the light of the Burning Forest, and Charles pulled the trigger.

The force of the blast slammed his shoulder into the pile of baggage behind him, and the people around him screamed in the echoing boom. Charles pumped the air cannon as fast as he could and leveled it again. Something screeched in the darkness.

Charles stared at the next surge. The arched tail swam out of the black water and sands. He barely had time to scream a warning before the Tail Sword's entire body surfaced, water pouring from its back and legs and terrible, monstrous claws.

Its solid black body was a moving shadow but for the light glistening off its rough chitin. Fire and lightning danced across the back of the Tail Sword, reflecting off each plate of the beast as its six legs propelled it forward at a sickening pace.

Charles waited. The people around him screamed, scrambling for guns and swords, and any heavy object that might protect them. He tracked the Tail Sword as it closed. Charles pulled the trigger again, and the creature's head split open, spilling dark blood across the sands as its claws flailed and crashed into one of the carriage wheels beside him.

He'd been in war enough times that he didn't dwell on just how close that claw had come. Charles didn't consider the fact that if he'd leaned the wrong way, he'd be so much paste and blood smeared across the sands. He pumped the air cannon again and unbuckled the long knives sheathed on his thighs.

It wasn't his carriage that needed protection. Charles heard the screams and the screech, even over the thunder above and the downpour slamming into the carriage all around him. His goggles revealed a nightmare scene when he glanced to the north. One of the carriages rose into the air and impacted the sands hard enough to bury its wheels.

The inertia snapped the axels of the transport and spilled its riders into the river of death. Charles saw the tails rise and fall, striking and maiming and killing in a frenzy. The old man leapt off his carriage, screaming for the drivers to stop before he'd even hit the sands. The Bangers slid out of his pocket easily. He mashed the igniters and threw the black orbs as hard as he could.

Charles wished he had Jacob's skill and aim. His would have to do. The Bangers popped, and while they didn't do any damage, the Tail Swords backed away from the sudden flash and sound, not knowing what to make of it.

It gave Drakkar the opening he needed. Charles watched in awe as the Cave Guardian raised his blades and leapt from George's back. Drakkar struck like a whirlwind, slicing through parts of the Tail Swords with every movement. It was beautiful and terrifying, and it reminded Charles why the swords of the Cave Guardians were feared above all others.

The curved tails and claws lashed out at Drakkar, only to be struck down or parried or severed as the guardian screamed his defiance. Drakkar stepped onto the head of a Tail Sword before ramming his blade home and rolling across the chitinous back in one swift motion. He severed the tail and leapt for the next creature.

A flash of lightning revealed another line of surging water, and Charles ran harder. He'd seen a cave in the distance. It was a risk, but if they stayed in the open, they were all dead. Not even Drakkar could keep up with the mass of creatures closing on them.

"Make for the cave!" Charles screamed as he passed each carriage, each transport. Terrified faces begged him for help. It wasn't long before he came upon the trio of Steamsworn who had come with them. "Get them to the caves!"

The nearest Steamsworn nodded. He moved a lever on his torso before the man lifted one of the carriages out of a rut. Charles passed a huddled mass of young Bollwerks, youth looking for an adventure, no doubt. Charles figured this to be more of an adventure than they'd wanted.

The sands surged at his feet. He slid to a stop and waited for the claws to surface. That told him where the head was, and he fired the air cannon into the sands. The tail and claw twitched, and then fell still.

"Into the caves!" Charles shouted.

"We can't build fires there," one of the young Bollwerks shouted back.

"Shut your mouth and get into the caves if you want to live, boy! Now!"

He finally found Samuel fighting beside one of the Steamsworn. Samuel knocked a Tail Sword's strike to the side, and the Steamsworn swung a war hammer. The hammer found its home, smashing the creature's head flat, but not before the left claw stabbed into the Steamsworn's leg. If it hit an artery, Charles knew the man might not even make it to the caves.

He shouted it anyway. "Get them to the caves!" Charles paused and took three deep breaths. The time he could run for miles without effort had long passed. Now his knees ached and his lungs felt like they couldn't pull in an ounce of air. It didn't matter. He turned and jogged back toward the trailing carriages.

"There are caves, just up in the foothills," Charles said to the first driver he found.

The man shook, petrified as he stared at the remains of a Tail Sword on the sands.

"Listen!" Charles shouted, drawing the man's attention. "Get to the cave. Park the carriages in front of it. We'll hole up until this is over. Pull yourself together and save these people."

He went to each carriage he could find, skirting the remnants of the shattered transport. Blood soaked the sands, revealed in the flashes of lightning above their heads. The pounding rain would soon wash it away. The storm raged hard enough that he couldn't see more than twenty feet in front of his face. If they didn't get off the sands soon, even the best-equipped carriage was going to sink.

The last carriage was the one he'd been on. The man he'd been sitting next to had a gun in his hand and the driver carried a blade coated in gore. They'd killed another Tail Sword.

"Well done," Charles said. He gave them the same instructions he'd given the others, and then he stayed on the carriage. If anything came up behind them, he wanted to know about it first. He watched the boiling black waters surge with the oncoming Tail Swords, and for the first time in almost fifty years, he thought he might not live through the night.

The carriage lurched to the side and plummeted through the raging stream of water. It didn't bother the beetles as they plowed through the currents and surfaced on the steeper bank of the stream. The carriage shifted on the flooded sands, but the harnesses held on to the mounts, and the beetles dragged them up onto the rocky mountainside.

Charles glanced back at the point he'd seen the Tail Swords. He was relieved to see them stopped, but thunder crashed and a flash of lightning showed him the poor soul being devoured by the creatures.

"Dammit," Charles almost growled as he spoke the word. "There!" he said when one of the caves revealed itself in a stuttering chain of lightning. He leapt off the edge of the slowly moving carriage and sprinted out in front of the beetles. He slid a small Flasher out of a pouch on his vest and clicked the igniter.

He'd thought about using a Burner, but the Flasher would let him see more. He didn't second-guess his instincts. He'd seen what happened to men who did in times of war. They died. Charles hurled the Flasher into the cave as far as it would go before it detonated.

The burst of light showed an open cavern. A few short tunnels at the back could be hiding some nasty creatures, but not so nasty as a swarm of Tail Swords. He glanced back to the north, eyeing the closest carriages and transports. A small knot untied itself in his gut when he saw Samuel riding the Desert Stick and Drakkar jogging beside him.

"Is it clear?" Samuel asked, shouting through the thunder and rain.

"Yes!"

"Bring them!" Drakkar shouted, his voice as deep as the thunder overhead.

Charles tracked the caravan, as best he could in the bursts of light, and tried to see if any more Tail Swords moved toward them. A handful of the creatures paced on the opposite side of the raging stream, but none seemed to be crossing. It looked like they might move to attack the other carriages. He hoped the water didn't have an easier spot for them to cross.

A man rushed toward him, and Charles saw the wet golden gleam of a Biomech arm in the lightning.

"You!" Charles shouted as he lifted one of the larger Bangers out of his pouch. The man slowed to a stop as Charles asked, "How good is your aim?"

"Very good, brother."

Charles nodded and held out his fist. The other man grinned as he wrapped his fingers around the old man's hand. "Now," Charles said as he pulled away. He clicked the igniter on a small Burner, dropped it into the Banger's shell, and snapped the entire contraption closed. "Get this near the back of the caravan. You have ten seconds before it explodes and kills us all."

The Steamsworn shifted a lever down on his arm, and it began to shake. Charles knew he'd made the right call when the man pulled his arm back and whipped it forward like someone who had mastered the game of Cork.

The orb glowed, and Charles bellowed a war cry when it landed a few feet from where he'd hoped. The moment stretched, as though the Banger took a deep breath, and then the fires of hell consumed two dozen Tail Swords in one giant shadowy fireball. Sand and water and bits of charred gore rocketed into the air, falling down to splatter around them.

People around Charles screamed, and he could understand why.

They didn't know he'd created the fireball. He worried briefly about shrapnel-like chunks of Tail Swords hurtling through the air, but most of the people were shielded by the carriages.

"Into the caves!"

"What the hell was that?" the Steamsworn beside Charles asked as he readjusted his arm and matched the old man's slow jog to the cavern entrance.

"A bomb."

The Steamsworn shook his head. "I noticed." He gave Charles a nod and moved ahead, toward one of the carriages.

Drakkar moved near the entrance, helping get the carriages into place. Samuel led the Desert Stick into the mouth of the cave as more carriages closed in behind him. Charles could see a few Tail Swords still heading toward them. He knew the bomb wouldn't kill them all, but an old man could always hope. The thought jarred him, and he remembered his brother's words on the day before he died.

There's always hope, Charles. Newton will come around. Give him time.

A rage he hadn't felt in a decade bubbled up in his gut. If he'd followed his heart and killed the Butcher back then, none of this might have happened. He'd wanted to believe in his brother's words so badly, he'd let the Butcher live. He might have let a mass murderer all but take over Parliament.

"Charles!"

Drakkar's basso shout woke him from his thoughts. He caught a glimpse of Drakkar's collapsible sword unfolding out of its sheath with a snap of the Cave Guardian's wrist, a moment before it severed a Tail Sword's stinger. Charles swung the air cannon around and blasted the creature's head into so much pulp.

"Wake up old man!" Drakkar shouted as he got close to Charles. "Follow your own words and get into the cave. We are almost ready to close the circle. Now go!"

Drakkar was right. Charles knew he was right, but a terrible urge slithered through him. A darkness he'd choked down and buried so long ago he'd almost forgotten what it felt like—the urge to kill. It hadn't been there when he'd killed the soldiers who'd come for Jacob, but now …

Charles glanced over his shoulder and watched the last carriage move into place, its riders dismounting and hurrying into the cave. The time had come for the Steamsworn to bring back order in Ancora. Charles slid the air cannon into its holster and walked into the darkness.

It was time his brother was avenged.

CHAPTER TWENTY-EIGHT

C HARLES STOOD BESIDE SAMUEL AT the front of the cave. The chittering cries of the Tail Swords sounded on the other side of the carriages. The orange glow of the Burning Forest formed a halo across the horizon, glimpsed between the cave ceiling and the carriage roofs. If the creatures were smart enough, or grew curious enough, they could tear through the fabric shells of the less expensive carriages.

"Good thing they're not intelligent," Samuel said.

Charles nodded. "No one ever accused a Tail Sword of being strategic." He caught Drakkar's eyes on him. "I'm fine."

"You almost let yourself die, Charles von Atlier. Why is that?"

At first, Charles wanted to deny what Drakkar had said, but Drakkar's dark eyes seemed to burn into his very soul. Charles sighed and ran a hand through his beard. "Help me look for some Fireworms, would you?"

"All of you," Charles said. He looked up and raised his voice. "Gather up any Fireworms you can find. They'll keep us warm until the sun rises. The Tail Swords will leave once dawn breaks."

Two of the Steamsworn took up the call, asking people to look for Fireworms farther back in the cave.

"Let's clear the tunnels while we talk," Charles said. "I want to make sure we don't have a nest of Widow Makers farther in."

"As you say," Drakkar said, adjusting the wet cloak around his shoulders.

Charles looked at the huddled groups of men and women trying to warm up in the chill draft of the cave. They needed to find the Fireworms sooner rather than later. There wasn't anything to burn inside the cave other than parts of carriages, and they were going to need those to get to Dauschen.

He increased his pace until they reached the largest chamber that he'd seen with the Flasher. Charles clicked his lantern on and swept it across the far wall.

"It is solid," Drakkar said.

"Good," Charles said. "We won't have to worry about anything coming from here." He looked at the tunnel to his left, and the lanterns of the Steamsworn could be seen farther in. The smaller tunnels weren't being searched. Charles sighed and walked to the back wall of the cave.

The only tunnel that looked large enough for a Widow Maker came up to his waist. He turned his lantern to the side so there was nothing but darkness in the tunnel of rock. In the far back of the shadows was the pulsing glow of a Fireworm cluster.

"Of course," Charles said. "Why am I not surprised?"

"What is it?" Samuel asked.

"Fireworms."

"That's great!"

"I can barely see the glow," Charles said, "and they're a good three hundred feet into the mountainside."

"Oh."

"Feel like climbing down a dark hole, Drakkar?" Charles asked.

"I may live in Cave, Charles von Atlier, but I do not enjoy small places."

Charles nodded. "Good luck, Samuel."

"Gods be damned," Samuel muttered to himself as he lowered his hands to the stone floor.

"Best not to think about it, and just get it done," Charles said. He handed the Spider Knight a leather sack to carry the Fireworms.

"Aren't they going to burn this?"

Drakkar burst into laughter. "They do not literally burn, Ancoran. They only emit a great deal of heat."

"Oh, ha ha, make fun of the Ancoran." Samuel grumbled something else as he disappeared into the hole.

Charles exchanged a smile with Drakkar.

SAMUEL GRUNTED AND PUSHED HIMSELF through a narrow part of the tunnel. He twisted his shoulders, had a brief moment of panic, thinking he'd gotten himself stuck, and then sighed when his body moved forward again. The brass lantern hung from a loop on his armored vest, and his vambraces clicked against the stone walls, echoing through the darkness.

"Why in the hell did I agree to this?"

"What was that?" Charles shouted from the tunnel entrance.

"Nothing! Getting closer."

He'd only said it to let Charles know he wasn't in trouble, but he was actually getting closer. The orange glow had a red tinge now, and he could see where the tunnel bent around a corner far ahead.

It took another ten minutes of shuffling and crawling in an ever-increasing heat before he hit the bend in the tunnel. Samuel stared, struck dumb by what waited for him. He would have cursed, but there wasn't a word large enough for the moment.

The tunnel expanded all around him, to the point that he could stand up easily. The walls and the ceiling looked like a firestorm, draped in the worms he'd been hunting. They devoured a strange-looking fungus that dripped from the ceiling and piled itself across the floor.

A Fireworm pulsed in the center of the room and looked more the size of a house than any bug. Its wrinkled folds had the same bulging flesh of a Carrion Worm, and images of the Fall in Ancora came screaming back to him. Samuel closed his eyes and ground his teeth until the gut-wrenching sense of vertigo passed.

He'd seen a lot of dead men in his time with the Spider Knights, but those worms inside the city walls … it was a nightmare he hoped to never see again.

When Samuel opened his eyes, he found the face of the giant Fireworm a few feet from his own. Its head nodded slightly, slithering out of its fleshy hood while its jaws stretched to either side. Samuel froze as the thing seemed to sniff him before lowering and raising its head again. It slowly turned back to the small mountain of glowing fungus.

"Time to go, time to go," Samuel whispered to himself.

He tore a few handfuls of the fungus off the stones, cringed at the sour scent that wafted up from it, and then tossed it into the leather sack Charles had given him. He set the bag on its side and reached out to the nearest worm.

He recoiled at the creature's warmth, almost too hot to touch, but not quite hot enough to burn him. It was a strange sensation, picking up the fleshly, wriggling critter. He could feel its tiny feet digging into his hand. As soon as the Fireworm saw the fungus in the bag, it crawled right inside.

Two more followed the first one in without coaxing. Samuel carefully packed in about five more for good measure and then slid back into the cave. He knew it was a straight shot back out to the entrance, so he didn't bother checking every nook and cranny of the tunnel on the way back.

He should have.

✧   ✧   ✧

"How can you justify what you did?"

Charles slowly turned to Drakkar. "What do you mean?"

"The slaughter at Gareth Cave was not the only horror dealt by Ancorans."

Charles felt his stomach sink a little. He'd seen the way Drakkar had looked at him on more than one occasion. It wasn't the way you looked at a new friend; it was the way you assessed a threat.

"It was war," Charles said. "We fought to survive."

"You destroyed an entire village on the outskirts of Bollwerk. Do you remember that?"

"That wasn't me."

"They were your creation, those Tower Mechs." Drakkar crossed his arms, letting his wet cloak drape from his elbows.

"The only other man who knew their secret was Archibald. Not even the pilots knew how they worked."

"Our people called them City Breakers. Our villages may have been nothing to you but an obstacle to traverse, but to us they were home. It was *our* families that your Mechs trampled."

Charles looked Drakkar in the eye. The Cave Guardian had a deep stare, the look of a man who had seen too much but knew he had a long way to journey.

"I know it doesn't mean much," Charles said as he held the guardian's stare, "but I am sorry for what happened in Midstream."

Drakkar's stone-like expression faltered. "You know its name?"

"Yes," Charles said. His voice grew quiet. "I know the name of every city, every street, and every army that my inventions helped destroy. Did you not wonder why I don't make instruments of war anymore?"

"Why?" Drakkar asked without elaborating.

"There is enough death in this world. I spent decades helping governments wage war. Now I'd rather create things to help the people, the common citizens."

Drakkar unfolded his arms slowly. "These are not the answers I expected from you. You are different from the legends, Charles von Atlier. I wonder how wrong our stories were."

"What did they say about me?" Charles asked. He didn't really want to know, but he sensed that Drakkar was not done with the topic.

"They told stories of the Tower Mechs, great inventions of steel and steam that devoured the blood of children. They told us of the Tower Mech that stampeded through Midstream, scooping up our brothers and sisters and elders to feed a mechanical god as it crushed our homes beneath its mighty feet. I swore if I ever found you, I would remove your head and impale it upon the gates of Midstream."

Charles took up a casual pose and leaned against the wall, putting the blades sheathed on his legs within easy reach.

Drakkar frowned and crossed his arms again. "I will not strike you, Charles."

The old man thought he'd been subtle, but apparently he hadn't been subtle enough. "Would you like to know what happened? I won't hide the truth of that day, Drakkar."

The guardian nodded.

"The pilot was a new recruit. We never should have let him behind the gears of a Titan. That's what we named the Tower Mechs, Titans. He lost control during a training exercise. We don't know what happened, exactly. It appeared that one of the throttles stuck and the pilot lost control. It sent the Titan in a straight line, through Midstream. After that tragedy, the Titan continued its pace until it hit the ocean. We tracked the footprints in an airship, leading out to the sea beside Fel. We never saw the recruit again, or the Titan.

"You can make up your own damned mind about whether or not I'm telling the truth. I have nothing to hide."

Drakkar slowly unfolded his arms and watched Charles. After a time, he said, "I do not believe you were ever the monster we were raised to fear."

Charles frowned and glanced at the tunnel, trying to figure out whether he'd just heard something other than Samuel moving. When no other sounds echoed up, he looked back to Drakkar.

"Midstream was a turning point for me. Seeing what destruction those creations could wreak, even without intent …" Charles shook his head. "I was done with killing." He thought of the soldiers he'd killed in Ancora to save Jacob. "Or at least I thought I was."

"Death will always have its place in the world," Drakkar said. "I only hope to avoid my own until I am as old and gray as you."

Charles chuckled, but his humor died when he heard the shout followed by Samuel's scream. The old man dropped to the floor, banging his knees on the rock floor and sticking his head into the tunnel.

"Samuel!"

"Stone Dogs! Seal the tunnel! Seal the—"

A terrifying, chittering whine like a thousand nails on a thousand chalkboards echoed out of the tunnel, and then Charles could hear the chitinous footsteps stampeding across the stone-like logs dropped onto a rock floor.

"Start the fires!" Charles shouted. "Stone Dogs!"

Drakkar took up the cry, his deep voice echoing through the caves. "Stone Dogs!"

The controlled panic impressed Charles as he turned to look at the people around him. They knew how to respond in a crisis. He could only guess it had been Archibald who had drilled that into them, but to whoever'd done it, he was thankful. By the time he turned away from the Bollwerks and back to Drakkar, the Cave Guardian already had his sword in hand.

"We need to block the tunnel," Drakkar said.

"But Samuel—" Charles cursed, interrupting his own objection. He started to pull a Banger out to blast the Stone Dogs, but it might bring the cavern down on their heads. Even if it didn't, it might kill Samuel before he even had a chance. Charles pulled a Burner out of his pocket instead, clicked the igniter, and tossed it into the tunnel.

Drakkar nodded as the orange and red shadows lanced out of the tunnel. "Samuel is a Spider Knight. If anyone has a chance, he does."

Charles watched the flickering light, and something tightened in his chest. Stone Dogs would run from the flames, but they might be too much for any knight, even Samuel.

"Bring steel!" Charles shouted. The tightness in his chest turned to emptiness as he said, "Close the tunnels."

CHAPTER TWENTY-NINE

*C*HARLES MADE THE RIGHT CALL. *Charles made the right call. Charles made the right call.* It became Samuel's mantra as he pushed himself backward, away from the awakening Stone Dogs. He saw the flash of a Burner and the lantern light dimmed at the exit as his companions sealed the tunnels, leaving him to his fate.

The chittering screech grew ever more intense as Samuel felt his way around the corner. He had enough room to turn around at the intersection. The cavern of Fireworms waited ahead, and then his brain clicked back on. He dumped the satchel of Fireworms out at his feet and scrambled forward.

Something caught his foot, but he didn't stop. He pulled away from whatever it had been, adrenaline fueling his mad crawl for safety. Only it wasn't really safety. The Fireworms would only hold off the Stone Dogs until they decided they were hungry enough to brave the heat. Samuel knew the Stone Dogs hated heat. Charles's decision to toss a Burner into the tunnel had been a stroke of genius, and he knew it.

He didn't slow down when the cavern opened around him. Instead he tore up clumps of fungus and threw it at the tunnel opening. He felt his pockets for weapons. The short blade sheathed on his thigh was it— more length than a dagger but less than a short sword. Samuel cursed and pulled it from its scabbard, baring the steel in the light of the Fireworms' glow. He wouldn't call the blade a weapon of choice against the long reach of the Stone Dogs.

The screech of the Stone Dogs grew louder, and Samuel knew in his gut they'd passed the Fireworms. He backed up, keeping his eyes on the tunnel until he thumped into something warm, and huge, and squishy. Samuel turned to find the massive Fireworm staring at him.

"Sorry, ma'am," he mumbled.

The worm didn't seem to mind much, as it returned to grazing on an enormous patch of fungus.

Samuel took in a sharp breath when the first Stone Dog peeked out of the tunnel. It looked small, maybe half the size of one of the Pillies Alice used to raise in Ancora. If he had a spear or a halberd, he wouldn't be too concerned.

The rocky gray carapace skittered into the cavern. Samuel could see the mass of stingers rising along its back. More than a prick from any one of those could kill him. He'd be nothing but fertilizer for the Fireworms after that.

The Stone Dog's legs clicked on the rocky floor in rapid succession as it moved around a Fireworm and closed in on Samuel. It was easy to see where Stone Dogs got their name. Even the thing's feet looked like rocks. Before Samuel could finish his thought, the Stone Dog rushed him, all six legs pounding at the rocks before it smashed a small Fireworm under its foot.

Samuel raised his stunted blade. The Stone Dog was fast. It was so damn fast. He was only going to get one shot at—

Something roared—something huge, and orange, and fiery. Samuel could scarcely comprehend what was happening as the massive Fireworm lunged in front of him. Its thick flesh stretched as its head swung down and smashed the Stone Dog in its jaws. The Fireworm gave one mighty shake of its head, and the Stone Dog shattered on the cavern wall. Bits of the creature pinged off the floor and dripped into a pile of gore.

When the stream of Stone Dogs came tearing into the cave, the Fireworm opened its mouth.

Samuel screamed and leapt backward as a cyclone of fire singed his hair. He watched in shock, horror, and awe, as the mammoth Fireworm exhaled a maelstrom of death. The Stone Dogs burst and exploded like a kettle of popcorn in the superheated blast. Something lanced into his hand, but he couldn't stop to look at it.

He backpedaled, trying to escape the heat. Every breath felt like he'd inhaled hot coals. It was quickly becoming too much for him to tolerate. He turned and stepped around some of the smaller Fireworms while the largest in the cavern roasted the Stone Dogs.

It felt cooler on the opposite side of the massive cavern. The air felt warm and muggy as opposed to life-threateningly hot. Samuel leaned against the wall and slid down it. He raised his hand and frowned at how bad it was shaking. He plucked the Stone Dog quill from his wrist before the blade fell from his hand and clattered onto the stone floor. Samuel wrapped his arms around his knees and lowered his head. It was too much. Everything since the Fall had been too much.

He tried to fight back the pressure in his eyes, but he couldn't stop the tears once he let go. Visions of his friends and strangers being torn apart by Red Death and Widow Makers came roaring back into his mind. He was frozen, locked into a looping reel of horror in that cave beside the Burning Forest as the venom took hold of his mind.

This wasn't how he was supposed to die.

✧　✧　✧

DRAKKAR LEANED HIS EAR AGAINST the webwork of steel blocking the tunnel. He glanced at Charles von Atlier. Drakkar still found it hard to reconcile the man he would call a friend against the terrible legends of his people. It would take time to change that. There are two sides to every story, and some are just as terrible as the other.

"I hear nothing," Drakkar said. "The Stone Dogs are gone."

"They could still be eating him," one of the other Steamsworn said.

"He's too good for that," Charles said.

Drakkar thought the pain on Charles von Atlier's face betrayed his true feelings. "We still do not know what that light was," Drakkar said. "He may have had another Burner. Whatever the case, it is silent. Help me open the tunnel."

"We can't put all these people at risk."

"You will not. Seal it behind me."

Charles grimaced and ran his hands through his hair. "We can't lose you both, Drakkar. We don't have enough warriors."

"Then you will open the tunnel and let me bring back another."

Charles cursed and motioned to one of the Steamsworn. "Help me move it."

The heavily muscled man didn't so much as question why. He only grabbed an edge with Charles and slid the bulky assembly of steel away from the tunnel in a high-pitched squeal of metal and stone.

"Seal it behind me," Drakkar said.

"Take a lantern," Charles said.

Drakkar shook his head. "No, it will betray me to the Stone Dogs."

Charles reached out and opened Drakkar's hand. "At least take these."

Drakkar stared at the metal orbs. Burners, one of the tinker's most useful inventions. His first instinct was to throw them to the wind, but he slid them into a pocket inside his cloak and nodded to Charles.

He gathered his cloak as he leaned down and began to crawl into the tunnel. With the gray fabric tucked into the belt at his waist, it would not catch his arms or legs at an inopportune time. Inopportune … Drakkar almost laughed at the thought. If he was caught at the wrong time, he would be dead. Inopportune did not seem a severe enough word.

He heard the steel grinding against the stone behind him, and then there was only darkness. It did not take long for his eyes to adjust enough to make out the orange glow at the end of the tunnel. If that was the lair of a queen worm, there may not be anything left of Samuel to find, Stone Dogs or not.

Drakkar closed away those darker thoughts, locking them in a mental vault so he could focus on the task at hand. He took a deep breath, pressed a hand to either wall, and listened. No vibrations echoed through the tunnel or the wall. Only silence accompanied him, and the faint crackle of a fire.

He moved forward. His training as a guardian had taught him to be silent enough that he could surprise death in her own realm. Drakkar liked that. He liked having the advantage. He did not like crawling into a den of Stone Dogs to rescue an Ancoran. Samuel had become more than just an Ancoran, though. Samuel was a brother in war, a man he would be proud to call his friend.

Drakkar's lock on his emotions faltered, and he sped forward through the tunnel. He swung around the sharp angle, where the warm light pulsed and shifted. Drakkar's pace slowed again when he reached the edge of the tunnel. The stone was warm here, and the floor … He stared at the charred, exploded Stone Dogs littering the floor.

There were old stories of Fireworms that could breathe flame, but he had never seen it. Drakkar swept the remains to either side with his cloak, careful not to prick himself on any of the Stone Dogs' spines. Even a dead Stone Dog's spine could inflict terrible hallucinations, or kill.

Drakkar stood up and stared at the massive Fireworm in the center of the room. It raised its head and stared at him for a moment before shifting to the side, almost as if it wanted Drakkar to see Samuel collapsed on the far side of the cavern.

"Please let me pass," Drakkar said, scooping up a handful of glowing fungus. He took a few steps toward the massive worm and held out his hand. The Fireworm swung its head toward him and sniffed at the fungus.

Drakkar held his ground as the worm closed its mouth over his hand.

When it pulled away, the fungus was gone, and he still had all his fingers. "Thank you."

He stepped carefully through the cavern, careful not to crush even the smallest Fireworm. The creatures were intensely protective of their young. If they saw one harmed, there was a good chance everything around them would die.

"Samuel," Drakkar said. He crouched down beside the Spider Knight. He felt Samuel's neck, relieved to find a pulse. Samuel shook, and it was almost as bad as a seizure he'd once seen after a man suffered a terrible blow to the head.

It was then that he saw the glint of the Stone Dog's spine on the ground beside Samuel's short sword. Drakkar's hand fled to his cloak. He pulled a short knife out of a sheath and turned Samuel's arm over. He sliced the vambrace off and split the flesh beneath it. Blood began to flow freely. Drakkar packed the wound with a salve made from a cactus flower and the venom of a young Sky Needle. It was something all the Cave Guardians carried.

"You will not like me in the morning for this wound," Drakkar said. "Hold on, and you will live. Do you hear me, Ancoran? Exercise your legendary stubbornness and live."

Drakkar pulled Samuel's eye open. Only the whites showed. That was not a good sign. The guardian tied the vambrace back in place with a strip of leather twine. It would keep the blood flow in check while the salve started to work on the flesh beneath. He would not have needed to make such a large cut if he could have found the entrance wound, but there was no time. He sheathed the short sword on the Spider Knight's hip.

Adrenaline gave Drakkar all the strength he needed. Samuel almost felt light slung over his shoulders. The guardian picked his way back to the tunnel. He spared one last glance for the nest of Fireworms. The largest raised its head again, moving its jaw as it devoured another clump of fungus.

Drakkar nodded his thanks to the creature before he lowered himself into the tunnel. He removed his cloak and wrapped it around Samuel. It made it easier to drag the knight through the tunnel. He could get to his sword faster if he needed to, but he did not have any illusions about it. If they were ambushed by more Stone Dogs, it was not likely either of them would survive.

Drakkar waited until he reached the turn before he shouted, "Open the tunnel! I have Samuel! Open the tunnel!"

He was almost to the gate when he finally heard the squeal of metal on stone. Drakkar never thought he would be so happy to see the monster, Charles von Atlier.

✧   ✧   ✧

CHARLES WATCHED, AND A BLACK pit of helplessness opened inside his chest.

"He has been stung," Drakkar said as he dragged Samuel fully out of the cave. "He needs a fire, and what water we can get down his throat."

"What else can we do?" Charles asked.

"I have already applied a salve. We can only wait. If he has the stamina left, he may survive."

Charles looped his hands under Samuel's shoulders—shocked to feel how bad he shook—and Drakkar grabbed the Spider Knight's legs. He backpedaled toward the fire at the front of the cave.

"What about the Fireworms?" Charles asked.

"I have a few," Drakkar said, lowering Samuel's legs next to the fire. "They will not be warm enough for what Samuel needs."

Charles watched the guardian take Samuel's pulse.

"We need to keep him warm. His seizures are already slowing. It is a good sign that the salve is working, but he has a hard night ahead."

"I'll keep watch."

"Get some rest," Drakkar said. "I will watch over him. I know more of what he needs than you do."

Charles stared at Drakkar for a moment before nodding. "I owe you." He walked away while Drakkar wrapped Samuel's chest in a blanket. Charles didn't know much about healing salves, especially when it came to poison.

He wandered a few paces away and threw some extra bits of lumber onto the fire. Charles watched it snap and pop, flinging embers into the air. The rains still pounded the sands outside, but the Tail Swords seemed to have lost interest now that the fire had been stoked. Charles sat down by one of the sleeping rolls, but he knew he wasn't sleeping anytime soon.

CHAPTER THIRTY

J ACOB STARED AT THE WORKBENCH, aged manuscripts and books sprawled across the vise, the shelves, and even his lap. A week had passed. They still hadn't heard from Charles or Samuel or Drakkar. Jacob worried, but he also knew they planned to be gone at least three weeks. There wasn't any real reason to worry, yet.

He felt like he'd spent a month doing nothing but memorizing the metals and compounds that could drive a Biomech insane. Smith explained to him why they suspected some of the metals were so terrible, and why others could kill a man in months, just from running his blood through them.

"And do not forget," Smith said, "there are others that can drive a Biomech insane over a longer stretch of time. Never forge an implant out of lead. It might be fine for a while, even a few years, but by the time they start having seizures, it will be too late to save them."

Jacob caught himself starting to nod off when someone knocked at the door. "Uh huh." He wondered if it would be Mary again. He hadn't seen her since she came by last week. Or was that the week before now?

"Would you get that?" Smith asked.

Jacob yawned and nodded before he stood up and took a few steps toward the door.

He froze.

He'd taken steps toward the door without even thinking about it. He took another, and there was only a dull ache in his knee.

"Smith … it doesn't really hurt!"

The tinker turned around, his eyes darting from the wheelchair to Jacob. A slow smile crawled across his face. "You heal fast, brother."

Jacob took three more tentative steps and opened the door, and there was almost no pain at all. No sense of weakness or that awful feeling of an impending collapse. It wasn't Mary at the door. Archibald stared at Jacob's leg.

"Gods … are you … how … how are you?"

Jacob leaned on his leg a little more. It stung a bit, not more than he could handle. "I can walk." A broad grin stretched across Jacob's face.

"I came to see how Smith's lessons were going, but I didn't expect this …"

"I am not so surprised," Smith said. "His resistance is strong. The Tree Killer's venom did not take his life, so it makes a good kind of sense that he would heal quickly."

"Can he walk more than the distance to the Council Hall?" Archibald asked.

Smith raised an eyebrow and glanced from Jacob to Archibald.

Archibald rolled his eyes. "I mean, is it safe to take him out? I'd like to take him to Gareth Cave."

Smith nodded. "The Skysworn has an extra chair in case he gets worn down, but yes. He can walk."

Jacob said the words over in his head. *He can walk.* Before, yes, he could walk, but the pain was intense. It had been far more intense than he'd admitted.

"I want to show you a part of our history, Jacob," Archibald said. "I know you read my book, but sometimes a book is not the same as standing in the place where history lives. Smith," he said as he glanced up. "Can you let Mary know we're on our way?"

"Now?"

Archibald nodded.

"Let me gather a few things, and I will join you on the Skysworn. We have only had her in the skies twice since finishing the repairs, so I would hate to leave you stranded in the old city."

"We'll meet you there."

Jacob took a few tentative steps to his backpack, slung it over his shoulder, and walked out with Archibald. He couldn't wipe the grin from his face, even though he tried. There was almost no pain, and he was *walking.*

Before the door clanged closed behind them, he heard Smith talking into his radio.

"They will be there in twenty minutes or so. I will be right behind them, so keep that ship on the ground."

A burst of angry static sounded before the words were cut off. Jacob couldn't wait to see Mary and the Skysworn again.

✧   ✧   ✧

THEY WALKED A SHORT DISTANCE before Jacob's leg started bothering him. He wished they could have brought Alice, but Archibald only wanted a couple people with them. Jacob sat down on one of the old brass benches he'd seen scattered around Bollwerk and rubbed his thigh.

"Who keeps these polished?" Jacob asked. He looked at the shiny metal they sat on.

Archibald ran his hand over the armrest and smiled. "No one, actually. We have to wash them down occasionally, but Smith treated them all with a polish that keeps them gleaming for almost a year."

Jacob flexed his leg and leaned back. He knew Ancora had some strange, and somewhat inefficient, traditions. Like the lantern men? Did they really need an entire crew of men just to turn on the lights at night? Probably not. Shiny benches seemed a bit like a waste, but if they didn't take much extra effort, why not have them? It was so small a thing, but something about those benches reminded Jacob of how different

Bollwerk could be from Ancora.

"Can you continue on?" Archibald asked, breaking Jacob's focus on the brass benches.

Jacob nodded.

"Good. We'll take a crawler the rest of the way."

"I can walk," Jacob said. "It's not too bad, almost like a splinter in my knee."

A burst of steam and the squeak of treads shot into the air as one of the wide, dark crawlers careened around the corner.

Archibald groaned. "I told him not to hurry."

Jacob watched the crawler surge forward, spinning its treads and sending a great cloud of steam into the air as it accelerated down the stone street. Jacob could see the driver's exaggerated movement as the man pulled the brake up and came to a screeching stop by the curb.

The driver hopped out and placed his fist over his heart. "Speaker, sir. Your ride awaits."

"Where's Jones?" Archibald asked. He stepped onto one of the treads and slid across the cushioned seat in the back.

"He's asleep, sir. Not much of a morning person, sir."

Archibald rolled his eyes and glanced up at the sky. "I'll have to have a talk with that boy. It's nearly noon."

"He *really* doesn't like the morning, sir."

"Stop calling me sir."

"Yes, sir."

Archibald sighed and gave Jacob a weak smile. "Come on, then. The sooner we get to the docks, the sooner I don't have to be called sir. Gods know Mary doesn't feel the need to call me sir."

Jacob climbed into the seat beside Archibald. The driver closed the door behind him and vaulted into the front, settling behind the levers he used for steering.

"Would you like to get to the docks quickly, sir?" the driver asked as he started the crawler forward.

"I would like to get to the docks alive, Bakir."

The driver turned and flashed Jacob a smile. "Hang on, kid."

Bakir slammed two levers forward, and the crawler lurched before speeding down the smooth stone road.

Jacob laughed, and then his hand clamped down on the doorframe and the edge of the seat when Bakir swung the crawler around a corner at a speed that no one would consider safe. There was only a tiny squeal, and then they shot forward.

"It's a new kind of tread, sir," Bakir shouted over the roar of the wind. "Dad thinks it's the way of the future. I think he might be right!"

"Bakir is Jones's son," Archibald said.

Once Archibald had mentioned it, Jacob could see a bit of the other driver in the younger man. He had the same frizzy hair and the same kind eyes. It took him a moment to remember that Jones was Archibald's son.

"Jones named his son Bakir?" Jacob asked, skirting the relationship question. Bakir was a name fit for the desert clans, not one of the northern cities. "That seems …" He trailed off, not sure what to say without sounding like a complete jerk. Or sounding like a pompous Highlander. He almost choked on the thought.

"My mom named me," Bakir said. "She was from Midstream." Bakir slowed to a stop, throwing Jacob and Archibald against their harnesses. "Sorry, didn't want to run over the nice people."

"Quite alright," Archibald said.

"Uh, sir," Bakir said with a sideways grin.

As soon as the street cleared, Bakir slammed the throttle to the ground. Jacob watched Archibald turn green, and he couldn't stifle a laugh.

"Not you too," Archibald said. He tried to keep a stern look on his face, but it fractured as he laughed.

"Almost there, sir," Bakir said. He tore around another corner, and the towering airship docks consumed the sky above them.

It was a sight Jacob thought he might never get used to. The warships of Bollwerk made a terrifying sight. He didn't care if they were only used for defense of the city walls. One of those ships could level a city, and it didn't seem like any person should hold that kind of power.

"I wish we didn't need them," Archibald said, as if he'd read Jacob's mind. "There is evil in the world, Jacob. Don't ever doubt that. Just ... do your best not to become it. It's all any of us can do."

Jacob watched Archibald as Bakir slowed the crawler and entered the airship docks. He'd read *The Dead Scourge*, and that gave him some insight into the man who was the Speaker of Bollwerk. Jacob knew what kind of atrocities Archibald had witnessed. How the man could believe there was anything *but* evil in the world made Jacob want to call Archibald a friend.

"I will, sir," Jacob said.

Archibald smiled.

The crawler stopped and Bakir turned around in his seat. "We're here, sir."

"Bakir, don't ..." Archibald pinched the bridge of his nose. "Thank you."

Jacob and Archibald left the crawler behind. Jacob waved to Bakir as he pulled away, and then he turned his attention back to the lifts. His last trip out on the Skysworn hadn't exactly ended well. This time he was hoping for a less exciting trip.

CHAPTER THIRTY-ONE

J ACOB SMILED WHEN THEY STEPPED off the lift and the Skysworn greeted them in all its recently repaired glory. The last time he'd seen it, he'd been short a leg and figured he wasn't going to live through the day.

"Welcome back," Mary said as she lowered the gangplank.

Jacob's boots clanged on the metal walkway and then thumped when he reached the wooden deck of the airship.

Mary stared at him. "Smith told me you were walking, but I kind of thought he was exaggerating."

"He should be right behind us," Jacob said.

"That's what he says. We're not leaving him behind. We've only got a skeleton crew at Archibald's request, and I am *not* getting stranded in a hellhole like Gareth Cave."

Jacob noticed she didn't refer to Archibald as Speaker, or sir, or use any kind of formality. He turned around and stood beside Mary. Across the dock, he saw the lift begin to lower.

"His recovery has been extraordinary," Archibald said as he joined them on deck. "I'm going to grab a seat in the cabin. Need to rest the old bones before we walk through the cave."

Mary's hand tightened on the railing of the Skysworn. "Need to rest the soul before you walk into that cave."

"What?" Jacob asked.

She cast him a small smile. "It's a dark place, Jacob. When the Butcher left a mark during the war, he made sure no one would ever forget. Then the damned warlords had to raze the area after the fighting ended. That part of our nation has never known peace."

"In Ancora, I used to think we didn't have peace because we had bullies and thugs who preyed on the people. Some of them picked on kids just because they liked to read. Alice had problems with them for a long time."

"You help straighten them out?" Mary asked, turning to Jacob.

"The bullies?" Jacob shook his head. "No, Alice kicked them in the nuts and broke their noses on her knee."

Mary chuckled. "She's a warrior, that one."

"You have no idea," Jacob said, a slightly exasperated edge to his voice.

They stood there for a time, with the scent of fresh stain on the decks and the cool breeze rocking the airship docks. Jacob knew he could get used it. Being in the skies was like being in a different world. Sometimes you needed to be in a different world.

"Here he comes," Mary said.

Jacob looked across the dock to the lift and saw the gate slide open before Smith stepped off. It was easy to forget how big the man really was. He stood a head taller than anyone else around him and almost twice as thick. Smith still had an easy grace about him that Jacob usually associated with the Spider Knights. It probably meant Smith had been a soldier for a long time, or at least knew how to defend himself. Smith's boots thundered across the gangplank before he reached out and ruffled Jacob's hair.

"I'm not twelve."

"You are closer to twelve than I am, kid."

"You're closer to Charles's age than my age."

Smith paused and thought about that. "Oh, gods, the fact I am even considering that means I am old."

"Watch yourself." Mary crossed her arms. "I'm not that much younger than you."

"Of course," Smith said. He adjusted his backpack. "I only meant the wisdom that I learned at such a young age was a heavy burden."

"Uh huh," Mary said as she cocked an eyebrow. "Why don't you go check the engine one last time? I'd like to test the thrusters out, cut some time off our trip today."

"Of course, Captain. Youngest captain in all of Bollwerk, she is," Smith said, hooking a thumb at Mary.

"Just stop," Mary said. She smiled and started closing the gangplank. The metal plank retracted into the hull before the panel beneath it rose to complete the railing that ran around the Skysworn. "Let's go, Jacob."

He followed Mary into the cabin and took his seat, a sharp pain in his knee reminding him of the fact he was walking on a leg that wasn't what he was born with.

✦　✦　✦

"I said it should be fine!"

Jacob tried not to laugh at the irritation in Smith's tinny voice as it boomed over the horns.

"Don't turn into my eight-year-old niece, Smith. I've had enough whining to last me a lifetime."

"It will hold, Captain," came Smith's overly patient response. "Please, feel free to engage the thrusters at your leisure."

A metallic bang sounded over the horn, and Jacob figured Smith had slammed the cap on his end.

Mary did the same. She reached out and put her hand on the wider lever that engaged the thrusters. "Everyone harnessed in?"

"Yes," Archibald said.

Jacob glanced at Archibald, surprised to see the older man's eyes squeezed shut. "You okay?"

"I'm not the biggest fan of flying, Jacob."

"He hates thrusters," Mary said.

"I've seen what can happen when they fail."

"Well, let's hope Smith made some good repairs then, eh? Three …"

"Shouldn't you tell Smith you're engaging the thrusters?"

"… two …"

"Umm …"

"One!" Mary slammed the throttle forward.

There was a short scream from one of the horns and then the sound of metal rattling and banging against the horn. Jacob felt the now familiar pressure on his chest as the turbines screamed and the thrusters propelled them faster than any ship had a right to move.

Mary flipped the cap off a brass horn and shouted, "Should have buckled yourself in a little sooner."

Smith's normally composed voice screeched back over the horn, shouting every expletive Jacob had ever heard, and a few he thought might be curses in another language.

"He loves me," Mary said as she flashed a grin at Jacob. "Alright, we should be there in about an hour. It's just northwest of the Burning Forest."

"Is that the same way Charles and the others went?" Jacob asked.

"Almost," Archibald said. Jacob glanced over at him and was glad to see his eyes were open. Archibald looked less certain of his own demise now that the pressure from the thrusters had evened out. "They stayed to the east of the Burning Forest. The plan was to take the mountain pass up to Dauschen."

Mary squinted out the window, a deep frown etched across her face. She flipped the horns open and shouted, "Smith! Brace yourself. We're stopping."

"Go!" he shouted back.

Jacob could hear Smith grunt as the inertia slammed them all into their harnesses. Mary threw her harness off and was out the door before they'd even come to a stop. Archibald undid his harness with shaky hands, and Jacob followed suit.

"What is it?" Archibald asked as he stepped up beside Mary at the railing.

Jacob didn't need to ask. He could see the tattered canvas on the road between the Burning Forest and the mountains.

"Damn." Mary pulled the scope away from her eye and handed it to Archibald.

He raised it, his left arm near the larger lens as he panned down and froze. "That's the carriage Jones gave us for the mission."

"Looks like you owe him a carriage."

"I don't see anyone else down there. Do you think it got lodged in the sands?"

"No," Mary said. "If they had to abandon it, they would have taken the long range radio. The antenna is still sticking out of the canvas."

"Can I?" Jacob asked.

Archibald nodded as he handed Jacob the scope. "It's only one carriage. I'm sure the rest of them are fine."

Smith came up behind them, wiping his hands on a stained towel. "Well, she held together. There was a small leak in one of the hydraulic lines, but it is patched now."

Something tightened in Jacob's chest when he swept the scope near the creek bed. A monstrous creature sat there with a tail half the length of the carriage.

"There's something next to the carriage," Jacob said. "I've never seen anything like it. The claws look like they could cut somebody in half."

Archibald snatched the scope and raised it to his eyes. "Where?"

"Closer to the creek bed."

Jacob saw him shift the focus, and then Archibald cursed. "Tail Swords. They got ambushed by Tail Swords. Gods."

"Should we land?" Smith asked. "We can search for survivors."

Archibald shook his head. "There aren't any flags. If there were survivors nearby, they would have raised flags. That antenna explains why we haven't heard anything. When they reach a safe house in Dauschen they'll radio home. I'm sure of it." Archibald slid the scope closed and handed it back to Mary.

"As long as the safe houses are still safe," Mary said.

"Some of our best spies are in Dauschen," Archibald said. "I spoke to Nora not two days ago."

"Nora?" Mary asked. "She's not overly fond of Drakkar's people."

Archibald gave her a small smile. "She'll have to get over that very quickly."

CHAPTER THIRTY-TWO

J ACOB LOOKED DOWN AT THE earth, far below at the end of the landing lines. He snapped his belayer onto the rope and smiled.

"Bend your knee when you hit," Smith said from behind him. "You do not want to take the full force of the impact when you land."

Jacob leapt off the side of the airship, drawing the rope out as he fired a salute off at Smith. A small smile crossed the tinker's face before Jacob vanished below the deck, the wind tearing at his hair and pulling on his vest.

The wheels on the belayer whined as he pulled the mechanism closed, slowing his descent as the heat from the desert sands intensified. He'd nearly reached a complete stop when he found the bottom. The pain stabbed at his knee for only a moment after the soft impact.

Jacob pulled off the belayer and looked back up at the Skysworn. He could see Archibald peeking over the side, and it sounded like they were arguing about something.

The last thing Jacob heard was "Fine!" and Archibald rode the rope down to land beside him.

"You okay?" Jacob asked as Archibald pulled his own belayer off the landing lines.

"I thought they were going to get a little closer to the ground. I'm not terribly fond of heights, Jacob."

"Why?"

Archibald frowned and adjusted the gleaming silver and leather jacket he wore. "I was on an airship that crashed in the Deadlands War. It rather took away my taste for flying."

A passage from *The Dead Scourge* leapt to the front of Jacob's mind.

```
    I could hear their screams and see their shadowed
forms burning in the fires of our ship, and there was
nothing I could do. I saved myself, and the dying, ter-
rified screams of my friends will haunt me until the end
of my days.
```

"I'm sorry," Jacob said. "I … I forgot."

Archibald nodded. "That was a long time ago." He offered up a smile. "Sometimes I forget you know so much of my past. It seems odd that someone as young as yourself would have any interest in history."

Jacob shrugged. "I like knowing where I came from. Everyone comes from somewhere, and we're all part of history in some way."

"You're not wrong," Archibald said as he squinted up at the Skysworn. "I think Smith will be joining us, or at least following us to the cave. I know he doesn't like to go in."

"Why not?"

"Smith believes in the old spirits. I don't mean that as any one particular spirit, or even a particular god, but he believes in ghosts and gods and all the terrible things that dwell in the darkness."

"Like what?"

"I'm a little behind on my theology, Jacob. I've always found humans to be the most frightening thing that lurks in the dark." He walked away, toward the sheer bluff in the side of the mountain. Jacob followed him.

"You can study history all you like, Jacob, but you'll usually only get one side of the story. That's the tragedy of it, I suppose. Whoever loses has no say in what history remembers."

"Like Midstream?"

"Midstream was different. No one was at war with Midstream, not really. They just happened to be in the way of a Titan."

"But who pays for that?" Jacob asked. "An entire city getting destroyed can't go unpunished."

"It can," Archibald said as they reached a small set of sandy stairs, "and it did."

"Why?"

"Where do you place the fault? At the time, we suspected the Titan had been stolen, but it ran from here to the Black Sea. Its pilot likely drowned, as surely as if he'd been tied to a stone. Charles blamed himself for that, saying it had to be a malfunction in the hydraulics. I'm not so sure.

"The town of Midstream was not far from here," Archibald said as they closed on the entrance. "It's no more than ruins and a graveyard now, lost in the stampede of a Titan."

"Didn't Bakir say his mom was from Midstream?"

Archibald nodded. "Some of the families stayed there. They had water and a decent supply of food. That's enough for some folks. It wasn't until about ten years ago that a warlord named Rana destroyed even that last vestige."

"Bakir's mom? Your grandson?"

"Yes," Archibald said. If he was surprised at Jacob's question, he hid it well. "Jones escaped, but his wife was not so fortunate. It's one of a thousand tragedies, Jacob, but I'm afraid I must show you a thousand more. Come."

Archibald slowed to a stop and frowned at the arched entryway to the cavern. The entire entrance was outlined by a bronze framework, chased by five words.

The Forgotten Will Never Be.

"This is a place of truths, Jacob. One of our darkest memories, and one of our greatest strengths, all within one cave. Come."

Jacob didn't speak, he only followed Archibald on the stone path. The sands covered a great deal of the stone, the winds creating dunes and small hills, but the path to the entrance remained relatively clear. It did not seem natural. It was either clear from the people who visited it, or someone kept the worst of the sands off the stone.

A light shone inside the cave. Jacob could see it, even in the bright sunlight of the desert. The light glowed deep inside Gareth Cave, like some long forgotten hope.

Jacob followed Archibald into the old cave. Bronze and copper and gold glinted in the lantern light. The bright desert sun seemed to abandon them when they crossed the threshold, leaving them to a darkness older than any man who walked upon the earth.

The beds came out of the darkness, tattered and rotted by time. Rusted heaps left to decay into some awful memory of what Gareth Cave was meant to be. Glass from a shattered medicine cabinet glinted in the shifting light.

A weight hung in that place, a feeling of dread hiding in the flicker of shadows. Jacob looked at the walls, peppered with broken, chipped stone that didn't look like any kind of natural blemish.

He reached out and ran his fingers over one of them. Where the cave wall was smooth, the wound in the stone was rough and uneven, almost jagged. Jacob had seen impacts like that before in the city wall of Ancora, behind the rifle stands where traders would hold contests with their firearms.

The realization twisted Jacob's stomach. Bullet holes littered Gareth Cave.

"It was called a chain gun," Archibald said, his voice echoing in the cave around them.

Jacob pulled his hand away from the walls and focused on the light deeper inside the cave.

"They call it the Slaughter of Gareth Cave, but it was far worse than that. Some men called it a massacre. That's more appropriate, I think."

"How many?"

Archibald shrugged. "I don't mean to seem casual about it, but we really don't know. Most of the kids were from Midstream, taking shelter after that town had been destroyed and their parents either went to war or were buried in the cemetery."

"Kids?"

Archibald nodded. "Over a hundred, cut down by the Butcher's chain gun."

Jacob tried to wrap his head around that number, so many people dying in one place. How could that *not* leave a mark on the world?

The walls evened out. The smooth, pockmarked cave gave way to marble slabs, perfectly squared away to form a hall. There was a table with a lantern that Jacob thought was the end of the cave, but Archibald led him past it, and down another path. It grew darker, the hallway clear of the hospital wreckage that had littered the earlier parts of the cave. A glimpse of gold and orange light waited around the corner.

The walls rose and Jacob's steps slowed as they walked into a massive cavern. The ceiling stretched away to the point he couldn't see it in the dim light. Only the specks of Fireworms lit the darkest recesses of the cavern, high above. Far away, at the other end of the cave, stood a towering monument. A shrine was the only word Jacob could find that fit the enormity of the golden sculpture.

"The worst of it was here. Charles's brother died here, trying to protect the innocents from the Butcher's rampage. Charles was out tracking down that rogue Titan. I don't know if he'll ever forgive himself for that. Most of these people were asleep when the Butcher struck. Gareth cave was filled with men and women and children, Jacob. No one survived."

Hulking old machines and rows of aged biomechanics peppered the room, as dead as the doctors and tinkers who once operated them.

"But why?" Jacob asked. "Why kill all those people?"

A sad smile crossed Archibald's face. "Newton lost his younger brother to a Berserker. Some madness made him believe anyone with a Biomech implant would be a Berserker. There was a truth to that, I suppose. It was the metals that drove his own father mad. I suspect he's attacked Dauschen because of the medicines they make to combat the madness."

"And Ancora because we mine the metals?" Jacob asked.

"Indeed. And now he will make for Bollwerk. A place that has come to accept Biomechs."

A face, barely lit by the Fireworms' glow, revealed itself as Jacob's eyes adjusted to the darkness. He stepped closer until he could make out the dark wood frame and the careful brush strokes. Jacob gasped when he realized paintings and photographs of the dead covered the entirety of the wall. There was no question in his mind that these were the victims who died in Gareth Cave.

Archibald stayed silent while Jacob followed the curve of the wall, gazing at the faces frozen in paint and glass and metal. For every one that he stopped and studied, there were a dozen more that he didn't even have a chance to glance at.

The room overwhelmed him.

After a time, he reached the far back of the wall. Jacob studied the golden shrine, bathed in the warm light of the Fireworms and the nearby lanterns. The shrine itself had been sculpted to look like the raised fist of the Steamsworn, names carved into the stone around it. Hundreds, if not thousands, of names were carefully etched, evenly spaced all around the sculpture.

"You see, son," Archibald said, "the Steamsworn were not founded for the sole purpose of violence. We were founded on the ideal of peace."

Jacob glanced up at Archibald before turning back to the names on the wall. "Why do you call it an ideal?"

Archibald sighed. "Mankind will always be mankind, Jacob. It fights what it fears, it rages against change, and it kills almost without conscience. This sculpture and these names … What happened in this place ripped away almost a hundred years of Bollwerk's pacifism. It was the slaughter in this cave that gave rise to the Steamsworn Berserkers.

"So we set out to hold on to that peace through violence. I hadn't been raised as a pacifist, Jacob. You know, I lived the first seventeen years of my life in Ancora. Here, when the war was over and I was older, I argued with Bollwerk's leaders and eventually won. I still remember the words that swayed them."

Jacob studied Archibald as he spoke. The man's eyes seemed unfocused, like he saw something that Jacob couldn't. Maybe, somewhere in his memories, that is exactly what he was doing.

" 'If you don't join our resistance now, Bollwerk will fall. You'll be erased from history as if you never existed, or at best remembered as a footnote in some great conqueror's story. Your ideals of peace will die behind a curtain of your own people's blood.' "

"Until we become something more than we have always been, Jacob, I'm afraid peace will always be an ideal."

Jacob looked back at the wall of names and thought. The losses here reminded him of the Fall, and the same man had set both tragedies in motion. He thought about the people he knew, the good people like Alice, and Samuel, and Charles, and his parents. And what about Reggie and Bobbie? Would they be so fast to kill? Would they forgo peace so easily? "I think you're wrong."

Jacob could feel Archibald's eyes on him, studying him. He didn't understand why older folks always assumed everything was exactly how it appeared on the surface. The acts of a few bad people didn't turn peace into an ideal. It only turned it into something you had to fight a little harder for.

"How can we give hope to the powerless?" Archibald asked.

That was a question he'd heard in school. A question one of the

Highland guests had asked Miss Penny. He always did like Alice's answer. "Practice." He slid the stiff photo out of his pocket, studying Alice and the Jumper back in Ancora.

"What do you have there?" Archibald asked.

Jacob glanced up and then slowly lowered his gaze back to the photograph. "It's Alice and me, back in Ancora.

"A photograph isn't going to change the world, but it *can* change the lens you see the world through. It can lift your spirits, and be a reminder of who you are. All that, and it is nothing but a frozen image on a dead tree."

Jacob smiled at the photo. "When Smith and Charles cut my leg open again. I thought … I thought I wasn't going to make it."

Archibald nodded.

"I thought of Alice. There, when I thought it was the end. I thought it would be my mom, or my dad, or even that crazy old tinker, but it was Alice."

"She's one of the most irritating people I've ever met."

"Mmm," Archibald said. "You should have met my late wife. Much the same, I fear."

Footsteps sounded behind them, and Jacob turned to find Smith lit by the dim glow of the Fireworms. Jacob slid the photograph back into his pocket. The tinker stayed silent as he passed Archibald. He stepped behind the shrine and Jacob heard stone shift before a loud squeak of metal hinges filled the air.

"Smith," Archibald said, "we don't have to show him that."

"He needs to see it," Smith said, stepping back around the shrine. "He needs to understand what can happen when safety and sanity are placed behind the sheer joy of creation." Smith held up a monstrous mechanism.

"It is too large and too heavy for most men to carry. Almost impossible to aim while you turn the crank, but that does not matter as much when you can send two hundred bullets into your enemy in a minute."

"Two hundred …" Jacob stared at the wide gears and the brass crank mounted on the side of the barrels. "That's a *gun?*"

Smith nodded as he turned the long cylinder to the side. "It is called a chain gun. You will usually only see them mounted on airships or armored transports. This is one of the first."

Something clicked as Smith turned the crank, and the entire assembly of eight barrels spun in its housing.

"Is that safe?" Jacob asked.

"Yes. I removed the firing pins many years ago. I want you to understand, just because a thing *can* be built, does not mean it *should* be built. Charles helped design this. Did you know that?"

Jacob folded his arms as a small frown crawled across his face. "Why would he do that?"

"For the airships, originally," Archibald said with a sigh. "They were mounted on warships, sent to eradicate infantry in a hail of gunfire, or defend against an enemy's gliders. War in the sky has its own unique concerns. The Butcher reduced the scale of the design and created *that.* His own personal slaughterhouse."

Smith ran his fingers over the wide, blocky initials carved into the base of the chain gun.

NVB.

Newton Victor Burns.

Jacob thought back to the toy he'd bought at Festival before the Fall. Those same initials were scratched into it. The same man who built such a beautiful, delicate machine, created something that slaughtered families.

Why?

He didn't realize he'd spoken out loud until Archibald replied. "For a fool's errand. Revenge against a people who had no hand in his pain."

Jacob frowned. "Why would Charles help him build that?"

"He didn't, really," Archibald said. "Burns stole the designs and made his own changes. Charles had created the chain guns to face a threat that never came."

"What threat?"

"Far across the seas, there are other nations. Other gatherings of cities and people and murderers. The pirates of Belldorn and Ballern, you've heard the tale?"

Jacob nodded. "It's a bedtime story for kids."

"Not entirely," Archibald said. "Both cities are quite real. Ballern is far more organized than any band of pirates. Early in the Deadlands War, they brought their airships across the great sea and struck Fel. The people there were lucky to have ballistae large enough to bring down those ships."

"They lost many men," Smith said. He hooked a wide rope through the barrels of the chain gun and hung it from his back.

"What are you doing?" Archibald asked.

"I want to show Jacob the gear ratios and the locking mechanism on this. It is a terrible weapon, but a beautiful machine."

Archibald nodded. "I suppose it won't do any harm to take it from the shrine."

Smith shivered. "Can we head out? I do not like it here."

Instead of answering, Archibald led them back toward the entrance of the shrine. Imaginary scenes flashed through Jacob's head, of the people on the walls screaming as a madman stormed their shelter and killed them all. He remembered the terror he felt when soldiers came to cut his hands off. The awful scenes that unfolded during the Fall—the dead, the dying, and the lost.

"I could never be a soldier like them."

Smith glanced down at Jacob. "There is no way to know that until you must. I have known many soldiers. You are strong, and brave, and surrounded by friends. You would make a terrible adversary, Jacob. I hope you are still yourself at journey's end."

"I'd rather just build things."

Smith laughed and patted Jacob's shoulder. "Me too, my friend. Me too."

CHAPTER THIRTY-THREE

S AMUEL GROANED AND SQUINTED AT the light trying to invade his eyes. He started to roll over before he noticed the ground was soft. That didn't make any sense. He'd fallen asleep in the cave after …

Samuel shot upright as his heart slammed against his ribcage, memories of the Fireworms and Stone Dogs, and of Drakkar trying to drag him to safety, bubbled up to the surface. Now it was light outside the window.

"Window?" Samuel asked as he tried to remember where he was.

It didn't take long for his eyes to adjust to the dim light. He was in a bedroom, somewhere. Not a terribly large bed, but sizable enough that his feet didn't hang over the edge. Samuel put his feet on the floor and ran his hands through his hair. He felt like someone had run over his entire body with a carriage, or two carriages.

He groaned and turned to the side.

The door handle rattled before the entryway opened with a creak. A cloaked form stood silhouetted by the bright sunlight behind it.

"Drakkar?"

"It is I."

"Where's Charles?" He glanced around. "Where are *we*, for that matter?"

"Charles is with some of the other Steamsworn, on their way to another safe house."

"This is a safe house?"

Drakkar walked across the room, letting the door click closed behind him before he cracked the shutters open on the window. "Not exactly. We are at an inn, though it is owned by one of Archibald's … men."

Samuel nodded. If one of Archibald's spies owned the place, it was probably as good as any other safe house.

"We were worried for you."

Samuel blew out a breath. "So was I. I was pretty sure that was the end of the road." Samuel paused and looked up at Drakkar. "Did you drag me out of there? I think I remember someone talking." He grimaced and rubbed his forehead.

"I did. By the time I found you, the Stone Dog poison was already deep within your blood. I had to cut your arm to apply the salve."

Samuel had heard stories about the desert folks' healing skills. He hoped he'd never need another demonstration. He rubbed at the bandage tied around his throbbing forearm. "Thank you."

"We are as good as brothers in this fight. I do not need your thanks."

"You're stuck with it," Samuel said as he arched his back until it popped. "How long have I been out?"

"Several days."

"Gods."

"It was a near thing. I believe you owe more thanks to the Fireworms than to me."

Samuel laughed and gave Drakkar a sideways smile. "I'd never seen anything like it." Samuel stood up and made his way to the low wooden dresser where his armor was folded. He started to slide the vest on.

"Are you well enough to venture out? We are in Dauschen now, and I am afraid things may be worse than we feared."

"Worse than we feared?" Samuel said. "I kind of doubt that. We already know they shut down the trade routes and stopped the flow of medicines to Ancora and Bollwerk. How much worse could it be?"

"We have seen soldiers from Fel stationed at several guard posts."

Samuel paused and blinked, considering the long feud between

Dauschen and Fel before he said, "Damn."

Drakkar nodded. "It is unlikely, if not impossible, that those soldiers are here by permission."

"Then …" A dozen scenarios flipped through Samuel's mind. That Dauschen had taken a new ally would seem the most likely occurrence if he hadn't personally seen the city's hatred for Fel. If it wasn't an alliance, it was an invasion. If Dauschen had been overthrown …

Samuel looked up at Drakkar. "If they're here by force, then Dauschen may not have set the embargo against Ancora."

Drakkar nodded. "Yes, that is what Charles is out to discover."

"We have to find him."

"He knows how to handle himself, my friend."

Samuel shook his head. "He doesn't understand the climate here. People are volatile, vicious. They're almost as territorial as those damn Fireworms. If they aren't fighting back, something's happened … something big."

Samuel leaned over to pull the loops of metal together on his greaves, cinching them with a leather tie. The metal skirt, as the Spider Knights liked to call it, went on next. Two long plates of metal latched over the front of his legs with matching armor on the sides and back. The vambraces came on next, hooking into his vest. He grimaced at the pressure on his wounded arm.

"Do you think it wise to wear that armor here?" Drakkar asked.

Samuel nodded. "The soldiers from Fel will be joyful about a Spider Knight defecting. They've despised Ancora since the Deadlands War."

"Why was I not aware of this?"

"Fel keeps to itself. Why *would* you know about it? Their views on the Deadlands War are quite different from our own. You've heard stories of the Ballern invasion?"

Drakkar nodded.

"Right, no one came to help Fel when those airships struck. They withdrew from the war after it happened, blaming both sides for casualties that could have been prevented."

"Why would that affect us now?"

Samuel let out a short laugh. "The way Charles tells it, they blamed Dauschen above all others. At the time, Dauschen had the grandest fleet of airships. Charles said they wouldn't have been able to stand up to the Ballern fleet, but Fel didn't seem to care about that little detail.

"Fel sent a group of politicians to Dauschen to negotiate what would become our trade routes. They weren't politicians. The entire Trade Council was murdered when they were introduced."

"I would assume the soldiers from Fel never made it home?"

Samuel nodded. "The ones who failed to kill themselves before being captured died terrible, slow deaths. Charles saw some of it. I think that's what turned him away from Dauschen for so long."

"Did he live here?"

"No." Samuel scratched his head. "I think he helped introduce the city to the trade routes, or helped establish trade with Ancora. I can't remember exactly."

"I have heard stories of what Charles von Atlier can do when he has no love for a place. We should find him before he destroys this city."

"What?" Samuel said as he finished attaching the plates to his boots. "I don't think he'll take it that far. He's still a reasonable guy."

Samuel could tell by the look on Drakkar's face that the Cave Guardian wasn't so sure.

✧　✧　✧

THE HEAVY, KNOTTED DREAD GREW ever larger in Charles's gut with every step he took across the rough cobblestones of the city. Soldiers clad in the gray and silver armor of Fel stood on alternating street corners. The farther away from the others he got, the more he thought they shouldn't have split up. It would be faster with the other Steamsworn checking the two other safe houses, but if anyone caught a glimpse of their biome-chanics, it could get bad fast. Whoever found the first radio was to make contact with Bollwerk. He'd hoped to have good news for Archibald, but he couldn't think of anything to say that wasn't grim.

Charles's steps slowed when he reached the old military base on the cliffside. He'd seen it built a great many years ago, steel plates riveted to a thick stone wall. It was the best sort of protection, but now it was only horror. Dead, rotting corpses hung from the walls every few feet. Each one was decked in the garb of a Dauschen soldier, or the robe of a Trade Council member.

The winds shifted, and the thick, rancid stench of the battlefield struck his nose. It was something he hadn't smelled in almost fifty years, and his first instinct was to reach for the air cannon mounted on his back. The air cannon he'd left with Drakkar.

"Move along."

Charles glanced up and saw one of the Fel soldiers standing in a watchtower.

"Unless you'd like to join your fellow fools, I would suggest you move."

Charles had no real love for Dauschen, but he wanted to kill that soldier. Slowly. He moved forward, hurrying to give the illusion that the man actually frightened him.

It wasn't long before Charles reached one of the gates to the base, and when he saw what waited inside, he had to brace himself against the vision. A pyramid of charred bodies smoldered next to the husk of a burned-out airship. They'd been tossed there like rag dolls and left to burn in the sun. He kept moving, but watched as soldiers milled around the bodies like macabre ants, picking up pieces and people and carting them away to be dumped over the cliffside.

There are moments when things become incredibly clear. When your path, no matter how terrible or how frightening, solidifies before your eyes. As Charles looked upon those bodies and the masses of Fel soldiers barricaded inside that base, he knew. Dauschen was already dead. He just needed to bury it.

Charles stopped briefly at the corner of the base, beside the pool of blood and gore beneath a young soldier. No older than Jacob, and possibly younger, someone had split the boy open like a melon, his face ruined and showing the early signs of decay. It meant they were still killing people. Still putting them on display. A single dry flower withered below the boy. Who'd left it? Family? Friends? A young lover?

Charles took deep breaths as he left that atrocity behind him, barely containing the rage that threatened to take over his actions. He saw at least three soldiers he could kill before anyone would know something had happened. Charles ground his teeth and turned away instead. He'd seen things during the Deadlands War that were probably worse, but the fact this could even *compare* tore at his heart. No one deserved this. This was not an age of war, but clearly it was no longer an age of peace.

He was ready to kill, and the realization sickened him.

Charles saw only a handful of Dauschen natives on the streets. He suspected the rest were either hiding in their homes or dead.

"I still don't understand why they let that warlord live."

The brief snippet of overheard conversation drew Charles's attention. He slipped into an alley not ten feet from the soldiers guarding an old bank.

"Rana?"

"Yeah, that guy's insane. I wouldn't be hard-pressed to believe he actually drinks out of a skull.

"Why'd they let him live?"

"Rumor is he pledged himself to Fel. His father helped one of our old kings in the Deadlands War or some such nonsense. He'll probably just go back to raiding villages and terrorizing the desert."

"They should have strung him up on the walls with the other rebels in this city."

Charles peered around the corner and saw the other soldier nod.

"I heard he marries his wives young."

"At least he's got something right."

Charles had heard enough. He slipped out of the alley and continued up the winding cobblestone road. It wasn't long before he came to the only two-story home with a weathervane on top, cast to look like a man with his fist extended. Charles pursed his lips. That didn't seem like a very subtle signal.

He walked behind the building anyway. It didn't appear that he had a choice in the matter. What he heard from outside the back door sent a shiver down his spine.

"You give us the other spies, and you live."

Some part of Charles's mind shut off. He knew what had to be done. It was like an old switch. He just had to turn off his humanity.

The solid thump of fist on meat whispered through the door. If the door squeaked, he'd have to be fast. If the door was silent, this would be a hell of a lot easier.

"She's not talking. Let's just string her up with the other insurgents. Dangle her from the wall."

"Not before we have some fun."

Two voices. Two men. The second was quieter. It could mean there was a wall or a hallway. No windows. Enough waiting. Charles gently applied force on the lever handle and the door whispered open, as silent as the dead.

The dead would soon have company.

A short, L-shaped hallway concealed Charles as he slipped inside the safe house. Two gliding steps took him to the edge of the doorway. One man had his back to Charles. The other was at an angle where he could potentially see Charles coming. That must have been the louder voice.

A young girl sat tied to a chair. Blood and tears ran down her face, but the sheer promise of violence in her eyes made Charles proud, and he didn't even know her.

Charles slid one of the Flashers out of his pocket, depressed the igniter, and threw it across the room. The men turned to look at the click when it hit the wall, and then the little black orb detonated. Charles was already moving by the time the men started screaming and rubbing at their eyes.

He wrenched one man's head back and jerked the knife through cartilage and arteries until it hit bone. Charles let the flailing man fall to the floor. He knew the corpse would be unconscious before it hit the ground. The next man he just kicked in the balls as hard as he could. The soldier didn't even scream. His eyes bulged and he passed out.

Charles turned to the girl and tried to untie her. When the rope wouldn't loosen, he cursed and sawed at it with the knife.

"Can you walk?"

"Who are you?"

"A friend of Archibald's," he said as the first rope fell away and he moved to the next. "Do you have the radio here?"

She nodded. "It's upstairs. Hidden behind the old bookcases."

A small wave of relief washed over him as he finished cutting the second rope and quickly sliced through the last between her ankles.

"I need to borrow your knife."

Charles glanced at the man on the ground and slowly turned back to the little brunette girl with hard green eyes. He didn't say anything else, only handed her the blade.

"I'll meet you upstairs," she said.

"Keep it quiet," Charles said as he nodded. He headed for the staircase closer to the front door. Keep it quiet? He laughed at his own words as he pounded up the carpeted staircase. The safe house had already been discovered; it didn't much matter what she did to that man at this point.

There were two rooms on the second floor. One was empty of anything, save a bed and an armoire. Charles opened the door to the armoire and checked under the bed, just to be safe, before he moved to the other room.

Two bookcases sat against the far wall. He didn't see any telltale scratches on the wall, but there were a few on the light hardwood floor. "Piss-poor design right there," he muttered as he hunted for a latch. He almost laughed when he realized there wasn't one. The right bookcase swung forward with a little tug, clearly on some kind of wheels. If it would have swung inward, there wouldn't have been a hint of a false wall.

The space inside, no larger than a closet, held a sprawl of leather-bound notebooks and pens and broken pencils. Sketches of cats and Pillies and even a few Fire Lizards hung on the wall. Whoever had drawn them was a gifted artist.

Charles turned his attention to the tangle of wires and tubes set in the corner. It looked like the antenna coiled around one of the steel beams of the house. It was brilliant, but it was also risky. Some spies knew how to track a radio signal. Maybe that's how the safe house was compromised in the first place.

Charles spun the three dials to find the signal. It was always the same. It had been the same since the Deadlands War.

N ... 5 ... 2.

Charles pressed the transmitter down and said, "Victor calling Burns, Victor calling Burns."

No answer.

They were supposed to be listening twenty-four hours a day. Charles clicked the button again and repeated the words, "Victor calling Burns."

"Burns here."

Charles was surprised when Archibald's voice came back over the speaker. "I didn't expect Burns himself."

"I was summoned by a monitor."

Charles nodded to himself. It made sense. It's not like Archibald had the time to sit around waiting. "The house was compromised. This will be the last transmission."

"Is Nora alive?" Archibald asked, his quick words betraying his concern.

Charles was a bit taken aback at the use of Nora's real name. At least, he assumed that was her real name. He realized he hadn't even asked. "She's a little worse for the wear, but she's alive."

"Thank the gods. What of her captors?"

Charles heard an unholy, piercing shriek from the first floor before the sound cut off. He listened for a moment, and then footsteps thudded on the stairs.

"Nora?" he asked, projecting his voice.

"Yes," came the low reply.

"They're dead," Charles said as he clicked the transmitter again. "Very, very dead."

"I need you to get her out of there. Get her somewhere safe. Bring her home."

"I'm pretty sure she can take care of herself," Charles said. He looked at Nora as she walked into the room. Blood, and a lot of it, had sprayed across her chest and neck. It wasn't hers.

"Hit the button," Nora said.

Charles did.

"Burns, we still have two vaults remaining. Recommend a full recall. It's only a matter of time until they're cracked."

"Understood. Stay with Victor, gather the others, and come home."

"If they take Ancora, they won't stop there." Charles snapped his finger off the transmitter.

The radio crackled and Archibald said, "Get them home."

Charles tossed the transmitter onto the table beside the radio. He sighed and looked up at Nora. "Do you have the plans to the city's substructure?"

She pointed to the pile of rolled up documents on the top of the desk. "It's one of those."

"How soon can you be ready to run?"

"I'm always ready to run."

Charles nodded.

"Let me rinse off and change. We need to bring the house down."

"Do you have charges set?"

Nora nodded quickly and then left the room.

The old man ran his hand through his hair and looked over the desk and shelves. Nora was going to torch the whole building. All that would be left was rubble and ruin. He'd done that a dozen times during the war, and almost always wished he'd saved something. He started taking down the sketches from the wall and placing them into a neat stack.

He heard pipes rattle and guessed Nora had decided to clean herself off a little more thoroughly once she'd seen the gore. A small pyramid of rolled papers sat high up on the narrow desk. Charles unrolled one and laughed quietly to himself.

"Well done, Nora. Well done." He stuffed the sketches and three of the paper rolls into his backpack. He didn't like the thoughts running through his head, terrible ideas of how to wreak destruction on a scale unseen since the war. What was the alternative? Let Fel walk into Ancora and kill off half the city?

Charles curled his hands into a fist. Never again.

CHAPTER THIRTY-FOUR

CHARLES FROZE WHEN HE OPENED the back door to the safe house. He exhaled in relief a moment later.

Samuel's hand hovered in front of the doorway, about to knock on the old wood.

"What are you doing here?" Charles asked.

"Looking for you. Drakkar tells me the situation is a lot worse than—"

"Move," Nora said as she elbowed past Samuel.

"Excuse me, but you could at least introduce your—"

Charles grabbed Samuel's shoulder, spun him around, and led him away from the house. "We can't be here." He lowered his voice to a whisper. "It's been compromised."

"I am surprised it remained standing," Drakkar said as he stepped out of the stone alley beside them.

Nora almost squeaked when he appeared beside her without warning. "A Cave Guardian? You brought a Cave Guardian here? Unbelievable. Don't you know anything about keeping a low profile?"

There was a muted boom, followed by a rumble that shook the cobblestones beneath their feet. Charles looked back at the cloud of dust and dirt billowing up from the collapsed safe house.

Drakkar took a deep breath. "*That* is more what I expected."

Samuel just said, "Oh."

"What's that supposed to mean?" Charles asked as he ushered them along the back alley.

"He only thought you'd opt for leveling the city," Samuel said.

"Hmph," Charles said as he increased his pace away from the destroyed safe house. People shouted a block over. Once Charles and the others turned a corner and crossed over two more blocks, he was pretty sure they were away from any immediate danger.

"Gods," Samuel said. "You *are* thinking about leveling the city!"

"Keep your voice down," Nora hissed. "There are guards on almost every major street corner, and ears in more places than that. Follow me to the other safe house."

"When did this happen?" Charles asked.

"It's been happening for a while," Nora said. "We didn't realize where the soldiers were from, frankly. We'd been reporting back with news of an uprising, not an invasion. Most of the soldiers have masked their accents. None of us knew who they were until we managed to breach one of their camps. They didn't bother with subtlety once they realized the camps had been compromised."

"When did they take Dauschen's children?" Charles asked.

"How did you know?" Nora asked, her voice quiet, showing an edge of something more broken than angry for the first time. "Two weeks. It was the last time the citizens tried to fight back."

"I saw them strung from the walls of the base."

Nora made a tiny sound that wasn't a moan and wasn't a cry, but it was full of pain.

"Kids?" Samuel said. "They killed kids?"

Nora glanced at Charles, and he could see the moisture glazing her eyes, lips drawn into a tight line. He didn't press her for any more information.

Charles heard something like a growl. It was low and deep, and promised a world of pain. He looked back and found an expression he'd never seen on Drakkar's face.

"I will help you, Charles von Atlier. For the Dauschen and Ancoran dead, I will help you send this city into the black."

THEY ONLY CROSSED PATHS WITH one pair of guards after they emerged from the smaller alleys of Dauschen. Nora led them past while she hung on Samuel's shoulder and laughed and smiled like everything was right in the world. The guards barely gave them a glance, occupied as they were harassing a street vendor for free sausage.

Charles had to steel himself against the violence he felt rising in his bones. The man he'd been some fifty years ago wasn't really dead. He'd only been sleeping, waiting for the time the world needed him once more. Charles didn't miss the way Drakkar looked at him, how he saw the monster instead of the man. In some ways, Drakkar was right, but sometimes you needed the monster.

"Here," Nora said, breaking the dark spiral of thoughts in Charles's mind. She knocked on the door, three short bursts and two spaced raps on the wood.

"Do you smell that?" Drakkar asked.

Charles took a deep breath and then cursed. He'd been smelling it for blocks now, and he hadn't put the pieces together. Charles placed his hand on the door. Warmth greeted his touch, but it wasn't fiery yet. He pulled the door open and Nora gasped.

"Guard the door," Charles said with a glance at Samuel and Drakkar.

The interior of the safe house was mostly ash. It looked like small controlled explosives and firebombs had been used to clear it out. Face down near the front door, on the opposite side of the room, lay one of the Steamsworn men from Bollwerk.

"I didn't even know his name," Charles said. He stared at the smoldering corpse. The gears and pistons of the man's biomechanics were singed and stained with ash. "They know whose spies are here now." There wouldn't be any doubt where a man with that many biomechanics had come from.

"They already knew we were here," Nora said. "No one else would have used the radios. Come on, we need to check the last house."

When Charles didn't turn away from the dead man, Nora said, "It's okay, Archibald is ready for anything."

Charles followed when he felt the pull on his fingers. Nora wanted him to follow. He could do that. It'd been a long time since he'd lost an ally to war, and here he was again. They'd lost two men to the Tail Swords, but somehow this was worse. This was done by soldiers and killers, and they'd taken someone Charles could have called a friend one day.

He ground his teeth together and looked up at Nora. She mounted the stairs, and he followed behind her. The second floor held a dead Fel soldier. He'd taken four bolts to the chest and neck. Charles felt his lips curl into a satisfied smile as he studied the fiber feathers the Steamsworn used on their wrist bolts.

"At least he got the bastard."

"Someone smashed the radio," Nora said. "Looks like they tried to burn the safe house down, but something went wrong."

"Fuses may have been too old, or the explosives."

Nora nodded and tossed a tangle of wires and cracked tubes onto the floral rug. The reds were a gruesome contrast to the soldier's blood.

"Let's go to the last safe house," Charles said. "If anyone's left, we need to help them get out of the city."

He didn't wait for Nora's response. His mind shifted gears, plotting and planning and digging up the layout for weapons he hadn't built in half a century. He had no real love for Dauschen, but if this city could fall to Fel, there would be no hope for Ancora. The Butcher had seen to that when he helped scale back their weapons stores not ten years ago. Now there were only a few ballistae mounted on the city walls, nowhere near enough to fight off an invasion before Ancora's defenses would collapse.

Charles pulled the back door open and found Samuel waiting below, shifting his steps and rubbing his thumb over his wrist.

"Are you okay?" the Spider Knight asked.

"We have men to kill," Charles said. He didn't like the dark look that crept over Drakkar's features—the profound distaste for the path they were now forced to walk. "It's them or us, Drakkar. They've taken enough of us. Lead the way, Nora. We'll hit the last house and get the hell out of here."

"What about the people who came here with us?" Samuel asked.

"They're prepared." Charles looked around at the vacant street before he said, "They have radios and they're well armed. Fresh eyes in the city that no one knows, we need that."

Samuel nodded. Charles knew the Spider Knight was a soldier. He wouldn't question what needed to be done.

"Very well," Drakkar said.

Some tight knot of worry untied itself in Charles's gut at Drakkar's words. A part of him thought he'd have to confront the guardian, and the thought alone made him sick. If he'd learned nothing else this trip, it was how noble a man Drakkar was.

"Nora, lead the way. We can't afford to be seen at any of the safe houses."

She left the door open at the top of the stairs and led them to the east. The sun neared its apex, lighting a path for the terrible new purpose brewing behind the tinker's eyes.

✧　　✧　　✧

SOMETHING MOVED ON THE OTHER side of the door to the final safe house. Drakkar placed his ear against the gap between the door and its frame. Footsteps faded, and then boots slammed against a wood floor, rushing toward him.

"Move!" Drakkar shouted. He shifted his stance away from the entrance and snapped his collapsible sword out in the same movement.

Wood cracked and the door swung out violently. The tip of a spear lunged through the gap, piercing the guardian's cloak but not the man himself. Drakkar jerked on the shaft and sent one of the Fel soldiers sprawling onto the stones behind him.

"Two more!" Charles shouted to Drakkar.

At some level, Drakkar knew Charles was right. If they did not fight back, they would only die.

"Cave Guar—!"

The soldier was forever silenced when Drakkar rammed his sword through the man's face. There was enough force behind the blow to impale the man behind him as well. Drakkar thought he'd barely clipped the other soldier, but an arc of blood said otherwise. He raised a booted foot, pressed it against the dead weight, and jerked his sword free as the bodies settled on the floor.

"Bring him."

Drakkar turned to find Samuel dragging the other soldier into the house—the man who'd almost managed to impale the guardian with his spear. Nora sprinted past.

"Wait!" he said. "There could be more …"

He trailed off when she froze at the entrance to the small living room. Drakkar took a few steps forward and looked over the roomful of bodies. The bonds and the small cuts and the bottles of acid lined up along the mantel were clear to see. These people had been tortured. There, in the far corner, slumped in a long gray cloak, was a young Cave Guardian.

"No," Drakkar said as he stepped across the bodies. "I know her." His voice cracked. "She was … she trained with my son. Gods, she can't be more than eighteen." His eyes trailed down her tunic where it was cut open, exposing far more flesh than was proper. Her pants were eaten through with the acid, her legs and abdomen a ruin of boiled flesh. Drakkar's knuckles paled as his grip on the sword threatened to crush the metal.

There are times when the mind of a disciplined soldier comes unraveled, and Drakkar embraced it.

"Drakkar, don't."

The guardian almost laughed at Charles's words. He wrapped his leather-gloved hand around the neck of the last surviving soldier and dragged him coughing and spluttering into the roomful of corpses.

"Don't. Move."

The man tried to roll away.

Drakkar stepped on the soldier's knee and lifted the man's foot until a gristly pop filled the room. He walked away, his eyes trailing back to the dead guardian as he wrapped his hand around a bottle of acid.

"You murdered my son's friend, Dead One." Silence choked the room. Drakkar had never uttered that phrase, never promised death to a human before. It was an oath unlike any other. Two little words, and the man on the ground froze.

"Tell my friends what they wish to know, and I will consider leaving your face recognizable for whatever family has had to endure your miserable existence."

"Who is leading the invasion?" Nora asked. "And what is their goal?"

The man didn't take his eyes from Drakkar.

"Answer her, or this will become unpleasant."

The man shivered and turned his attention to Nora. "Fel is. They've allied with the desert warlords through Rana."

"Who in Fel?"

He looked away. Drakkar shifted the cork in the acid so it squeaked and drew the man's attention. "Mordair," he said. "The King of Fel is set on taking Bollwerk."

"Where are the spies from?" Nora asked.

"Bollwerk," the man whispered. "The entire network here was from Bollwerk. Even our spies were planted in that city."

Nora hesitated. "How many are left?"

"Just you, you bitch." The soldier's eyes flashed to the rest of the group, and it looked as though he was reconsidering that declaration.

"I don't need anything else," Nora said quietly.

"Do your people accept cremation as a form of burial?" Drakkar asked Nora.

She nodded.

Drakkar fished around in his cloak and pulled out a Burner. "I am sorry to mix the ashes of these heathens with your brethren."

"Wait!" the soldier screamed. "You said you wouldn't!"

"I said I would consider it," Drakkar said. "And I have."

"Mordair will run your precious Cave into the earth," the man snarled. "What we did to that Cave Guardian will be done to every man, woman, and child in—"

The glass bottle of acid shattered against the man's face, and he screamed as his flesh smoked. Drakkar clicked the igniter on the Burner and threw it onto the thrashing soldier. The acid was flammable. He went up like an oil-soaked rag.

CHAPTER THIRTY-FIVE

"S MITH?" Jacob asked.

"Hmm?" he said without looking up from the tangle of wires he hunched over.

"What do you know about the Forgotten?"

Smith pulled two tiny filaments through the braid he'd created and then leaned back to look at Jacob. "My father was a Forgotten."

Jacob had wondered why Smith's skin was so much lighter than a lot of the men and women in Bollwerk. It would make sense that his father had been Ancoran. "Why were they chased out of Ancora?"

"For what we are doing at this very moment," Smith said. "Working in biomechanics was considered embracing a great evil during, and after, the Deadlands War. My father, much like Charles and even Archibald, learned the trade to save lives. Archibald refused to give it up, but Charles did so he could return to Ancora.

"Charles could have been the greatest biomechanic that ever lived, Jacob, but he was not willing to make the sacrifice."

"Why not? I'd live here in a heartbeat."

Smith smiled. "Bollwerk was not always the haven it is today. There was a great deal of time spent building the walls and restoring order after the war. It was not a safe place to be, if our historians are honest. What do *your* people say of the Forgotten?"

"They don't talk about them," Jacob said. "I'd never heard of them until I found a copy of *The Dead Scourge*. You know, Archibald's book?"

Smith nodded.

"It seems like the older people in Ancora are the only ones who knew anything about the Forgotten."

"It is not unusual for a culture to try erasing an atrocity from their past."

"What do you mean?"

"The Forgotten were sentenced to die in the desert. Your Parliament sent a death squad after them, not even a day after the last of them left the city."

"What?"

"They were trying to ensure that 'evil perished' in the sands. The death squad met their end between the Horns. Bollwerk had sent a detachment to escort the last of the Forgotten. You see, not all of the Forgotten had been captured, or ever returned home to even face a trial. Word spreads quickly in times of war. Archibald and his men persuaded the leaders of Bollwerk to help bring the Forgotten to the city in safety."

"Why did Bollwerk help?"

"They knew of Archibald's skill, and my father's. The Forgotten helped build the walls and improve Bollwerk's biomechanics. They helped turn this city into what it is today, helped forge its government, as much as its defenses."

Jacob thought about that, and how much fear Ancorans had for Mechs. He ran a hand over his knee and wondered if he'd have trouble going home again with his Biomech implant. He thought about Boll-werk's pacifism, and how it must have influenced the Forgotten, and how the Forgotten must have influenced Bollwerk. It's the only way he could see one of the most peace-loving cities in the world having the largest warships he'd ever seen.

"Was the Butcher's brother one of the Forgotten?" Jacob asked.

"No," Smith said. "I have heard that rumor before, but there is no truth to it."

"Charles said a Berserker killed him in the war."

"It would fit with what I know of the story," Smith said with a nod.

"That was before the Butcher murdered Charles's brother."

"I know that story," Smith said with a sad smile. "The old man hides it well, but I fear what he would sacrifice for a chance to destroy the Butcher."

"You're wrong about him," Jacob said.

"How so?"

"Charles could have killed him a hundred times over by now. He's even purchased parts and supplies from him."

"Truly?" Smith asked as he narrowed his eyes. "Why would he do that?"

"The Butcher is the best smith in the Highlands. People think he's a war hero in Ancora. Charles buys parts from him because they're the best parts he can find without forging them himself."

"That does not sound like the rash man my father talked so fondly of." Smith turned back to his wires and began braiding them again. "Time changes everything, I suppose, and men are no different."

JACOB TWISTED THE CRANK AND watched the hammers rise and fall, metal clicking against metal as the chain gun's mechanism spun. He slowed it down and slid the thin copper plate out of the breach once it had cycled through all the barrels.

He held it up at an angle and studied the small indentations. "Smith, the third on the right isn't hitting as hard as the others," Jacob said, handing the copper disc to the tinker.

Smith glanced at it and nodded. "I think that may just be a shorter striker," he said as he ran his finger over the dents. "Here, measure it with this."

Jacob took the strange-looking thing out of Smith's hands. It was something like a brass wrench, but it only had one jaw and a set of tiny lines etched into the base. Jacob pulled one of the hammers back and set the jaw against the striker. He turned the knob, which seemed to be the only moving part of the gadget, and a small piston descended until it tapped against the hammer where the striker was mounted.

Jacob squinted at the lines on the wrench-like tool. "Looks like it's just over eight lines?"

Smith nodded.

Jacob moved to the next and repeated the process. "Eight and a half." He shifted to the next. "Barely over seven on the lighter strike."

"That should still be plenty hard," Smith said. "I think we will be ready to take it out to the range sooner than Archibald would like."

Jacob smiled when Smith flashed him a broad grin.

"This thing is a lot more complicated than those bolt guns," Jacob said.

Smith reached up and grabbed the bolt gun Jacob had been tinkering with. "I do rather like the change you made on this one. Using a bandolier as an ammo chain was brilliant."

Jacob shrugged. "The chain gun gave me the idea. You can still reload it like a normal bolt gun though. I did loosen the spring a bit so it's easier to arm with one hand."

The door to the lab rattled in its frame with a flurry of knocks, a brief pause, and then someone screamed, "Open the door! Jacob? Jacob!"

The knocks resumed as Jacob's mind caught up with his ears. "Alice?" He leapt off the stool, wincing at the sharp needle of pain in his knee when he landed, and took a few quick steps to the door. He threw the bolt open, and the heavy iron-banded door almost smacked him in the face.

"Alice, what's wrong?" Jacob had only seen that look on her face a few times, like when she'd slammed a bully into the ground to help one of their classmates.

"We were back at The Fish Head and they just, they just took her."

"Took who?" Jacob asked as he reached out and grabbed Alice's shoulders.

"Gladys. They took Gladys."

"The Desert Princess?" Smith said.

Alice nodded and the tinker cursed.

"I'm going after her," Alice said. "They knocked George out and there's no one to help her."

"Is George okay?" Smith asked.

"One of the street vendors was with him. Said she was a healer. I don't know if she was lying, I just … We have to help her!"

"Who took her?" Smith asked.

"I heard them say they were taking her to the desert."

"Son of a … Jacob, take your bolt gun. I will grab the bags. Alice, are you armed?"

She nodded, opening her vest to reveal the cotton shirt beneath and a series of short knives. Jacob saw the red welt across her other cheek when she turned to the side. Someone had hit her, and hit her hard.

"What happened?" he said as he reached out toward the wound.

She slapped his hand away. "I'm fine," she snapped. "We have to find Gladys."

"I did not know you threw knives." Smith paused, picked up one of Charles's heavy nail guns, and tossed it to Alice. "Take that with you too. It may come in handy against Rana and his soldiers."

Alice didn't ask questions. She slid her hand through the webbing and up into the fingers of the glove. Jacob picked up a jar of the thick anchoring nails and handed them to Alice. She filled one of the pockets on her pants and readjusted her vest.

"Before they knocked George out, he started saying things that didn't make sense." She drew her eyebrows drew down and ran her hands through her hair. "He said … he said it was disgusting how they consummated their marriages on Midstream's tragedy. The fist is a sacred place that should never be …" She shook her head. "That was it. They knocked him out with a staff. I thought they'd killed him."

"Was the staff wrapped in black leather?"

"Why does that even matter!" Alice shouted.

"It matters," Smith said, his tone calm.

Alice closed her eyes and moved her head slightly from one side to the other. "I think so. I think it was."

Smith pulled a small copper grid out from beneath the collar of his vest and clicked a button on the side. "Mary, come in." He resumed packing the backpacks, tossing one to Jacob once he finished.

Something crackled and Smith flipped a switch on the little box.

"This is Mary."

"The Desert Princess has been kidnapped by Rana's men. Get the Skysworn ready. We are ending this."

"Archibald won't sanction that, Smith."

"That's why we're going."

"She'll be ready in twenty."

"We'll be there." Smith almost snarled as he stared at his workbench. "Screw it all." He started slamming pieces of the chain gun together. Metal clicked and squealed and clanged until the entire assembly gleamed in the light of workshop.

"Give Alice your backpack."

Jacob did, and Alice threw it over her shoulders without complaint. Smith handed Jacob his own backpack, and Jacob grunted as the weight pulled on his shoulders. The tinker fastened a strap to the chain gun and slung it across his own back. He dragged two enormous belts of ammo out from under the workbench and wrapped each around his shoulders.

"How heavy is that?" Alice asked.

"As heavy as the burden I bear for not killing Rana when I had the chance."

Smith scrawled something on a piece of paper and then walked to the door. He held it up and rammed a knife through it. There were only three words.

RANA HAS GLADYS.

CHAPTER THIRTY-SIX

"HOW DO I LET YOU talk me into this shit?" Mary asked as she glared at the horn echoing with Smith's voice. "This is a good way to get dead." She rubbed her face and continued before Smith had a chance to respond. "Considering what George was rambling about, I'm guessing they'll be at Gareth Cave. I don't see why he would have mentioned the fist otherwise."

"We will check the cave," Smith said, his voice sounding over the brass horn beside Mary. "If they are not there, we will find them in the ruins of Midstream. Archibald should have let me kill him, Mary. How many people would be alive if I had killed him five years ago?"

"Those weren't your orders, Smith. None of this is your fault. Archibald would have hung you as a traitor if you'd broken that treaty."

"You may be right, but I am not wrong." The horn clanged when Smith slammed it closed.

"What treaty?" Jacob asked.

Mary pulled a lever toward her waist and shifted it to the right. The Skysworn accelerated, the turbines of the thrusters screaming louder than Jacob had ever heard. She glanced back at Jacob and Alice.

"Bollwerk had a treaty with the warlords. It declared Bollwerk's citizens off limits, but basically gave the warlords free rein over the native people of the desert."

"What?" Alice hissed. "What kind unconscionable monster would agree to that?"

"Archibald wasn't a monster," Mary said. "You can't understand what was happening here. If he hadn't signed the treaty, he would have been removed as Speaker. Bollwerk's government would have fallen into ruin."

"So you just give Rana permission to do as he wants with the people of the desert? You just let them die."

Mary's mouth tightened before she spun her chair around.

"Dammit, girl, I did what I could. I saved who I could."

"Five years ago," Jacob said over the roar of the turbines, "Bollwerk already had their warships. *Five years ago,* you could have saved every refugee in those towns."

Mary slumped back into her chair. "Archibald would have killed us."

Alice leaned forward and shouted, "Who the *hell* cares about that! Tell me! I want to hear it. Whose life is worth an entire people?"

"No one's," came the tinny reply from the horns beside Mary. "Kids are right. At some level, you know they are, or you would not be flying out with us. It is time to fix an old mistake."

Mary turned her seat back toward the windscreen. "We can never make it right, Smith. Never."

✧   ✧   ✧

THE SKYSWORN SLOWLY DRIFTED IN a small circle above Gareth Cave. Jacob looked up at the ship as it sailed around the stone anchor sunk into the earth.

"It's not going anywhere," Mary said.

Jacob nodded and looked back to the cave's entrance. It seemed darker now, ready to devour them instead of continuing its existence as a memorial and a lesson.

Smith adjusted the chain gun on his back and set a quick pace into the cave.

"Slow down," Mary hissed. "And keep the boots quiet."

"You think Rana does not know we are coming? He has taken

Gladys." Smith didn't slow down. His footfalls seemed to grow louder when they passed the first hallway and started the short walk to the cavern beyond.

Alice palmed one of her knives, and Jacob's hand moved back and forth to the safety catch on his wrist-mounted bolt gun.

"How far back does this go?" Alice asked.

"Not much farther," Jacob said.

"This is really Gareth Cave?"

Jacob nodded. "They have all the names. They're just … you'll see."

It wasn't long before the hallway opened up into the massive cavern and Alice gasped.

Smith stomped across the room, turned, and cursed. "They aren't here."

Jacob walked with Alice. She looked at the paintings and the names carved into the stone before she reached the Steamsworn fist.

"It's huge." Alice froze and covered her mouth. "There are so many …"

"I know," Jacob said, not knowing what else to say. It really was different standing in front of the monument, knowing what happened in that place. Books and stories could only translate so much horror. The rest, you felt it in your bones.

"They were here," Alice said, raising her voice as her arm snapped forward. She bent down and picked up something silver that glinted in the dim light.

Smith walked over and held out his hand. He curled his fingers around the bracelet when Alice handed it to him. "This belongs to Gladys."

"So, did they leave for Midstream?" Mary asked.

"I doubt it," Smith said. "Get back to the ship, we may have walked into a trap."

Jacob knew that was a possibility, chasing after Gladys like they were, but to hear Smith say it out loud gave it a terrible weight in his mind. He tugged on Alice's sleeve, and she followed without protest.

The walk back out of the cave seemed to take forever. Smith paused every few feet in the bend and listened. If an ambush came, Jacob doubted Rana would suddenly be exposed because Smith had stopped to listen.

It wasn't until they turned the corner to face the front of the cavern that they froze.

"Ah, Smith," one of the shadowed silhouettes said. Bright sunlight kept their features obscured, but Jacob could still make out a little detail from the lights inside Gareth Cave.

"Rana," Smith said with no inflection as he pulled the chain gun off his back, holding it even with his waist. "Give me the girl."

"You hit nothing but girl with shotgun like that," Rana said. "A trade, perhaps? Give me fiery girl," the warlord said as a broad, sickening smile split his face. "I let princess go free."

"No!" Jacob said. He stepped in front of Alice.

"This is not your fight, boy," Smith said.

Jacob didn't agree. Gladys was a friend, no matter how short a time they'd known her, and Alice wasn't going with a monster like Rana. Alice didn't have a great deal of friends back in Ancora, but the ones she did have were good, kind people. Jacob had no doubt Gladys would be the same, and he took another step forward. He turned his head when he felt a pressure on his arm.

Alice's eyes looked hard. "Midstream's people have suffered enough. Let me go with him. You can find me some other time."

"Are you insane?" Jacob asked, unable to hide the anger bubbling beneath his words.

"Girl smart," Rana said, gesturing to the semi-circle of men around him. "Come now and we release princess."

Alice turned to Smith, her eyes trailing across the chain gun. She exchanged a nod with the tinker and then walked toward the warlord's line.

Jacob felt sick. He was letting Alice walk into the arms of that monster. What would he do to her? A hundred horrible, twisted things burst into his mind and Jacob whispered, "Alice, don't."

She didn't stop. She made it within arm's reach of Rana before he held up his hand.

"Stop there, girl. Take off weapons, then we trade."

A small glimmer of hope blossomed in Jacob's mind. Maybe she could hit Rana with the throwing knives at that range. The knife in her hand clinked against the stone floor, as cold as the hope that died with it.

Alice opened her vest slowly, showing the warlord her remaining knives. They clattered to the ground one at a time, and each metallic clang took away Jacob's hope that she'd stab Rana with one of them.

"Listen well," Rana said with a half smile. "We will have much fun." He gestured for her to come closer, and she did. "Bring princess. She can go."

Jacob watched as Gladys walked away from the line of Rana's men and came to stand beside Alice. "Don't do this, Alice. You don't understand what he'll do." Gladys was bruised and beaten but kept her posture rigid and regal.

Rana bent over slightly and cupped Alice's butt, dragging her closer and inhaling her hair.

The rage in Jacob's gut was not a thing to be contained. His hand slid the safety catch off the bolt gun mounted on his wrist.

Smith raised the chain gun.

"What are you doing?" Jacob hissed. "You'll kill them all."

Jacob watched Alice as she leaned in and kissed the warlord. He almost retched, and he barely heard her whisper …

"You should have taken *all* my weapons."

Alice slammed her fist into the side of Rana's head. There was no scream of pain or cry of protest as the anchoring bolt fired through the warlord's skull with a crack. One of the spring-loaded legs of the anchor protruded from Rana's left eye as he fell backward.

By the time the warlord hit the ground, Alice had tackled Gladys to the sandy stone.

Something screamed, a roar unlike anything Jacob had ever heard, as Smith spun up the barrels of the chain gun. Smith's muscles bulged as his biomechanics kicked in, and he moved the crank faster than humanly possible. Fire and bullets and death stormed out of the cave's throat. Some men tried to run, some tried to draw their own weapons, and a few managed to get their swords unsheathed or their crossbows partially raised. They all died as Smith swept the spinning barrels back and forth, shattering swords and shredding men in explosive bursts of gore.

When the ammo belt expired, Smith stopped turning the crank to the chain gun. "Gladys?" He winced as he threw three of the Biomech switches on his arm. The gun smoked, but something in Smith's arm was blown too.

The princess raised her head slowly, her face splashed in blood. Her hand shook as she wiped some of it away. "I'm okay." She turned to Alice and shook her shoulders. Alice folded her arms underneath her and kept her head down. Jacob could see she was shaking far worse than Gladys.

"Alice?" he asked as he ran forward. Panic ate away at him. Had she been hit? How bad? "Are you okay? Alice, say something!"

He rolled her over gently, looking for any blossoming wounds or damage or breaks. There was blood sprayed across her chest, but he didn't think it was hers. It was probably Rana's. When Jacob met her eyes, he realized she was crying.

"I killed him." It was only a whisper, but the tears on her face betrayed the depth of those three words. "I killed him."

Something moved behind them. Jacob turned to find one of the swordsmen trying to prop himself up, a massive wound torn through his abdomen.

"The treaty will not stand up to—"

Jacob watched, somewhat fascinated at how well the crossbow bolts from his wrist penetrated the chest wall and neck and face of Rana's man. The swordsman fell over into the pile of gore that had been his allies.

He heard Smith say, "Make sure the rest are dead," but he was only interested in Alice.

"Get the kids back on the Skysworn," Mary said.

"Jacob will help," Smith said. "They are fine."

Fine wasn't the word that came to Jacob's mind. He slid his hands beneath Alice. "You didn't have a choice. You saved Gladys. You may have saved us all." She was heavier than he expected, but the adrenaline pumping through him made everything seem easier.

She sniffed. "Smith would have shot them all anyway." Jacob smiled when Alice buried her head in his shoulder, and they left Rana's ruin behind.

✧　✧　✧

SMITH STOOD IN THE DOORWAY to the sleeping quarters for a time, watching the young man and the two women. They were not kids, really. Not anymore. They had lived through the Fall of Ancora and a warlord's wrath. There is a point when you have seen so much, you can never be a child again.

Smith always enjoyed the beds on the Skysworn. They were a bit cramped for someone of his size, but walking into them felt like walking into a bedroom in Bollwerk. Mary had even decorated with copper artwork bolted to the walls and red curtains that didn't actually cover a window. Mary could be a tough-as-nails adventurer, but she had quite the knack for decorating too. Smith thought she'd missed her calling as an artist.

"You left your knives in the sand," Smith said. He stepped forward and handed them to Alice. "I rather hoped you were going to stick that bastard with one."

The fiery-haired girl offered him a weak smile. The tearstains on her cheek made him sad. He should have killed Rana for her.

"Thank you," she said.

"We are going to make the jump soon. Would you like to stay here? There are harnesses in the beds if you would."

Alice glanced at Gladys and then Jacob before shaking her head. "No, I'd like to go back to the cabin. It's … it's beautiful there."

Smith smiled and offered his hand. She took it and followed him out of the sleeping quarters, trailed by Jacob and Gladys.

Smith paused to check a cluster of gauges as they walked toward the ladder that would take them above deck. The pressure and heat still looked normal, and that was an impressive thing so soon after a run with the thrusters. They were already good for another jump.

He hopped up the ladder rungs first before offering his hand to Gladys. She was one of the last members of the royal family that used to rule over Midstream. A lot of the native peoples of the desert had a great respect for her and her late father. Smith hoped one day the natives would be treated as equals to the citizens of Bollwerk. Eventually they would need a leader, and Smith thought Gladys would fit that role well.

Alice came up next, followed by Jacob. The girl seemed better. She was not shaking nearly so badly now, but she was still withdrawn. Smith could understand. The first time he had been forced to kill, it was an awful thing. He was not proud to say it got easier, but it definitely did.

Mary was in the captain's chair when they walked into the cabin.

"Grab your seats and fasten your harnesses," Mary said. "We'll be back home in no time. You want to check the gauges, Smith?"

"Already did. Everything is normal. We are ready to jump when you are."

"You're a damn good mechanic." Mary started the countdown as she shifted the Skysworn, angling the nose back toward Bollwerk.

It was not often Smith got to watch the windscreen when the thrusters engaged, and he could not stop the smile that crawled across his face as the clouds raced by beside them.

CHAPTER THIRTY-SEVEN

THE CARRIAGE BOUNCED OFF SOMETHING hard buried in the desert sands, and Charles looked at Samuel. The Spider Knight rubbed at his injured arm. Charles realized he hadn't asked how the recovery was going since they'd left Dauschen. "How are you feeling?"

Samuel squinted into the sun and grimaced. "Like crap."

"At least that means you're alive."

Samuel grunted and flexed his arm. "Ever have one of those days you kind of wish you weren't?"

Charles grinned. "Yes, in fact, I have."

Samuel eyed him and then looked away. "I guess if *you* lived through it, I'll live through it."

"You wouldn't have lived through it without Drakkar."

"I know. I still can't believe he dragged me out through the Stone Dogs."

Charles nodded and looked out the small gap at the front of the carriage. The sun grew low on the horizon. They were going to beat nightfall to Bollwerk, but not by much. "I was there when he did it."

Samuel shook his head. "Every time I let my mind wander, it comes back to that giant Fireworm burning the Stone Dogs when they ran into the cavern. I figured I was next." He paused until Charles looked over at him. "I didn't think I was going to make it."

"We've all been there," Charles said. "Steamsworn, Spider Knight, it makes little difference. We've all had narrow escapes."

"Some closer than others," Drakkar said, leaning down to peek through the canopy's gap.

"How close are we?" Charles asked.

"The wall has been on the horizon for a time."

Charles laughed. "How much longer do you think it will be until we're inside the gates?"

"Half an hour at most. I can already see the docks."

Another half hour. That gave Charles a little more time to figure out how to approach Archibald about his plan for Dauschen. The soldiers from Fel had to be dealt with, and he had an idea that would drop the floor from beneath their feet.

✧   ✧   ✧

CHARLES COULDN'T BE SURE WITHOUT his watch, but it didn't seem like it had taken more than an hour to drop off the carriage at the stables and take a crawler to Council Hall. He led Samuel and Drakkar down the hallway leading to Smith's lab, their footsteps echoing through the empty corridor.

A short time later they reached the iron-banded door. It stood open a crack, and Charles didn't knock as he pushed the door wider.

"Smith, we …"

It wasn't Smith sitting at the workbench. Archibald stared at a piece of paper with a hole in the middle.

"Where's Jacob?" Charles asked.

"He ran off into the desert."

"What? Why?"

"Gladys, one of the last descendants of Midstream's Royal Family, was taken by the warlord, Rana. Smith means to rescue her."

"Son of a bitch. Him and what army?"

Archibald's eyes rolled up to meet the old tinker's gaze. "The Skysworn."

Charles dropped onto a stool and leaned on the workbench. Smith and Mary against a warlord? "Can we go after them?"

Archibald bent the paper in his hand and shook his head. "Whatever is going to happen has happened by now. There's nothing we can do."

"Have you hailed them?" Drakkar asked. "I know you have the radios here."

Archibald nodded. "When I found the note, I tried. They aren't responding, but I wouldn't assume the worst. Smith has a long history with Rana." Archibald laid the paper on the bench and rubbed at his forehead.

"Let's try the radio again," Samuel said.

Archibald waved at the pile of wire and speakers and glowing tubes on the bench beside them. "Go ahead and try. It's already set to the Skysworn's channel. Just hit the transmitter and talk."

Samuel clicked the small black transmitter and spoke into the wire mesh. Some part of him hoped Jacob or Smith or Mary would respond. A darker part of him thought it was already too late.

✧   ✧   ✧

ALMOST THIRTY MINUTES PASSED BEFORE Charles had finally had enough. "I'm going after them. I can't just sit here and wait!" He slammed his palm on the bench beside Samuel as the Spider Knight released the transmitter and the radio crackled to life.

"Skysworn, over."

Charles snapped the transmitter out of Samuel's hand and pushed the button down, hard. "Skysworn, where the *hell* are you? Is Jacob safe?"

"Charles?"

"Yes, Smith, it's Charles. Now answer the damn question so I can decide whether or not to cut your head off with a toothpick."

"We are ... well, we are docking."

Some terrible knot of dread unwound itself just a little in Charles's gut. "Is everyone safe?"

"Ask him about Gladys," Archibald said.

"And Gladys?"

"We are all safe," Smith said.

Archibald pressed the transmitter and said, "Get Gladys back to George at The Fish Head. He already has a detachment of guards stationed there. As soon as you're done, meet us at the Council Hall."

"I will bring Alice and Jacob with me."

"Alice was with them too?" Charles asked, his voice rising. "I should have known."

"And Mary," Archibald said, turning his eyes on Charles. "We need … we need to talk."

Charles smiled when he heard Mary cursing at Smith in the background. Apparently she didn't want to be involved either. Charles knew how she felt, but sometimes you didn't have a choice.

Archibald tossed the transmitter onto the bench and it landed with a thunk. He looked up at Charles with a frown. "What's your plan?"

Charles didn't hesitate. He'd need Archibald on their side if his plan had half a chance in hell of working. Keeping things from him wouldn't help.

"Dauschen has fallen to Fel. It was silent and deadly, and both those facts scare the hell out of me."

"Me as well," Drakkar said, calling the focus of everyone in the room. "How is it none of us knew of that? How could they have kept an operation so silent at such a scale."

"I think I know part of it," Samuel said. "We started having trouble with folks disappearing on the mountain trails when they traveled between the cities. We assumed it was Widow Makers, or maybe bandits from the Deadlands."

Charles cursed and slammed his fist against the workbench. "Mordair's men killed them."

"Not all of them," Archibald said. "We lost caravans, but there were always survivors. They told us it was Tail Swords."

"I would not be quick to dismiss *that* possibility," Drakkar said. "We found our fair share of Tail Swords on the road to Dauschen. Cave also saw an unusual amount of missing travelers."

"And Stone Dogs," Samuel grumbled. He flexed his arm and grimaced.

Charles ran his fingers through his beard. "We've kept our cities so isolated from each other we didn't even see it happening. The trade embargo did most of the work." He blew out a deep breath through his nose. "If it's been Mordair for months—"

"Or longer," Drakkar said.

"—then the survivors are either just that—survivors—or they're something more insidious."

"Gods," Archibald said. "We could be harboring dozens of them."

"Dozens of what?" Samuel asked before he hesitated and then cursed.

"Spies," Charles said, nearly spitting the word out. "It's the only thing that makes sense. The only way they could have covered it up. Every one of our cities is covered in spies."

✧   ✧   ✧

"THAT'S INSANE," ARCHIBALD SAID, CROSSING his arms and leaning away from the bench. They'd moved into the Council Hall, a more secure room, away from curious ears.

Charles couldn't hold back the frown on his face as he mirrored Archibald's posture. "What choice do we have? Do you understand that they've set up an entire *army* inside Dauschen's base? Do you understand what that army could do to Ancora? Or Cave? Or even Bollwerk?"

"You can't just *blow up* the goddamned city, *Charles!*"

Charles slammed his palm onto the schematics he'd taken from the safe house in Dauschen. "Then send one of your warships! What would it take? Fifteen rounds from those cannons to turn that base into a crater?"

"That would be an act of war," Archibald whispered as his face turned into a snarl. "And if the Skysworn comes back with Rana's head, I'm in two wars."

"It's all the same war, Archibald, and if you don't do something, your city is going to get burned to the ground while you watch."

"Is that a threat?"

"No!" Charles shouted. "It's me begging you to open your eyes! This isn't fifty years ago, Archibald. You can't walk away from this! Bollwerk will rise to power and take the seat it should have borne half a century ago, or everything we love will perish in the ashes of this invasion."

"It's not …" Archibald said as he slumped onto the bench.

"Not what?" Charles snapped. "Not an invasion? You didn't see the bodies in Dauschen. They built a pyramid out of the dead and set them on fire, Archibald." He couldn't stop the rage as he pointed his finger at the Speaker and shouted, "They hung children from the walls and cut the innards from their guts. They let them rot on the goddamned walls, Archibald! And they'll be here. They'll come for you and your kids and your women, and your soldiers will hang from the walls of Bollwerk like so much meat!" Charles slammed his hand onto the schematics. "Is that what you want!" Spittle sprayed across the paper and Charles wiped his mouth. He leaned in toward Archibald and lowered his voice to a vicious whisper. "Is that what you want?"

The doors to the Council Hall squeaked quietly before they clanged closed. Charles turned to Jacob, standing wide-eyed, Alice's arm tucked around his waist. Smith and Mary stood behind them.

Charles took a deep breath and brought his gaze back to Archibald. He heard the footsteps echoing behind him as the others came closer. Charles whispered so no one else could hear. No one but Archibald. "Do you want them to witness the rebirth of the Deadlands War? What was it you said? 'Your ideals of peace will die behind a curtain of your own people's blood.' That's where we're heading."

CHAPTER THIRTY-EIGHT

Jacob had never seen Charles so angry. The old man was red enough that Jacob feared he might pop. The sight made Jacob a bit concerned for their immediate safety. He knew Charles would be mad about them chasing down Rana to save Gladys, but wow.

"Come on," Smith said from behind him. "Let us get this over with. I am sure they are going to be furious with us all."

Alice drew away from Jacob as they walked toward Charles, passing the massive pillars supporting the cavernous ceiling. Jacob missed Alice's warmth as soon as the chill in the air replaced the curve of her hip.

Jacob thought he'd preempt the imminent lecture by saying, "I'm sorry, but we couldn't leave Gladys out there with that monster."

Charles waved his hand in dismissal and took a deep breath. "It's good to see you all. It's been a hard time for everyone." Charles stepped away from the bench and wrapped his arms around Jacob, stabbing Jacob's cheek with his beard.

"Alice," Charles said, releasing Jacob and turning toward her. He hugged her before nodding to Smith and Mary.

"Rana is dead," Smith said. He pulled a silver chain out of his pocket and laid it on the bench before Archibald. Blood stained the intricate knots.

Archibald sighed and prodded the thick necklace like it might bite. "Good riddance. Gladys is alive?"

Jacob felt at a loss as to why he wasn't getting screamed at. Something was still wrong. Archibald didn't look happy about the necklace.

"Her wounds are superficial," Smith said. "Her mind …" he shrugged. "She seems to be okay, and she was very happy to see George."

"Gladys is strong," Mary said, stepping up beside Smith. "I don't think we need to worry about her. She'll rally the desert clans to your side, Archibald. I let her know the entire rescue mission was *your* idea."

Archibald didn't speak. His expression softened.

"We're even," Mary said. "I owe you no favors, and I expect none in return."

"The Skysworn is yours in full," Archibald said without hesitation. Jacob wondered why the Skysworn wasn't already hers, but this didn't seem like the time to ask. When Mary didn't move, Archibald said, "We'll get the paperwork in order tomorrow."

Mary nodded.

"Will you come with us to Dauschen?" Charles asked.

Mary glanced at the old tinker. "If I can fly there," she said with a small smile.

Charles laughed and ran a hand through his hair. "Is that a maybe? Smith?"

"What is your intention?" Smith asked. He crossed his arms, causing the biomechanics in his right arm to click and shake when his biceps flexed. Smith glanced down. "I have some work to do on my arm."

Charles nodded at the schematics laid out across the wide Council bench. "We're going back to Dauschen. I aim to remove Fel's army by force."

Smith's eyebrows rose.

"That's insane," Mary said. She shook her head. "You'd need one of Archibald's warships to accomplish that. He won't leave Bollwerk unarmed with the warlords all but at our gates. Unless you're planning on stealing one? That would seem a stupid thing to discuss while the man is sitting right here."

Charles gave Mary a broad smile. "No, I've no intentions of thievery. My plan is somewhat more … severe. I wouldn't ask Archibald to move the warships. Not now that we know Mordair has allied Fel with the warlords."

Archibald started to say something, but Drakkar cut him off. "It's a good plan, Speaker. The risk is nothing to you and your city. There is more risk in resting on your laurels, waiting for Fel to tear down your walls."

"They'd never get past the warships," Archibald said.

"They could," Drakkar said, "if they have their own fleet. Or if they allied themselves with Ballern. Or a spy cripples one of your key defenses. Or one of a hundred different scenarios." Drakkar's accent broke "scenarios" down into four distinct syllables.

"Ballern will never set foot on this continent again," Archibald said. "Fel handed them enough of a defeat in the Deadlands War to assure that."

Charles shook his head. "You underestimate the stubbornness of youth and their need to prove themselves. If you truly believe Ballern will never set foot on our soil again, you're not paying attention."

"Well that's not exactly our largest concern at the moment, is it?" Archibald said with a tight frown.

"No," Charles said. He laid his hand on the schematics spread across the Council's bench.

"You might as well tell everyone your plan," Archibald said. "Get this insanity out in the open."

"It could work," Samuel said. "The soldiers stick to regular posts. The cliffsides are unguarded, and really, why wouldn't they be?"

Charles rifled through the schematics until he found what he wanted. The papers cracked and crinkled as he pulled one sheet out and smoothed it over with a broad sweep of his hands.

"You're all familiar with the base inside of Dauschen? They use it to store a great deal of foodstuffs, medicine, and most anything essential to the survival of a city."

Jacob leaned forward and looked at the hexagonal layout of the building Charles pointed at. The schematics had a surreal amount of detail written in, and Jacob could scarcely guess how anyone managed to write something in such a small hand.

"The northern food silo was burned to the ground," Charles said.

"Why?" Samuel asked. "Do you think the soldiers did it, or the citizens?"

"Could be either," Charles said, "but I'm betting on the soldiers."

Archibald nodded. "It's a good tactic. They force the citizens to rely on rationed food distributed by the soldiers. It doesn't earn trust, really, but people are generally not keen on killing off their food supply."

Charles pointed to the edge of the base. "The southwest corner hangs off the mountain."

Smith harrumphed. "Hangs off the mountain? They had to sink hundreds of supports into the stone to extend that out. It was originally planned as an airship dock. Did you know that?"

"Yes," Charles said. "I was there the first time they tried to land an airship. The mountain winds picked up and slammed it into the cliff. No one survived that fireball."

"So, don't try to land an airship there," Mary said. "Got it."

Charles flashed her a weak smile. "So, the plan …" He tapped his finger on that overhanging section of the hexagon. "There are air vents beneath the base built around those supports. We need to get in, deliver a payload, and get the hell out. The passages are small. Extremely small. I doubt even Samuel could squeeze through them, as wide as his shoulders are."

"You have a bit more of a gut than you used to," Archibald said as he raised an eyebrow.

Charles grinned. "Well, you're right about that." He patted his stomach. "I should still be able to get through."

"I could fit," Alice said.

"I could too," Mary said as she looked over the schematics.

Charles shook his head. "I don't want to put anyone at risk that doesn't absolutely *have* to be there. Jacob knows more about bombs and wires and metal than any of you, save Smith and Archibald. Smith won't fit," Charles said as he looked up at the tinker. "Smith *really* won't fit. Archibald can't go for obvious reasons."

"Charles, I still don't see how you can go back," Archibald said. "It will raise too much suspicion. If anyone saw you …"

"The only soldiers who got a good look at us are dead. Our return will only reinforce the idea that citizens are defecting from Ancora and Bollwerk."

Jacob had heard Charles talk about payloads before. He only said it when he was talking about … "Charles, do you mean we're going to crawl up under Dauschen and plant bombs?"

"Big bombs."

Jacob's stomach soured and flip-flopped. He felt Alice squeeze his arm, and he wrapped his hand around hers.

"What happens if you don't do this?" Alice asked.

"Maybe nothing," Archibald said. "Either way, I can't send a party with you again. We need our people here."

"Maybe nothing?" Charles said, his voice hardening as he spoke. "Maybe Fel marches on Ancora, and then Cave. You know what happens then? They come here. Get it through your head, Archibald. You fight them in another city, or you fight them here. Either way, you can't run from this."

"That's why we need our people here," Archibald said. "I can't let you take another group into a war zone." He glanced at Jacob before locking his eyes with Charles.

"Not Jacob," Samuel said as he leaned forward. "*Not Jacob*. Send me.

You want these kids to fight like Steamsworn soldiers, but they're just *kids*."

"We're not kids," Alice said. "I killed a warlord single-handedly." Her hands curled into fists.

"We shouldn't involve them in this," Samuel said.

There was a time Jacob wanted to sit with the adults and share in their plans and tragedies and victories. Now he longed for the time he could sit with Alice in the Lowlands. No more a care in the world than whose pocket he'd pick next so they could buy a handful of strawberries and pay for his father's medicine.

It was a sad thing, realizing that those days were gone.

"I'll go," Jacob said. "I'm doing it, Samuel."

Samuel deflated as he began to comprehend his loss of the argument.

"Jacob is the only one I trust to deal with a complicated bomb, Samuel," Charles said before he glanced at Smith and Archibald in turn. "He's the only one small enough to fit through the vents and reach the pillars, at least. If something goes wrong with the bomb, Jacob can fix it without my help."

There was a burst of pride in Jacob's chest, hearing Charles talk like that. It didn't completely overcome the sickening thought of killing again, but it was something.

"Charles," Samuel said as he opened his palm, "if something goes wrong with the bomb, it could kill him."

"You think I don't know that?" Charles snapped. "The last thing I want is to put him in danger, but you know something, Samuel?"

The Spider Knight didn't respond.

Charles took a deep breath and said, "We're all in danger now."

CHAPTER THIRTY-NINE

"I CAN'T BELIEVE YOU GOT him to agree to that plan," Samuel said, pulling the door open to The Fish Head. Jacob couldn't help but stare at the giant rusted fish head hanging above them.

"It's why I jumped on the warships after Mary brought them up," Charles said. "Archibald will never send those into battle. He sees them as Bollwerk's greatest defense."

"Aren't they?"

Charles nodded and filed past the Spider Knight, followed by Smith and the others. Jacob watched them all from behind, walking with Alice.

"Yes," Charles said, "they are, but they could be much more. One of those ships is more than enough to defend the walls of Bollwerk. Anything short of a fleet of airships wouldn't stand a chance."

"Ballista could take them down," Mary said. She pulled one of the stools out at the rounded wooden bar.

"It is possible," Smith said, "but they would need to hit at least half the gas chambers. No small thing with all the armor."

"Archibald will keep them ready," Mary said. She twirled a pair of chopsticks between her fingers. The little slivers of wood clicked and squeaked when she rolled them back and forth.

Alice sat down beside Jacob and rubbed his forearm. He grabbed her hand on instinct alone. It felt nice to be back in a city, back behind the walls. He hadn't been sure if they'd survive Rana's ambush, much less share another meal together.

Charles shook his head as Drakkar sat down beside him. "Look, Dauschen and Fel don't have the airpower between them to threaten Bollwerk. None of their ships, at least none that I've seen, are armored enough to withstand the ballista towers on the city wall."

Drakkar tapped his chopsticks on the table while something crashed to the floor in the back room. Jacob heard George cursing about burned bread before the conversation returned to a normal level.

The Cave Guardian watched Charles until the tinker looked at him. "You could be sending Jacob to his death."

Alice squeezed Jacob's hand, and he wrapped his fingers more tightly around hers.

Charles nodded at Drakkar. "I could be sending all of us to our deaths. If we can't remove the threat at the base, we may need to bring the entire city down."

"How would you propose that?" Drakkar asked. "I will not help you kill thousands of innocents."

Charles laced his fingers together and stared at his hands. "There are times, Drakkar, when we don't have a choice. If you don't take an opportunity when you have it …" He shook his head. "We could lose Ancora and Cave and even Bollwerk. The Butcher would have an entire kingdom of his own."

"I will not help you kill innocents."

Charles nodded. "I'll do everything I can to make sure it doesn't come to that."

Drakkar extended his fist and Charles smiled as he wrapped his fingers around it.

"We are brothers," Drakkar said, "and I will fight for my family."

"No!" came a shout from the back. "It's burned, ruined. Just throw it away and make a new batch. We have customers!"

George stomped around the corner that led to the kitchen, rubbing his hands on a towel that looked to be covered in ash. "Girl can't cook to save her life. Good thing you were all there to save her."

Something crashed in the kitchen again and George shouted in a language Jacob didn't recognize.

"Is that Gladys?" Alice asked.

"Yes, it is," George said, the irritation plain on his face.

"Don't you think she should be resting?" Jacob asked.

"Resting!" George said as he waved his hand at the thought. "I have a huge bump on my head because she had to go and get grabbed by Rana. If we'd left for Cave when I told her to, two weeks ago, it never would have happened. So no. No rest. Flatbread."

Jacob couldn't help but smile at George. The man was as deadly as could be, guardian to a princess, but he looked intensely irritated by her incinerating a tray of flatbread.

"Oh, so now you laugh?" George said. "Laugh at my pain. You tinkers and Biomechs are all the same. No compassion!" George winked at Alice. "Go on, I'm sure she'll be happy to see you."

Alice squeezed Jacob's hand before she hopped off her stool and jogged into the kitchen.

"I kind of thought this place was going to be a dive," Samuel said. "Your sign is all rusty, you know?"

"Oh, thank you, wise and powerful Spider Knight," George said. "Without your great insight, I may never have realized my aged iron sign was showing *rust*."

Samuel stared and blinked at George, but Jacob choked back a laugh.

George leaned forward, raising one of his eyebrows. "I've heard rumors of a crazy plan, yes? Concocted by some crazy tinker?"

"Do you have spies in the Hall?" Smith asked. He sounded calm, but Jacob suspected there was a promise behind the words.

"Spies? Why would I need spies? Archibald himself told me about it on the radio."

"Oh," Smith said.

"Yes, ohhhh," George said. "You are a man of many words, Smith." George's stern expression slipped and he let out a smile. "Well, since you all did help keep Gladys alive while I was napping, let me get you a round."

"Of what?" Samuel asked as he eyed the bar with great suspicion. "I don't like fish."

"Oh, you're going to pay for the fish and be glad you did." George pulled a set of small white cups out and set them on the bar. He poured a clear liquid into each one from a vessel that looked a bit like a teapot. "Now, we drink to Gladys, and to my new friends." He slid one of the cups to everyone at the bar.

"Drinking on the job?" Charles asked.

"On the job?" George asked. "Drinking while awake. It's a long and honored tradition of my people."

"I don't mean to be critical," Samuel said, "but aren't most of your people dead?"

"Ah, again with the wisdom! I see why you keep the Spider Knight around. It would be hard to notice obvious things without him."

Jacob sniffed at the small cup and winced before setting it back down on the bar. "What is that?"

"Sake," George said. "It's a recipe passed down through the royal family." He frowned and squinted. "I think they said it was eight thousand years old."

"Hopefully the recipe and not the sake?" Samuel asked.

"Not that you'd be able to tell a difference," Charles said.

"Now you insult our oldest traditions?" George asked. "Think of the children."

"Don't know if the boy's parents would approve of that," Mary said with a nod toward Jacob's cup.

"No man should die without a taste of sake," George said. "You are sending him into great danger, so I say drink. I would like to speak.

Alice! Gladys! Come."

"We're not Pillies," Alice said when she rounded the corner of the kitchen, followed by Gladys.

"No doubt about that," George said. "Never had a Pilly get me ambushed and knocked unconscious before."

"He's going to milk this for months," Gladys grumbled as she slid onto the stool beside Jacob.

Alice stepped between them with one hand on Jacob's shoulder and the other around Gladys.

"Now, raise your glasses."

Gladys sighed and picked up the small white cup when Jacob did.

"Normally I would say to sip this fine sake, but we have Steamsworn brutes with us. Drink it all at once and savor nothing. Isn't that one of your oaths?"

Smith groaned, but his smile betrayed him.

"More serious," George said as his smile faded. "Thank you for rescuing Gladys. I was in no condition to move for many hours. By the time I would have gotten to her, she may not have been herself anymore. So I drink to you, my Steamsworn friends and my Ancoran friends, and to the most beautiful pilot of the Skysworn."

Everyone turned to look at Mary.

She stared wide-eyed at George. "Umm, what?"

"The most skilled pilot of the Skysworn. Is that not what I said?"

George raised his glass and winked at Mary. "Thank you, my friends. You have our alliance, for whatever good may come of it."

Jacob exchanged a glance with Alice as she raised her cup. She shrugged and Jacob returned the gesture before they both threw the sake back with the rest of the group.

It was disgusting. Jacob coughed and spluttered. It felt like the venom from the Tree Killer was working its way down his throat. It settled in his stomach and burned its way out through the rest of his body.

"Oh, gods!" Alice said as she frowned and stuck out her tongue. "Oh oh oh. Why would you *drink* that?"

A smile raised George's cheeks until it looked like someone had stretched his face out. "It's good, yes? Give me a few minutes, my friends. You will feast this evening." He paused and looked out the narrow front window. "Well, this very late night."

"That is good," Drakkar said. He slid the sake cup back toward the edge of the bar. "Much more friendly to the palate than the white fire they serve in Cave."

"Oh, yes," Charles said, wincing at the mere mention of white fire. "Compared to that, anything's a good drink."

"Amen," Mary and Smith said together.

"That's not a good drink compared to anything," Jacob said.

"It's not like it'll kill you, kid," Samuel said with a sideways grin.

"So you say," Jacob said, not sure if Samuel knew what he was talking about, considering the burning in his stomach.

"Did you have the new dress here?" Alice asked as she turned to Gladys and leaned against Jacob.

Gladys nodded and her deep stare lightened when she looked up at Alice. "You want to see it?"

"Yes! Let's go."

Jacob watched the pair head toward the kitchen, and part of him longed for Alice just to lean up against his arm. He'd come to love her warmth when she was close, ever since that time in the old abandoned station.

Alice paused and turned back to Jacob. She leaned over, wrapped her arms around his shoulder, and kissed his cheek before she smiled and hurried after Gladys.

Jacob blinked and stared after her, dumbfounded, while Samuel and Charles exchanged a low chuckle.

✧   ✧   ✧

"I FEEL LIKE WE HAVEN'T accomplished anything," Jacob said, leaning on the bar top. He watched Alice and Gladys for a second, now that they were huddled at a table in the far corner, talking with a hooded Drakkar. The bar had several late-night patrons, most belonging to Gladys's royal guard. Jacob turned his eyes back to Charles when the old tinker released a humorless laugh.

"Haven't accomplished anything?" Charles said. "That might be the sake talking." He glanced down at the empty chirori, as George had explained the name. "Is that my third? Damn, maybe the sake is talking for me." Charles grinned, and it lifted his blushed cheeks. "Don't forget, you're alive, and Alice is safe, and we have allies to fight with us against Fel. We've accomplished a great deal."

"It's not over, though," Jacob said, sipping on a Sweetwing Tea. Maybe the sake *had* gone to his brain, because he thought the sugary drink tasted delicious. "Alice killed Rana, and I killed that other man, and Smith … Smith killed everyone." Jacob shivered at the memory of that chain gun tearing away flesh and blood and ending lives in a storm of metal. "It's not over."

"No," Charles said as he raised his hand and pointed at Jacob. "You know the worst thing about fighting? About war? It's never really over. Doesn't seem to matter who wins, or who dies, someone always decides to start another one."

Jacob snapped a piece of juicy white meat off some strangely shaped creature on his plate. He didn't know what it was, but it had six legs, so clearly it was some kind of bug. It was tender and salty and delicious, and Jacob didn't much care what else it was at that point.

He swallowed and looked up at Charles. "Last week I thought you could keep the peace as long as you had the biggest weapons."

Charles shook his head. "Well, now you know better. I wish Archibald would get out of that frame of mind. He's going to get a lot of folks killed relying on those warships. If the war gets worse …" Charles sighed.

A chorus of laughter went up from the table where George sat. Charles glanced at the circle of men. Smith had his shirt off and worked on his arm with a little help from Mary. Charles had done the same thing in the war, and it was never a good idea to drink before working on biomechanics. Charles smiled before turning his attention back to Jacob.

"You like the Scrambler?"

Jacob's chewing slowed. "The what?"

Charles laughed and patted him on the back. "It's a delicacy for the old Midstream folks."

Jacob swallowed and stared at the shredded chunk of meat on his plate. "It's a Scrambler?"

Charles nodded. "Pretty tasty though, eh?"

"I can't believe I'm eating a parasite off a Walker."

"A deep-fried parasite!" George shouted as he walked past them and headed into the kitchen. "I saved you the fattest one, my friend."

Jacob smiled and took another bite. He'd eaten stranger things, if he was honest with himself, and the Scrambler *was* delicious. Jacob and Charles ate and drank in silence for a while, letting The Fish Head live and breathe around them. There was something homey about the bar. The noise and laughter reminded him of the Lowlands, and in turn of his parents. He hoped they were still alright, and that his father still had enough medicine to get by.

"Charles?" Jacob said. He waited for the old man to meet his eyes. "Is it going to get worse?" He almost whispered the question.

"It may, but it will also get better, and those are the times that must live in your heart to chase away the darkness." Charles raised his glass to the heavens, nodded, and drank the rest of his sake.

Note from Eric R. Asher

Thank you for spending time with Jacob and Alice! I've been blown away by the reader response to this series, and am so grateful to you all. The next book of Jacob and Alice's adventures is called Steamsworn, and it's available now.

If you'd like an email when I release a new book, sign up for my mailing list (www.ericrasher.com). Emails only go out about once per month and your information is closely guarded by a ravenous Pilly.

Also, follow me on BookBub (bookbub.com/authors/eric-r-asher), and you'll always get an email for special sales.

Thanks for reading!
Eric

Please enjoy the following excerpt from

Steamsworn

The Steamborn Trilogy, book #3

By Eric R. Asher

The world dies in war only to be reborn. It is the way of things, and always will be.

Forged in the Deadlands crucible, and armed with the knowledge of their true enemy, Jacob, Alice, and their allies bring the fight back to Ancora. The wounds cut deep in their darkest hour, but in the end, vengeance will light their path.

JACOB WATCHED THE desert sands drift by as the crawler's treads pulled them over dunes and rocks alike. The grains of sand in the gusts of hot wind stung his face, but the ride was far smoother than that of a Walker. Here, on the northwest edge of the Burning Forest, the cacti towered higher than any he'd seen before.

A halo of fire erupted from the stone trees in the distance. It looked like the world burned, and the cacti shimmered and danced in the waves of heat. The place bore an apt name.

"Do you really think stopping the army in Dauschen will be enough?" Jacob asked, his thoughts trailing from the fiery landscape to the flames of war.

Charles scratched his wide gray beard. "I know what Archibald said, and he's not entirely wrong, but strapping all of his forces down to protect Bollwerk is a fool's gambit. We don't have the manpower to attack Fel directly. Destroying their army—not just stopping it, but destroying it in Dauschen—should be enough to force a retreat."

Jacob nodded. He wished Smith had traveled with them, but Jacob knew Mary needed the tinker more. Smith had helped build the bombs, and that was more than most anyone could do.

Jacob was going to miss Alice, too. She'd stayed behind with Gladys and George to train, so if something like Rana's abduction happened again, they'd be ready. The royal guard from Midstream had signed on with Archibald to help prepare the city for the worst. Jacob thought it was probably unnecessary, with the two giant warships docked in Bollwerk, but he knew enough to know he didn't know much about preparing for war. If all went well, it wouldn't be long until he saw her again. Until then, he at least had the memory of her lips on his cheek and the warmth of their parting hugs.

Jacob frowned and studied his hands for a moment.

"I've seen that look on a dozen soldiers," Samuel said, shifting in the front seat of the crawler to look back at Jacob.

"What?" Jacob said as his brain registered that Samuel had been speaking to him.

"You're either sick about not getting Cocoa Crunch until this little campaign is over, or you miss her."

"No," Jacob said. He gave Samuel a half frown. "That's not …" Jacob sighed and rubbed his head. "Yeah, I miss her. It's dumb, I guess, but I didn't really realize it until Rana. After she killed him? I just wanted to take it away."

"Take what away?" Charles asked.

Jacob glanced at Charles and Samuel in turn. Drakkar stayed silent behind the levers of the crawler. Jacob took a deep breath and a small crease deepened between his eyebrows. "I didn't want her to have that memory."

Charles wore a gentle smile as he turned back to the landscape. "You're a good man, Jacob. You don't need to worry about Alice. She has a fire in her that will weather any storm."

Samuel propped his arm up on the back of his seat. The crawler jerked and bounced over a small, nearly dry creek, and the Spider Knight grinned at Jacob before turning around. The mountains soared into the sky beyond the Burning Forest. Beyond them lay the meadows, and then Dauschen.

It was there, below the streets of that fallen place, they would launch the first counterstrike.

✧　✧　✧

"This is a hell of a lot nicer when the Tail Swords aren't trying to kill you," Samuel said.

Drakkar let out a slow laugh. "It is a good rule to find shelter when the rains come to the desert, and not to be slow about it."

"It doesn't hurt to be driving around in a giant metal beast, either."

"No," Drakkar said as he pulled one of the brass levers and adjusted their angle into the mountain pass. "It does not."

The metal treads of the crawler slammed into the stone foothills with a squeal before they gained enough traction to lift the crawler's bulk at a forty-five-degree angle. Jacob threw his arms out against the seat as he feared getting tossed out the top of the open cabin.

"No need to worry," Charles said. "There's a gyro that detects an overbalance. It can fail if you hit something too quickly, of course, but it's designed to release the gears and reverse automatically."

"What if you really needed it to try anyway?" Jacob asked. "Like if you're getting chased by an army of Tail Swords and your only hope is to crawl up a steeper wall?"

"There's an override," Charles said.

"Yes," Drakkar said as he pointed to a plunger with a ruby top. "Although, if it was only Tail Swords, and you were in a crawler of this size, run them down. They are not the smartest creatures in the desert. They will strike the metal of the crawler instead of its passengers."

"Why the hell didn't we take crawlers last time?" Samuel muttered.

"Things turned out alright," Charles said.

"Tell that to the dead people," Samuel said. "I didn't exactly have a fun time getting poisoned by Stone Dogs either."

"You lived," Drakkar said. "Be thankful for that life, and do the best you can with it."

"I get what you're saying, Drakkar, but I kind of feel like I lived just to die somewhere else."

"We all live to die somewhere else. We die when there is nowhere else for us to be. You, Spider Knight, you still have somewhere to be."

"Or he's just a stubborn bastard," Charles said.

Jacob laughed at the cutting look Samuel threw in Charles's direction.

"You're one to talk, old man," Samuel said. "I've already broken my oaths to the city and the Spider Knights. It seems a bit daft to put my life on the line for them now."

"It's not for them, though," Jacob said. "We're doing this for our family, and our friends, and the people who aren't strong enough to do it for themselves. Like my dad. I mean, if he could, he'd be out here fighting with us. I know it. But he can't, so we have to."

"Kid's right," Charles said.

"I'm not a kid."

"He did have sake," Drakkar said.

Jacob's mouth twisted at the memory of the awful drink they'd had at The Fish Head. He didn't think he'd ever want to taste something that terrible again.

Charles patted Jacob's shoulder. "It's an acquired taste, boy."

"Why bother acquiring it?" Jacob asked.

"You will change your mind when you're older and have less sense," Drakkar said, shifting the steering levers to swerve around a boulder.

"I thought I was supposed to get *more* sense as I got older. At least my mom seemed to hope so."

"Jacob," Charles said as he set his arm on the edge of the crawler's door. "If men gained more sense as they got older, I would be a damn genius by now."

"You kind of are," Jacob said.

Samuel snorted and turned in his seat again. "Now I know why you needed Jacob on this trip, old man. Pad the ego a bit, eh?"

Charles gave the Spider Knight a knowing smile, but Jacob knew why Charles really had him along, and that burden came crashing back into his mind. They were on their way to Dauschen to lay waste to the military base on the southwest cliff face. Jacob's actions would kill men, and women, and whatever else was standing inside.

Jacob looked back at the Burning Forest before it vanished beyond the mountain pass. Those old stones had burned as long as history could remember, and they'd be burning long after he'd been lost to time. It was hard to reconcile that such a thing as war could seem trivial to a future generation. Now, at this moment, there was nothing more important to Jacob than freeing Ancora from the war it didn't know was coming.

The darkness of the pass closed over them, and the Burning Forest slipped into a shadowed oblivion.

Steamsworn

The Steamborn Trilogy, book #3

Available now!

Also by Eric R. Asher

Shop ebooks, audiobooks, and paperbacks at ericrasherstore.com

The Theme Park at the End of the World

The Steamborn Series

Steamborn

Steamforged

Steamsworn

Skyborn

Skyforged

Skysworn

Stormborn

Stormforged

Stormsworn

The Vesik Series
(Recommended for Ages 17+)

Days Gone Bad

Wolves and the River of Stone

Winter's Demon

This Broken World

Destroyer Rising

Rattle the Bones

Witch Queen's War

Forgotten Ghosts

The Book of the Ghost

The Book of the Claw

The Book of the Sea

The Book of the Staff

The Book of the Rune

The Book of the Sails

The Book of the Wing

The Book of the Blade

The Book of the Fang

The Book of the Reaper

Dreams of the Forgotten Dead

Garden Gnome Graves

The Vesik Series Box Sets

Box Set One (Books 1-3)

Box Set Two (Books 4-6)

Box Set Three (Books 7-8)

Box Set Four: The Books of the Dead Part 1

Box Set Five: The Books of the Dead Part 2

Mason Dixon: Monster Hunter

Episode One

Episode Two

Episode Three

Episode Four

Want to receive an email when one of Eric's books releases?
Visit ericrasher.com to get started.

About the Author

Eric is a former bookseller, cellist, and comic seller currently living in Saint Louis, Missouri. A lifelong enthusiast of books, music, toys, and games, he discovered a love for the written word after being dragged to the library by his parents at a young age. When he is not writing, you can usually find him reading, gaming, or buried beneath a small avalanche of Transformers. For more about Eric, see: www.ericrasher.com

Enjoy this book? You can make a big difference.

If you've enjoyed this book, I would be very grateful if you could take a minute to leave a review on the platform of your choice. It can be as short as you like. Thank you for spending time with Jacob and Alice.

Connect with Eric R. Asher Online:

Facebook: @ericrasher

Instagram: @ericrasher

TikTok: ericrasher

ericrasher.com

ericrasherstore.com